TRACE

Copyright

First Original Edition, March 2015
Copyright © 2015 by Deborah Bladon
ISBN-13: 978-1508705734
ISBN-10: 1508705739
Cover Design by Wolf & Eagle Media

TRACE

The Complete Series

New York Times & USA Today Bestselling Author
Deborah Bladon

Thank you for making my biggest dreams come true.

TRACE

Part One

ONE

"There's a word for men like you." I try to sound as civilized as I can.

"Handsome?"

I look to the left to avoid eye contact with him. The man is devastatingly handsome. I can't say I'm surprised he realizes it. "No."

"Charming?"

I glance at his face. He's smirking at me. He's actually standing in front of me, smirking. "No."

"Well-hung?" His gaze drops down to the front of the hospital gown he's wearing.

In instances like this I need to be professional. I'm a nurse. I've been trained to deal with virtually every possible medical scenario and to keep my composure. If my eyes follow the path of his, there's no telling what I'm going to see. "No."

"You didn't even look," he teases. "Your eyes haven't left my face even though I'm here because I have a pain in my ass."

It's too easy. He's handing it right to me on a silver platter but I'm on duty so I can't react at all.

"Mr. Ryan." I glance down at the chart in my hand. "I get that you can't sit on the exam table because of the pain in your backside, but you need to stay within this cubicle. Dr. Foster is going to be here shortly and if you're out roaming the corridor, it's just going to prolong the process."

"It's Garrett." His eyes settle on my nametag. "Vanessa, I'm in a lot of pain here."

"What exactly happened to you?" I already know the answer to the question. He crashed his bike and knocked himself out cold. It's worth hearing how he'll put a spin on it though. According to his chart he's a lawyer. Every lawyer I've ever known blurs the line between fact and fiction effortlessly.

"I was riding my bike in Central Park this morning." He shifts on his feet slightly. "I like to do that to keep in shape."

"It's important to exercise." I don't look up from his chart.

"I was riding along and turned a corner and that's when I saw them." He shakes slightly.

If he falls over on my watch, I'm going to need to write up a report and I hate writing up reports. "Maybe you should lean against the exam table."

He nods as he pushes his hand against it. "I was riding and I saw them, and after that everything went black."

"The paramedics that brought you in said you hit a tree." I wince at the imagined image of that. "They said you were lucky you were wearing a helmet."

"I could have been luckier."

"How so?" I turn towards the curtain. Dr. Foster should have been in here by now. I'm going to need to find him.

"If I would have caught what I was chasing when I crashed, I would have been the luckiest guy in Manhattan."

"What were you chasing when you crashed?" I lean in waiting to hear the part of the story everyone in admitting has been dying to know. How does a grown man veer so far off the assigned bicycle path that he hits a huge tree head-on?

"I was chasing the most perfect pair of tits I've seen in a long time."

"Are you serious?" I lean closer to have a look at his eyes.

"I'm dead serious." His hands bolt to the air in front of him. "They were round and plump. She was jogging on the path and I saw them bounce and then they bounced again."

"That's just..." my voice trails because anything I want to say may result in my being suspended. Offending a patient is a definite no-no and I've already had two warnings. I only have one more before I'm out the door for good.

"I'm going to get Dr. Foster." The sooner we get this guy out of here the better.

"Her tits can't compare to your ass, Vanessa. It's seriously the best looking ass I've ever seen."

I can't resist. I know that there's a chance I'm going to regret this but I do it anyway. "No, I'd disagree with that."

"You can't." He shakes his head slightly even though it's the worst possible thing for him to do after slamming it into a tree. "I'm an ass man and your ass is the best looking one I've ever come across."

2

"Actually." I take a step closer to him. "You're the best looking ass I've ever come across. No, wait. That came out wrong."

He starts to turn to reveal his naked ass beneath the hospital gown.

"I meant to say that you're an asshole," I spit out through clenched teeth.

"Nurse Meyer?"

I don't need to turn to recognize that voice. It's Dr. Foster. That only and only chance I had left to keep my job just disappeared into thin air.

I look down at the floor. I feel him brush past me as he walks into the exam room. I brace myself when I see his black shoes stop almost directly in front of me.

"I'm sorry, Dr. Foster." I exhale softly as I level my gaze on him. I don't grovel. It's not something I normally do but I need to pay my rent and New York is an incredibly expensive city to live in so if I have to beg to keep my job here, I'm going to do it. I know that Dr. Ben Foster is a compassionate man. I've seen it myself. Right now, I just need him to throw some of that benevolence in my direction.

"I need a moment in the corridor, Nurse Meyer." There isn't an ounce of anger in his voice as he turns to look at the patient. "Garrett, what are you doing here?"

"Ben?" Garrett's brows pop up.

I watch the back of his head as he nods once before his hand flies into the air. "Sit down. I'll be right back."

***

Dr. Foster knows the patient. My luck can't get any worse. I know that he heard me call Garrett Ryan an asshole. I wouldn't be surprised if everyone in the emergency department heard it. I didn't tone it down at all.

"Before you say anything, Ben," I begin as I look up into his kind face. "He's been belligerent since they brought him in."

His eyes focus over my head at where another nurse is standing in the corridor. "You're hanging by a thread here, Vanessa. We've talked about this in the past."

We have. I love my job. I've never wanted to be anything but a registered nurse, but since I've been thrown into the emergency room, I've seen things I couldn't have imagined. I lost it two months ago on a guy my age who had shaken his baby daughter so hard that she was still recovering in intensive care. His cavalier attitude about her injuries and his frantic attempt to leave the hospital resulted in me wrestling him to the ground. The police thanked me for restraining him but my supervisor wasn't quite as complimentary.

"I have been trying to take his vitals since they brought him in," I say quietly. "I urged him to remain still and he kept getting up from the exam table, so I gave up. He's more than a foot taller than I am and he's at least a hundred pounds heavier. The man is as solid as a brick wall."

"Why didn't you call for another nurse?"

It's a logical question and it's not one that I expect him to know the answer to. He's overworked, just as every doctor in this emergency department is. "We're short staffed today, Ben. I called but no one came."

"He's a friend of mine, Vanessa. What was with the asshole comment?" he whispers the question as he leans in close to me. "Where did that come from?"

I don't know Ben well enough to tell him word-for-word what his friend said to me. I'm not about to start talking about tits and ass in the middle of this bustling hallway. "He made some sexist remarks."

"Garrett did?" His brow cocks.

He doesn't believe me. I see it in his eyes. "He's arrogant, Ben. He wouldn't let me exam him. He sent the lab tech running out of the room when he tried to draw his blood. He's incredibly uncooperative."

"Why is he even here?" He glances down at the tablet in his hand. "What's wrong with him?"

"He ran his bike into a tree." I shrug my shoulder I'm going to leave the details about the tit chasing up to Garrett.

"I need to get back in there, but be more careful." He pats his hand on my shoulder. "I'm not giving you a warning, but anyone else would."

I nod just as Ben pulls the curtain open with a flourish to reveal Garrett Ryan falling face first onto the hard, tiled floor with a thud.

***

"I'm impressed, Vanessa." I feel Ben's hand on my shoulder. "You were a real asset earlier."

I was too shocked to do anything but let my training guide me. The sickening sound of Garrett's head hitting the hard tile floor keeps replaying in my mind. The blood that was flowing rapidly out of his nose when Ben turned his head to the side was jarring, but more than that, the evident edge of panic in Ben's voice when he was trying to get his friend to open his eyes was disorienting. I've never seen the impenetrable façade of Ben Foster break until today.

"Is he going to be okay?" I hang my head towards the floor. After two other male doctors had rushed into the room, they were able to lift Garrett onto the exam table. I stood by, assisting Ben with whatever I could, even though now, three hours later, I'm still shaking as much as I was then.

He lowers himself into the chair next to me in the nurse's lounge. "He'll be fine. He didn't suffer a concussion or any broken bones from either incident. There are a few lacerations on his face but nothing that will be permanent. His blood sugar was dangerously low. That's why he fainted."

"I should have been more insistent on having his blood drawn." I push the toes of my shoes together. "I would have realized before he fell."

"I spoke to the paramedics who brought him in earlier." He pats my knee. "They had a hell of a ride over here with him."

I curb the urge to chuckle because I can only imagine what went on inside that ambulance. I was in admitting when they wheeled him into the ER. I watched, along with two other nurses, as Garrett jumped off the stretcher when the paramedics turned their backs. He didn't want to be here but the insistence of the nurse in charge had been enough to convince him that a doctor had to look him over. The man thinks he's made of steel.

"I'm glad he'll be okay." I whisper with a small, weak smile. "I didn't realize you two were friends when they brought him in."

His gaze meets mine. "He's one of the good ones. We met at a mutual friend's engagement party. Her name is Lilly. Garrett is her attorney."

"I read in his chart that he's a lawyer." I turn my head to look at him.

"He helps with the foundation. He does all of our legal stuff for us pro bono. I've never met a nicer guy."

He's talking about the Foster Foundation. Ben and his twin brother, Noah, established it in honor of their late mother. It provides medical care for anyone who can't afford it. It began as a small project and has since taken on a life of its own. Just last month, a national news crew was in here, interviewing Ben so they could showcase the good work he does.

"I had no idea he even knew you," I say truthfully. "I wouldn't have pegged you two as friends."

"Why not?"

I scratch my cheek as I weigh his question. Bringing up what Garrett said to me serves no purpose at this point. He's tucked safely away in a bed on the third floor and it's likely by this time tomorrow, he'll be at home resting comfortably. I'll never see the man again.

"You two seem very different," I offer before I continue. "I'm just happy that he'll be alright."

"I'm going back up to see him before I leave for the day." He leisurely rises to his feet. "Do you want to come with me? He was asking about you."

"About me? Why would he ask about me?"

"I don't know." His eyes narrow. "He just said that he needed to see the beautiful nurse from the ER."

"That could be anyone." I stand and adjust the left leg of my pants over my shoe. "He wasn't exactly lucid when I was trying to help him. I doubt he remembers me at all."

I say it as much out of hope as belief. I don't want Garrett to remember me. I'm optimistic that his face first fall into the floor will erase from his memory what I said to him. He's an attorney. If he goes to the hospital board with a complaint about me, my job is history.

"He remembers." He turns to walk out of the lounge. "He told me he remembers everything about you."

TWO

I'm on the third floor. Visiting hours are over. My shift is over too. It's actually been over for more than an hour but I hung around in the cafeteria debating whether I should go see what Garrett Ryan wants.

In a perfect world, I want him to forget about me and about what I said. Internally I feel justified for calling him an asshole, but there's no way in hell my supervisor, or the administrative board, would view the situation the same way I do. If he reports me, I'm going to be out on the street and trying to find another nursing job won't be easy.

"Vanessa," Carla calls to me as soon as I exit the elevator. "What are you doing up here?"

Carla was the first friendly face I saw when I started working here. She was working in the ER then and fortunately, our shifts almost always overlapped. We hit it off instantly and when she told me that her and her roommate needed a third wheel to make rent, I'd jumped at the chance. It got me out of my small apartment in Brooklyn. Living in Manhattan may be expensive but I'm close enough to walk to the hospital every day and I get to hang out with Carla whenever our shifts allow it.

"There's a patient in your ward." I gesture down the dimly lit hallway. "He was in the ER earlier. I thought I'd check on him."

"Garrett Ryan," she slides his name over her lips with a purr. "That's the one, right?"

If my mouth isn't hanging open, it should be. "Why would you think I'm up here because of him?"

"Let me count the ways," she begins before she taps her index finger on her forearm. "The man is absolutely drop dead gorgeous. That's reasons one through five."

"Very funny."

"Reason number six is because of his voice. Have you ever heard a voice like that? Number seven is because he's single."

That tidbit of information doesn't surprise me at all given the fact that he was on a breast catching mission when he rammed his bike into a tree. "I assumed he was single."

"Number eight is because he's a lawyer? Have you ever seen a lawyer in that great shape?"

I shake my head slightly. "I can't say that I have."

"I caught a glimpse of what's under his hospital gown earlier when he was walking down the hallway, " she lowers her voice to a whisper as she leans in close to me. "That's either reason number nine or it could even be ten. If you know what I mean."

I know what she means. I have no doubt what she means judging by the way she's holding her hands almost a foot apart and nodding with a cocked brow. "I don't care what's under his hospital gown."

"Then why are you up here?" She pushes against my shoulder with her hand. "You're just like the rest of us. You want a moment to bask in all his masculine glory."

Technically I want a moment to convince him not to report me. "I actually just wanted to talk to him about something that happened when he was in the ER."

"What happened?"

I can tell by her tone that she's craving a juicy piece of gossip she can share on her coffee break tonight.

"Nothing." I shrug it off. "I just needed clarification on something for one of my reports. I'll just talk to him briefly."

"You can't." She gestures down the hallway with a tip of her chin. "Ben prescribed a sedative to keep him quiet. He's sleeping like a baby."

Great, that's just fucking great. The man who holds the power to ruin my career is tucked away in dreamland while I'm living in the nightmare of not knowing what his next move will be.

***

"How's your friend?" I ask as I settle into a chair next to Ben in the cafeteria. I should know the answer myself but when I went up to the third floor before my shift started two hours ago, Garrett wasn't there. The charge nurse told me they'd taken him for more xrays and although I'd hung around hoping to talk to him, I had to bail. I couldn't be late for work.

"He's good." He grins as he looks up at me. "He'll be discharged today."

"Did you see him this morning?"

He pushes a rectangular, disposable plastic tray of fruit towards me. "Do you want some?"

I reach across to snag a piece of an apple. "Thanks. I'm glad he's going home today."

"Not as glad as he is." He pops a grape into his mouth. "He was back to normal this morning. His glucose levels are stable and there are no signs of head trauma so he's good to go."

I breathe an audible sigh of relief. If Garrett leaves the hospital without mentioning what happened between us yesterday to any of my superiors, I may be able to escape with my job.

"When I went up to see him he asked about you again."

My stomach drops instantly. "He did?"

"He did," he answers. "Your name was actually the first word out of his mouth when I walked into his room."

I take a gulp of water from the bottle I bought when I walked into the cafeteria. "What did he say?"

He picks up a piece of pear and holds it in the air. "He wanted to know if you were seeing anyone. I told him I didn't know."

It takes me a minute to absorb the words. They're so completely unexpected. "He didn't talk about what happened yesterday?"

"He's way too proud to talk about that again. Garrett wants to forget that yesterday ever happened."

He's not the only one. "I'd like to forget it too."

He scans his smartphone's screen as he gives me an absentminded nod in return. "It was intense when he collapsed. I think we all want to leave it behind us."

"I hope that we can," I mumble under my breath.

"How's your mom?"

To anyone listening to our conversation, it would seem like an unnatural segue. It's not. Each time Ben and I have lunch, or dinner, during a shift, he asks about my mother. "There's no change. I'll go see her after work today."

He glances at the silver wristwatch he's wearing. "Kayla and I are having dinner with some friends in Brooklyn tonight. I'll stop in and check on her."

Ben's fiancé, Kayla, has become an unlikely friend. We shared a short exchange in the hallway one night when both Ben and I were working a late shift. Since then whenever she stops by to see Ben, she'll find me to ask about my mom. Her heart is limitless.

"You don't have to." I catch my bottom lip between my teeth. He doesn't have to, but I want him to. "She's responding well to the antibiotics you prescribed for her last week."

"I want to follow-up," he says graciously. "I love seeing your mom."

I wish that I could say that she loves seeing him. I doubt that she even knows who he is. The majority of the time when I'm sitting next to her in the extended care center she lives in, her eyes are vacant and she can't remember my name. The bitter journey of watching her sink into the clutches of Alzheimer's has been wrenching for me. I'm an only child of a single mother who has essentially disappeared within herself. I wish I could have just one more lucid moment to say all the things that have gone unspoken.

"We'll try to stop by when you're there." His eyes brighten. "Around eight, okay?"

"I'll be there," I say through a stilted smile. It gets harder every single day to see her like that, but I'll be there. I need to be. She's still my mother.

THREE

"Have you given any thought to searching for your biological mother, Van?"

I look over my shoulder to where Zoe Beck, my best friend is standing with two paper cups in her hands. I already know what's inside. It's cocoa. It's Zoe's favorite and I have to admit, although I don't crave the taste the way I do a strong cup of coffee, I like the reminder of the cocoa my mom used to make for me when I was a little girl growing up in Maine.

"I haven't." I reach for the cup she holds out for me. "I don't know if I can do it."

She carefully lowers herself into the chair next to me. Zoe is six months pregnant. She and her husband, Brighton Beck, are expecting a son in just a few months. The beautiful curve of her belly beneath the pale printed dress she's wearing only adds to my bittersweet feelings regarding my biological mother.

"I love you like a sister so I need you to listen to me." She pats her hand on my knee. "The first time I saw you here with her I could see the love between you. You adore her. Finding your birth mother won't change anything between you and Rowena."

Zoe is my voice of reason in all of this. We became fast, and close, friends after meeting one afternoon when she was volunteering here at the extended care center my mother lives in. She was helpful, caring and would always spend more time than she could probably spare with my mom. Our friendship naturally transferred to the world outside these walls and we devote at least an hour a day to texting or talking on the phone.

"She never wanted me to search." I motion towards where my mother is sitting in her wheelchair in front of a square plastic table covered with the pieces of a never completed jigsaw puzzle. "I'm betraying her if I start looking now."

"Rowena gave you a beautiful life." She rubs her hand over her swollen stomach. "Finding your birth mother now won't change any of that."

I know she's right. When I was younger I couldn't comprehend my mother's unbending reluctance to discuss the details of my birth and what brought me into her arms. There was never a moment where she sat down to explain to me that I was adopted. It wasn't necessary. I knew from the time I could absorb my reflection in the mirror that my straight blonde hair, blue eyes and pale complexion were in direct contrast to her wild mane of black hair, her exotic brown eyes and her olive skin. She was as old as the grandparents of all of my friends and she told me that I was chosen to be her last chance at happiness. I felt special every day of my life.

"I can go to Maine with you to get your adoption records," Zoe offers. "We can do it tomorrow if you want."

It's an offer she makes at least once a week. I sometimes regret telling her that all I need to do to access my original birth certificate is to go to Augusta, Maine, fill out a few forms, pay a fee and I'll have my birth parent's names in my hands.

"Once you have your birth mother's name, I can help you do research to find her," she says quietly. "Beck can help too. He knows a lot of people."

My brows pop up. Zoe's husband is an artist. His watercolor paintings are hanging in some of the most prestigious galleries and museums in the world. To say he knows a lot of people is an understatement. The man has connections that I can't even begin to fathom. "He knows everyone, Zoe."

She laughs so heartily that a small splash of the dark, rich liquid in her cup spills onto her lap. I reach quickly into my purse to pull out a tissue.

"Thanks, Van." She glides it along her dress, carefully pulling up as much of the cocoa as she can. "I'm so clumsy now that I'm pregnant."

"I think you're perfect." I reach to rest my hand on the top of her belly. "Clumsy or not, you're the best friend I've ever had."

"I always will be." She cups her hand over mine. "Let us help you, Van. Let us help you find your mom."

***

After Ben and Kayla had stopped by the center, I took Zoe up on her offer of a ride home. We used to take the subway from the extended care center in Brooklyn into Manhattan together, but now that she's pregnant, a driver is always waiting out front for her and when she insists I join her in the car, I'm quick to accept. The ride is more comfortable, less crowded and it gives me and my best friend an extra chance to talk before we have to say goodbye.

"You're sure you don't want us to wait to take you home?" Zoe dips her head a touch so she can see me standing outside the open back door of the car. I had quickly slid across the seat after hugging her goodbye once we stopped in front of the hospital.

I'm tempted to say yes to escape the walk to my apartment in the chilly spring air, but I want her to get home. "I just need to grab my tablet from my locker and then I'll call you once I'm home."

"Promise?" She cocks a dark brow. "I worry about you when you walk alone."

She shouldn't. I've never felt unsafe in Manhattan although my adventures are generally confined to a twenty-block radius around the hospital. I live only a few blocks from work with two other nurses. It's a sublet that affords all of us the chance to live in one of the most vibrant cities in the world, while still saving for a rainy day. "I'll be fine."

I spin on my heel and stare at the front of the hospital. This is my dream. This is what I've worked for my entire adult life, and yet, each and every time I walk through the front doors I question the irony of my ability to help people get well every day, while at the same time, my mother is slowing slipping away from me and there's absolutely nothing I can do to save her.

FOUR

"I come in peace." A deep smooth voice resonates from behind me.

I don't turn. I'm standing next to a crowded nurses' station in the ER. There are at least six of my co-workers within a few feet of me. If one of the doctors needs help, I'm going to sit this one out. I've been on my feet for close to ten hours and I'm counting the minutes until I can finally go home to soak in a warm tub.

"Vanessa." There's a rasp in the tone that's oddly familiar. It can't be a doctor. I don't work with anyone who has a voice that sounds like that. Please don't let it be one of the three men I've slept with in the past year. I dated two briefly and the third disappeared into an excuse about having a sick friend. He may have been good in bed, but I don't look back once I've said goodbye.

A faint tap on my shoulder is enough to turn me around. There's the hint of a smile on his lips as I soak in his features. He's incredibly good-looking. His dark hair slicked back from his face, which is chiseled and clean-shaven. His green eyes are keen and intense. He's tall. I'm suddenly aware that the sneakers I wear to work aren't doing me any favors. I feel miniscule. He towers above me. He has to be at least six foot two and judging by the way the black dress shirt and matching pants he's wearing are clinging to him, he's muscular, toned and more than likely well hung.

Wait. No. It can't be.

"Do you remember me?" he asks with a low growl. "We met last week."

My lips are so dry that I have to run my tongue over them, twice. It does little to help. "Yes. I remember you. You're Garrett Ryan."

"I brought these for you."

There's a flash of color in front of me and a chorus of gleeful squeals from some of the other nurses as they catch sight of the large bouquet of flowers he must have been holding behind his back when I was checking him out.

I reach for the flowers and his fingers brush against mine. A burst of energy flows between us. It's not electric or dynamic. It's more restrained, but intense. He holds my gaze as I inhale the lavish scent of the flowers.

"I can't accept these," I lie not because I don't welcome the gift, but because with it comes with the promise of a favor in return. I see that within his gaze and the way his tongue darts out over his bottom lip.

"Yes, you can, "Rosalie, my supervisor, pops into view. "These are beautiful, Vanessa. Your boyfriend has excellent taste."

"No," I whisper through a scowl. "He's not my boyfriend. I don't even know him."

"I'm a grateful man." He rests his hand on Rosalie's shoulder and I watch the heave of her chest at his touch. "Nurse Meyer took extra good care of me last week."

"She's a wonderful nurse," Rosalie says. "We're so lucky to have her."

"You're very lucky to have her," he continues with a nod. "I'd like a few minutes alone with her if you can spare her."

"I have to get back to the patient in exam room five," I wave the flowers in the air before I shove them into his firm chest. "You should take these back. I don't need flowers. I was doing my job."

"They're yours to keep." He raises his hand to gently push them back at me. "I just need five minutes, Vanessa. I promise I won't take any longer than that."

The breath I draw in is so heavy that it's audible. "I can spare five minutes."

"You lead the way." His hand jumps to my elbow as he falls in step beside me.

***

"I don't remember everything that happened last week." He leans back against the wall in the private waiting area I've taken him to. "I spoke to Ben about it this morning."

I cross my ankles as I sit on the edge of a chair. "What did he say?"

"He said I was out of it." His left hand jumps to his right bicep. "Apparently my blood sugar was low. I just remember being in a lot of pain."

"You hurt yourself when you hit the tree." I glance at my watch.

"I still have three minutes." He dips his chin towards me. "That's just enough time to apologize."

"You don't need to." I bounce to my feet, smoothing my hands over the wrinkled legs of the blue scrubs I'm required to wear since I work in the emergency room. "You don't owe me anything. I was just doing my job."

"I'm worried that I said things I shouldn't have. I wasn't thinking clearly."

The cultured tone of his voice doesn't match the frenzied cries of the man who was in here last week, clinging to the edge of the exam table because of the pain he was. "You were in shock."

"If I was a jerk and I'd like to make it up to you." He taps his shoe on the tiled floor. "Can I buy you a coffee sometime?"

I'm wise enough to know when a man is wearing a hidden cloak of future regret around him. I've always based my decisions to meet men for coffee, or drinks, or even just sex on first impressions. He may have cleaned up remarkably well in every sense of the word, but the man standing before me, who is dressed impeccably and looks like he'd fuck me into tomorrow, is still the same jerk who I met last week.

"I don't think so." I move towards the waiting room door.

"You don't want to give it some thought?"

"I don't need to." I glance briefly at the plain gray, fabric colored chair where I left the flowers. "I appreciate the apology, but I'll pass on the coffee."

His full lips part slightly as he exhales loudly. "You forgot your flowers, Vanessa."

I narrow my gaze at him, noticing how completely in control he looks at this moment. It's the polar opposite of who I imagined him to be. "You should take them up to the nurse's station on the third floor. They took much better care of you than I did."

"I'd beg to differ." He walks across the room with confidence, scooping the flowers into his hand.

"You were only in my care for an hour." I swallow hard when he stands directly in front of me. "They took care of you the entire night."

"They may have watched over me through the night," he stops talking to lean down so his forehead is hovering close to mine. "But you're the only one I remember."

I inhale the luxurious scent of his skin combined with expensive cologne. He knows what he's doing to me. There's no way in hell that he's oblivious to the sheen of moisture on my lips or my labored breathing. I can't do this. I need to remember what a total ass he was when the paramedics brought him in. A bump on the head and hypoglycemia can't completely alter a man's personality, can it?

"I have to get back to work." I turn towards the door before looking back over my shoulder to catch him staring directly at my ass.

FIVE

"I went onto a few of the adoption reconnection forums that I was telling you about, but there wasn't anything." I scratch the top of my nose. "I think that is a sign that I shouldn't search for my birth mother."

"A sign?" Zoe pulls her fork through the salad she's been picking at for the past fifteen minutes. "It's a sign that you're wasting time doing that. We need to take a road trip to Maine."

I knew she'd say that. I thought it too. When I'd logged into the forum for Maine adoptees and birth parents, I had a sinking feeling that I'd turn up nothing. I based that prediction on experience. I've been on the forums on and off for months, and although a host of new members always pop up, I've never found a match for my birth date. The reassurance that I'd feel knowing that at least one of my birth parents is looking for me isn't going to come. I'm beginning to realize that now.

"I think I'll put the idea to rest until…" my voice trails. I can't bring myself to say the words even though the thought that fuels them runs through my mind every single day. My mother is seventy-five-years-old. If she were healthy, I'd be counting on having years with her yet. I'd feel safe in the knowledge that she'd be at my wedding, and be standing by my side when I gave birth to my first child. I'm schooled enough in medicine to know that her time is limited, and that it will be a miracle if I'm able to celebrate with her on her eightieth birthday. I'm going to lose her and the thought terrifies me to my core.

"Don't think about that, Van." Zoe reaches across the table to pull my hand into hers. "Think about all the fun the two of you had when you were growing up."

It's a notion that I should embrace. I try to and want to but the sad and tragic reality is that I miss the moments when I could talk to my mom about everyday things like a new dress I bought or the flower garden that she used to lovingly nurture in front of our apartment building in Maine every spring and summer. Those are lost memories now.

"I miss her," I say softly. "I don't want to disappoint her."

"You can't." Her head tilts to the side as her eyes hone in on mine. "You have a right to know your birth mother. You told me it's been nagging at you for years. You need to do this for you."

She's right. I've been volleying the idea of knowing versus not knowing around for a long time. My desire to know more about my birth parents was first ignited when I was in nursing school and one of my classmates had gotten ill. It was a genetic condition and the simple fact that I didn't have an understanding of my predisposition to medical issues worried me. It's much more than that though. I want to look into the face of the woman who gave me life.

"What if I find out who my birth mother is and she wants nothing to do with me?" The question is painful to ask.

She tugs on my hand to get me to look at her. "This will eat at you until you find out. You have to do it. You'll never know how she'll react until you find out who she is and you contact her."

"You're right," I agree. "I need to find the courage to go to Maine. I have to. It's time."

***

"It's time to party."

I disagree. It's time to sleep. The problem is that today is Rosalie's birthday and virtually everyone who works in the emergency department, who isn't on duty right now, is in this bar. It's more a pub, actually. It's Easton Pub and I've been here more times than I can count. That's because Zoe used to work here and she met her husband here. When she feels like taking a sentimental walk into her memories, we come here. She orders a club soda with lemon and I order the same thing I'm drinking tonight, a Tom Collins. It might not be what you'd expect a petite blonde nurse to drink but when I drink, I don't want to waste the effort. It always gives me a slight buzz, and I'm not going to shy away from that tonight. I don't work tomorrow which means I'm only responsible for myself for the next thirty-six hours.

I scan the room looking for a familiar face. I want someone who isn't going to engage me in a lengthy discussion about a patient's prognosis. I get enough of that when I'm rushing between exam rooms during the twelve-hour shifts I pull. Tonight, I'm just Vanessa. I'm not Nurse Meyer and I want to keep it that way.

"Nurse Meyer," Rosalie slurs the words just as she embraces me from behind. "Let's toast to me."

I turn towards her and raise my glass in celebration of her special day. I would have brought a gift if she hadn't insisted that we don't mention the fact that it's her birthday. She actually called it a non-birthday party because she's not ready to age another year. She's beautiful and brilliant and by my best estimate, can't be more than fifty-years-old. Judging by the killer set of legs that she's sporting under the short black cocktail dress she's wearing, the woman is not only young in spirit, she's in great shape.

"You're so pretty, Vanessa." She pulls on the bottom of my hair. "You look so different when your hair is down like this."

I smile at the compliment. I doubt that she's ever seen me with anything other than a high bun on the top of my head or a ponytail. It's not only hospital protocol to have your hair pulled back, but it's my preference. I don't waste a lot of time fussing with how I look but tonight I took the time to straighten my hair and put on make-up. I needed a night out.

"You have the next two days off, don't you?" She races her hand up my exposed arm until it reaches my shoulder. She adjusts the strap of my white bra so it's hidden beneath the grey, textured lace tank top I chose to wear with black jeans. "What are you going to do?"

I'm going to get on an airplane and go to Maine, all alone. I haven't told Zoe because I know that she'd insist on going with me. Her presence would definitely add a comfort I'm likely going to need, but at the same time, the solitude will give me a chance to absorb the names of my parents.

The server walks by and Rosalie clings to her arm as she orders us both another drink, even though I've barely touched mine. I don't want to be rude, but hanging out for more than a couple of hours isn't in my plan. I want to get home and crawl into bed so I can try and chase a few hours of sleep before I jump on the bus that will take me to La Guardia airport.

20

"You invited him?" Her hand flies into the air. "I thought you said he wasn't your boyfriend."

I turn towards the entrance of the pub just in time to see Garrett Ryan embracing a beautiful brunette.

SIX

"Did you follow me here?"

I should be asking him that question, but he's beaten me to the punch. I lost sight of him soon after he arrived at the pub. I turned completely around hopeful that he wouldn't spot me in the growing crowd. I thought I could finish my drink, visit with a few co-workers and be out the door before he even spotted me. Now, he's whispering in my ear.

"Why would I do that?" I take in a quick, short breath as I pivot on my heels to face him.

"What are the chances that you'd show up at my neighborhood pub?" He motions towards the bar with his chin. "Manhattan's a big place. You could have gone drinking anywhere."

He wears arrogance with the same confidence that he wears the clothes on his back. He has to know that virtually every single woman in this pub, and likely most of the not-so-single ones, are checking him out. A quick glance to my left confirms my suspicion when I catch Rosalie giving him the once over.

"I'm here to celebrate a co-worker's birthday." I shoot back, wanting to justify my presence, even though there's absolutely no need for it.

"A birthday?" He taps his hand on the bar. "This calls for a drink. What are you having?"

I hold up my empty glass. "I was drinking a Tom Collins, but I'm afraid two is my limit."

"A woman with limits?" He rakes his eyes over my body. "That's a shame."

The hidden innuendo within the words isn't lost on me. "Your loss."

"I wouldn't say that." He raises his hand, motioning towards the bartender. "I owe you for what happened at the hospital. Let me buy you a drink and we'll call it even."

I look around the room before speaking. "You're not going to drop this grateful act, are you?"

"It's not an act." He gracefully lowers himself onto the bar stool next to me. "I make it a point to repay my debts. I owe you so I want to show my appreciation."

"You don't owe me anything, "I counter. "I told you I was doing my job."

"That's not the debt I'm referring to." He grabs the edge of a cocktail napkin sitting on the bar. "I think I offended you. I want to make that up to you, Vanessa."

I could give him a free pass and tell him that there are no hard feelings. It would be the truth. I don't know the man and how he acts when his blood sugar is plummeting is no concern of mine. If anything, I got to be witness to one of the most exciting emergency room visits I'll probably ever see. He's not the first man to comment on my body, and he won't be the last. I'm hardly the only nurse who has heard her fair share of sexually charged comments. It's par for the course.

"I forgive you." I pull my hands to my chest. "We're even now, okay?"

His eyes settle on where my hands are clasped together. "No. It's not okay."

"It really is." I reach to scoop my silver clutch up from where I rested it on the bar earlier. "You said some things you regret, and I forgive you."

He turns towards the bartender and orders a whiskey sour. I breathe a sigh of relief when he doesn't assume that I'm joining him.

"Can I ask you a question, Vanessa?" He looks at me carefully. "Just one question and then I'll leave you alone for the night."

I lean against the bar, dangling my clutch in my hand. "What's the question?"

"Tell me exactly what I said to you. Give it to me straight from the hip." His eyes settle on my right hip, which is jutting out.

He has to be shitting me. This must be part of some twisted game he plays to assuage his own guilt over being an arrogant, chauvinistic asshole. I doubt like hell that he doesn't remember every single word he said to me last week in the ER.

I take in a deep breath before I blow it out slowly. I like a challenge. I never back down from one and right now, I want desperately to have the upper hand in this even though I know he still has the power to get me fired. "You know what you said, Garrett."

"I don't." His voice is deep and low. "I remember bits and pieces of that morning but everything is hazy."

"Do you remember anything I said to you?" I grab the side of the bar for added balance.

"I vaguely remember the word '*asshole*' coming out of those lips."

I feel my back bristle. He's a lawyer. He's schooled in how to lead people down a path towards their own demise. If I confirm what he just said, I'm essentially guaranteeing myself a spot in the unemployment line.

"Vanessa." His index finger brushes fleetingly against my chin. "If you called me an asshole, I'd like to know why."

I glance briefly to where Rosalie is now pressed up against a man who just started working in the hospital pharmacy. If Garrett tells her what I said, there may be a flash of compassion within her, but she's as straight laced as they come. Rosalie is a by-the-book employee and she'd see to it that I was reprimanded.

"Ben told me you're the best nurse in the ER." His posture softens. "I agree with him. I would never do anything to jeopardize that."

I blink before I look directly into his eyes. "You wouldn't?"

"If you called me an asshole, Vanessa, there was a reason. Tell me why."

I shouldn't answer, but instead I lean forward so my face is hovering close to his. "You said something about my body."

He moves forward on the barstool. "What did I say?"

My eyes dart from his lips to his eyes. "You said I have the best looking ass you've ever seen."

I don't flinch when I feel both his hands jump to my hips. "I said that to you?"

I nod slowly knowing I should pull back and break free.

"You do," he whispers into the heated air between us. "I haven't stopped thinking about it or you since that day."

SEVEN

I wanted to kiss him and I don't know why. Wait. That's not entirely true. I wanted to kiss him because his lips were so close to mine and his hands were resting on my hips. His breath was sweet and intoxicating and the firmness of his thighs pressing against the outside of my own legs made me feel weak.

I'd pulled free the moment Carla came over to the bar. When I'd left our apartment to come to the party, she'd had her head buried in a book. I'd tried to coax her into dressing up so we could have a fun night together, but she wanted no part of it. I'm not sure if I was more shocked to see her standing next to Garrett wearing one of my little black dresses, or if the way she was pressing her tits into his shoulder was more jarring. Either way, the moment his eyes left me for her, I'd excused myself and made a break for the ladies' room.

I scrub my hands over my face when I hear the door to the bathroom opening. I slide my fingers apart to glance in the mirror at Carla's reflection staring back at me.

"You look better in that dress than I do," I offer with a smile. "You should keep it."

"I might." She rests her hands on my shoulders. "I couldn't find anything to wear. You don't mind, do you?"

I don't. I like the fact that she feels comfortable enough to go through my closet. I've taken care of my mother for so many years, that most of the friendships I did have when I was younger have drifted into the ether. I'm not as close to Carla as I am to Zoe, but we're comfortable and building a bond every day.

"He's looking for you." She gestures towards the door with her chin. "What's that about?"

If I had a reply to that question I might be tempted to answer it, but I'm not about to. Garrett Ryan is everything I don't need in my life right now. The man exudes intensity and if I'm going to jump into anything with any man it needs to be uncomplicated.

"We were talking about when he was in the ER."

"No you weren't." She pulls playfully on a few strands of my hair. "I know what I saw."

I know what I felt and I don't want to give it any merit. "You saw the two of us talking about what happened in the ER."

"No." She twists me around quickly by the shoulders. "I saw two people who were about to go at it on the bar."

"That's not going to happen. He's not my type."

"Not your type?" Her hands fall to her sides. "That man is every woman's type. Seriously, Vanessa? Who wouldn't want to be fucked by that?"

"Me," I try to say convincingly. "He's an arrogant lawyer, Carla. He uses women. I'm not into that."

"What he does for a living isn't relevant." She waves her hands in the air. "Who the hell cares if he uses you for sex?"

"I care," I point out.

"You're looking at this all wrong." Her voice softens. "You could be using him right now. You fuck him, you thank him and you walk away."

"It's never that easy. I guarantee you that Garrett Ryan is more complicated than that."

"You'll never know unless you try." She brushes past me to look at herself in the mirror. "I just know what I saw when I walked in the pub. The man wants you and you want him whether you want to admit it or not."

***

"You want me to, don't you?" He eyes me. "I'm a lawyer. You can trust me."

I shove my hand against his strong shoulder. "I told you that I can take a taxi from here. I know my way around the city."

His chest heaves with a sigh. "Vanessa, it's late. I'd feel better knowing that you got to your apartment safe and sound."

This gallant act is endearing, if not over-the-top. I'd tried to slide past his gaze when I left the ladies' room. I was hopeful that he would have set his sights on someone new by then, but he spotted me in an instant and before I had one foot out of the door of the pub, he was right behind him.

"I will get there safe and sound." I inch towards the street. "I've been taking taxis in this city for years. I'll be fine."

"Indulge me." His voice is thick and heavy. "I'll get in the taxi with you. I'll watch you walk to your building and I'll be on my way."

"There's no need." I wave my hand in the air at two approaching cabs. They both fly by without slowing at all. "I can handle it. You should stay here. The night is young."

"I'm on my way home too." He glances at his smartphone screen. "I have a full day in court tomorrow."

"What kind of lawyer are you?" I ask out of curiosity. I don't know the intricacies of the legal system but I do know that it takes a certain type of man to take on that role. "I'm just wondering."

"I'm a probate attorney." He dips his hands into the front pockets of his grey pants. "I handle estate law."

I arch a brow. "That's not what I thought."

"What did you think?" He leans slightly forward.

"I'm not sure," I answer honestly. "I hadn't given it that much thought."

"You can come by the courthouse tomorrow and see me in action." He licks his bottom lip. "I'll be on my best behavior for you."

"I can't." I glance at the street again, wishing a taxi would magically appear. "I'm going to Maine tomorrow."

"Maine?" His mouth curves into a smile. "What's in Maine?"

I heave a sigh of relief as a taxi rounds the corner and stops in front of the pub. I dart to the street just as a man and a woman slide out of the back seat. "Answers," I call back to Garrett as I duck inside the car. "Maine has all the answers I need."

EIGHT

"Can you repeat that?" I lean forward so my elbows are resting on the desk. The motion isn't just so I can get closer to her; it's also for stability. I can't believe what she just said to me.

"I'm sorry, Ms. Meyer." She pulls her glasses to the tip of her nose as she looks at the screen of her laptop. "We don't have a record of your birth in our system."

I scratch the back of my head. "Can you check again? Just this one last time, please?"

Turning her head quickly, she types something into the keyboard of her laptop before she lowers her glasses and sets them on the desk in front of her. "There wasn't a child adopted who was born the same day as you. In fact, there wasn't a baby girl born within a week of you who was placed up for adoption. Just two boys."

"My mother told me that she was at the hospital when I was born." I drum my fingers on her desk. "She talked about the nurses and how they handed me to her right after I was born."

"Perhaps she was mistaken about the state?"

It's a ludicrous question meant to placate me. "I was born and raised in Maine. There's no question about that."

"The only thing I can suggest is that you speak to your mother and tell her what I've told you." She opens the top drawer of her desk to pull out a small, white rectangular card. "This is my number. I handle all the records. Ask your mother to call me if she has any questions."

I want to tell her that the card will never reach my mother's hands. The woman is stuck in a prison of her own mind. If she were lucid, I'd be on the phone to her right now, asking what's going on. "My mother isn't available," I say to avoid the pity that is expected after I tell a person that my mother is ill. "Do you have any suggestions for my next step?"

"Does your mother have family?"

"I have an aunt," I tell her. "She lives here in Augusta."

"Talk to her." She closes her desk drawer with a thud. "Sometimes people are holding onto details they don't even realize are relevant."

***

"Your aunt stuck to the same story your mother gave you?" Zoe holds a paint sample card up to the wall. We're in the nursery that has yet to be transformed. Right now it's a blank canvas.

"Are you going with that shade of blue?" I nod towards the light blue card in her hand.

"I don't want to." She lets it drop from her fingers down to the hardwood floor. "I want Beck to paint this room. I want every inch of the walls to be colored with watercolors."

It's a beautiful idea. "I think that's amazing. It's really special, Zoe."

"It would be if I could tear him away from his studio to do it." I can hear the exasperation in her voice. "I'm worried that we'll run out of time to decorate and the baby will have to sleep in this plain room."

I'm not a baby, but I'd welcome the chance to sleep in this room. It's larger than any bedroom I've ever had and it has floor-to-ceiling windows with a view of Central Park. "The baby will love the room regardless of what it looks like."

"You're right." She bends down to pick up the sample card, cradling her hand under her belly. "Let's talk about your aunt."

"Technically she's not my aunt," I correct her cautiously. "She lived in the apartment next to ours when I was growing up and I called her Aunt Nora."

"She knew your mom before you were born though, right?" She twirls her finger around a red ribbon hanging from the front of her maternity top. "She would have been around during the adoption?"

"I can't remember a time when she wasn't part of our family," I hesitate because since my mother has digressed into the Alzheimer's, Nora has stopped coming to Brooklyn to visit her. "She was always around when I was growing up."

"What did she say when you asked about the adoption?"

It should be a cut and dry answer, but it's not. When I'd stopped by Aunt Nora's apartment yesterday to ask about my adoption, she'd become uncomfortable quickly. She went from welcoming me with open arms into her kitchen to telling me that she had an appointment with her hair stylist.

"Did she know why there's no record of it?"

I half-shrug my shoulder. "She said that she can't remember all the small details but she remembers what a beautiful baby I was."

Zoe sighs softly as she leans back in the rocking chair she's sitting in. I take in the sight of her, so peaceful and content with what life is about to offer her. She's going to be a mother soon. I'm going to watch her holding her beautiful, newborn son in her arms. I already know that it's going to be a poignant moment for me.

"I'm not sure what my next step should be." I squeeze my hands together. I've been thinking about it since I boarded my flight back to New York this morning. It's not just that I feel as though I've hit an impasse. It's much more than that. I never questioned the scattered and disjointed facts about my adoption that my mother did share with me. I always imagined that her impatience and reluctance to talk about my birth parents was based on her need to hold me close to her. Now, after visiting Maine and learning that my adoption records don't exist, I feel more lost than I ever have before.

"Maybe you need to talk to a lawyer," she suggests. "You don't happen to know one, do you?"

NINE

"I can't tell you how glad I am that you called me, Vanessa." His eyes blaze across the table at me. "I've been hoping to get that call for months."

I've been hoping to avoid the call for months. I had two choices when I realized that I needed to follow Zoe's advice and consult a lawyer about my adoption. I could confide in Garrett, but going to him with something so personal feels illogical given the fact that I don't even know him, or I could meet with Curtis, an entertainment lawyer I had sex with once when I was lonely and I was enamored with reruns of a courtroom drama. I realized in the middle of his missionary, jack hammering, fucking technique that not everything they say on television about lawyers is true.

"I'm glad you could meet me on such short notice." I pull a smile out of somewhere.

"I'd drop everything to help you." He reaches across the table to yank my hand into his. "I hope you know that."

I know that hand sweat is an actual thing. Curtis is the poster boy for it. I'm going to need to retreat to the ladies' room to scrub my hands clean before I dive into the sandwich I ordered for lunch. "You're very kind," I offer back because I need to.

I don't have room in my budget for a consultation fee with an attorney. I do have an appetite for lunch and an endless supply of forced smiles. If I can get Curtis to spell out for me what I need to do to find my birth parents, I can conveniently misplace his number again. I don't like using men, but Curtis owes me. At the very least, he owes me an orgasm or two so if I can cash that in for legal advice, I'm all for it.

"You said on the phone that you needed some advice?" He picks up the linen napkin next to his place setting and snaps it in the air. It narrowly misses my nose.

"It's about my adoption," I say tightly. "You remember that I told you I was adopted, right?"

"I remember that." He glances at me with a wide smile. "I remember that and a lot more about you."

The extra emphasis on the word '*you*' is duly noted by my brain and my body. "I need some advice about that."

"About you?" He sits up straighter in his chair. "My advice would be to start dating me again."

That's advice I'll never take. I've learned, through much trial and error, that when a relationship isn't working, I can't pretend it is. Curtis and I dated for a few weeks and had sex once. I knew it was headed nowhere so I ended it as politely as I could. He took it well and surprisingly, when I called him yesterday to ask if we could meet for lunch, he excitedly suggested this restaurant close to his office.

"Can we talk about the adoption, first?" I ask sweetly, knowing full well that there isn't going to be time to discuss anything beyond that. He made it clear, when we spoke on the phone, that he has exactly sixty minutes to spend with me. I'm counting on that because, right now, I realize it's all I can handle in one sitting.

"What about it?" His blonde brows dart up.

"I thought I was adopted in Maine." I trace a path along the edge of the table with my finger. "I went there to access my adoption records and there was nothing."

"Nothing?" He bites on the edge of a piece of bread. "What do you mean nothing?"

"The woman I met with at the registry office couldn't find any record of my birth." I fidget in my seat. "I don't think I was adopted there."

He assesses me across the table. "I remember you telling me that your mother picked you up from the hospital in Augusta the day you were born."

I don't need the reminder. My mother had said that, repeatedly, when I'd asked about my adoption. "She told me that."

He leans back as the waiter approaches with our food. "That's tough, Vanessa. I don't know what to tell you from a legal standpoint."

I was fearful of that. I'm not even sure why I arranged this meeting. "I was hoping there was something I could do."

"I know you can't ask your mother," he begins before he shoves a forkful of salad into his mouth and chews it quickly. "If I was you I'd start with looking for any records she kept from that time. People her age usually have a safety deposit box. Sometimes they a shoe box under their bed with all their important documents."

My lips purse together. "I hadn't thought of that. I'll see what I can find."

"I hope you find something." He digs into his meal. "It must feel like shit not knowing where you came from."

TEN

"I thought about talking to Beck about what's going on with you." Zoe leans forward on the stool she's sitting on. "I'm not sure you want me to do that though."

I don't. I'd taken the advice Curtis gave to me literally. The problem was that without a power of attorney in place, the bank wouldn't give me access to my mother's safety deposit box. The bank manager wouldn't budge even when I explained the situation to her.

I hadn't planned enough when my mother started to go downhill. I assumed there would be time or she'd find her way back to lucidity. I know she has a simple will in place, but that doesn't grant me any of the rights I need now to start searching for the answers to the questions about my adoption.

"The legal system is bizarre." I take a sip of the glass of house red wine I'd ordered when I met Zoe at Easton Pub. "I can access everything that belongs to my mother once she's gone but for now, I'm stuck in legal limbo."

"Legal limbo?" His voice wafts over my shoulder just as I catch of the startled look on Zoe's face. "I'm an expert at legal limbo."

I knew when Zoe invited me to the pub tonight that the chances of Garrett walking in were slim to none. He may live nearby but the fact that I hadn't ever seen him in here before the other night offered a comforting reassurance that he doesn't stop in for a drink that often.

"Zoe?" His hand brushes past my shoulder as he reaches out to her.

"Garrett." She takes his hand in hers. "I know you."

"I know you too," he says as I catch my first glimpse of him when he walks into my peripheral vision. "You used to work here."

"You used to drink here." She taps her hand on the table. "Right here actually. Wasn't this your favorite table?"

"It was because it was in your section." He motions towards the empty stool between us. "May I?"

"Please, yes," she says too excitedly. "Van, this was my best customer."

No, he was not. The world can't be this small. My best friend can't know Garrett Ryan.

"This was my favorite server." He studies Zoe carefully. "You're pregnant?"

"Pregnant and married." Her left hand proudly jumps into the air. "I married the man of my dreams and we're having a baby boy."

"Christ." He leans forward on his stool and brushes his lips over her cheek. "That's the best news I've heard in a long time, Zoe. No one deserves that more than you."

I finish the rest of the wine in my glass. "I need another drink."

"More wine?" He waves his hand towards the server.

"No. Get me a Tom Collins."

***

"You need legal advice and I'm a lawyer." He pushes both his hands against the edge of the small table. "I'll even waive my retainer for you, Vanessa."

It's a tempting offer. He's a probate attorney. He'd likely know better than anyone what I can do to gain access to my mother's safety deposit box but with his help comes an expectation. It won't be free. I already know that.

"One of my friends is a lawyer." I look down at my half-empty glass. "I'll just ask him."

"What kind of law does he practice?"

"He works in entertainment," I blurt out without hesitation.

"That's not going to work." He takes another swallow from the beer bottle in his hand. "He won't know shit about this."

"You don't know shit about it either," I counter with a smile. "All you know is what you overheard me saying to Zoe."

"I heard something about your mother and legal limbo." He tips the bottle towards me. "That adds up to a probate issue so I'm your guy."

I know I should end this conversation before it takes another step forward but I made a promise to Zoe on the street in front of the pub an hour ago when she left. I told her I'd ask him what I could do to get power of attorney.

"My mother is ill." I stop to look directly at him. "She has Alzheimer's."

"Shit." His hand slides across the table to cover mine. "That's rough. I'm sorry to hear that."

There's sincerity woven into the words so I continue. "I didn't think about legalities when she first became ill and now that her condition has worsened, I'm not sure what I can do."

"You don't have a power of attorney in place?"

"No," I shake my head lightly. "We didn't set that up."

"Does she have a living will?"

"Just a will." I heave a sigh. "It's a standard will she drew up years ago."

He scrubs his hand over his forehead. "Is she aware at all at this point? Would she be able to read and understand a legal document?"

She can't understand anything. "No. She wouldn't be able to do that."

"I'd need to look at her will to see if there's anything that can be done to give you more control over her assets. We might be able to set you up as a conservator." He pulls his smartphone from his pocket before his thumb slides across the screen. "Let me check my schedule to see when you can come into the office."

"I have the will at my apartment." I lean forward on the stool to glance at his phone. "I can stop by after work one day."

"Can you show it to me now?" He stands quickly. "I can give you my opinion tonight so you won't have to wait."

I hesitate only briefly before I slide to my feet and turn to face him. "Let's go. We can be there in ten minutes."

ELEVEN

"You're an only child?" He looks up from where he's sitting on the edge of my bed. "Your mother never married?"

Diving into the details of my mysterious adoption, at this point, seems like it will only complicate this already complex legal puzzle I'm in. "It was always just the two of us."

His gaze falls back down to the will. "It's very straightforward. Your mother's intentions are clear. You'll inherit everything once she…"

"Yes, I assumed that much," I interrupt, wanting to not only save myself from hearing the word, but also from having him feel obligated to point out something that is already so glaringly obvious. "Is there anything I can do now to gain access to her safety deposit box?"

"Is there something of importance in her safety deposit box?" His eyes scan my face. "Do you need to retrieve something from it for her now?"

The question only reminds me of how horrified my mother would be if she knew that I'm searching through her things. She's always been very private and growing up, I was never allowed access to her dresser drawers. I was scolded more than once for stepping foot into her bedroom without her there. Looking back now, knowing that the details of my adoption aren't as straightforward as I thought, I can't help but wonder what secrets she was keeping from me.

"I'm just trying to organize her things and I know she kept important documents in there," I lie as I shuffle nervously on my feet. "She may have left a note in there about what she wanted if she got sick."

I can see the trust in my words when I look in his eyes. "You need to gain access to that box. I think I can help you do that."

"Seriously?" I move forward without thinking. "You really think you can do that?"

"I haven't told you this yet." He rests the will on my bed before he rises to his feet. "I'm the best probate attorney in the state."

I smile at how arrogant the statement is. "You believe you're the best probate attorney in the state."

"No." He leans forward so his lips are close to mine. "Google it, Vanessa. I'm the best. There's no question."

I feel the familiar rush of heat run through me when he's this close to me. I twist my hands into the hem of the sleeveless black sweater I'm wearing. "Thank you for helping me with this, Garrett."

"Vanessa." His finger catches my chin. "I'll get you what you need."

I don't move as his lips brush softly across my forehead before he scoops the will back into his hand and walks straight out my bedroom door.

***

"With the signed affidavit I got from Ben and your written plea, the judge didn't see any reason to refuse my request." He adjusts his suit jacket. "I told you I'd get you anything you need."

I look down at my blue scrubs. I didn't have a chance to change before Garrett texted me telling me to meet him at the bank. It's only been four days since he took the will but now, we're standing in the bank manager's office waiting for her to take me to the vault.

"You look so nervous." He playfully pulls on my ponytail. "This is a step in the right direction."

He can't know the gravity of his words. Our correspondence the last few days has been completely focused on my mother and the safety deposit box. I was grateful when he told me that Ben wanted to help.

"Ms. Meyer." The bank manager breezes through the door, her eyes trained on Garrett. "Mr. Ryan, is it?"

"Garrett," he corrects her as he reaches for her hand. "You received the package I had delivered earlier, yes?"

"Yes." She nods a little too exuberantly. "We're more than happy to give Ms. Meyer the access she needs. We're here to help her."

Bullshit. The woman couldn't be more insincere if she tried. What is it about lawyers that makes people cave instantly?

"If you two will follow me, I'll take you back to the vault now."

"I have to run." Garrett's hand jumps to my back. "I have a meeting in twenty minutes at my office."

I feel an instant pit in the bottom of my stomach. I didn't want to do this alone and although Garrett wouldn't have been my first choice, he would be offering a sense of balance that I've been missing since I went to Maine.

"You can't stay?" I look up at him. "I thought you were going to stay."

"I'm sorry." His hand slides to my exposed neck. "I can cancel my meeting. If you need me to be here I can do that."

"No." I trace a path over my bottom lip with my fingers. "I can do this. I'll be fine."

"You're sure?" He leans down so his lips feather over my ear. "I'd cancel everything if you told me you needed me."

I know they're the words of someone just wanting to help. I saw the pity in his eyes when I first told him about my mother's condition and I know it's there now too.

"Please go." I tap him lightly on his chest. "I want you to go."

I feel his chin brush against the top of my head as he nods. "I'm only a phone call away."

The distance feels insurmountable the moment he turns to walk away but I don't stop him. I can't. I have to find out what my mother has been hiding from me all by myself.

TWELVE

I knew when I called in sick today that unless I spoke to Ben, I'd be subjected to countless questions. I've never missed a day of work. I love being at the hospital. The energy there fuels me in a way nothing else does but today, right now, all I want is silence.

The moment I came home from the bank last night, I'd hidden in my room with a purse full of my mother's things. I'd emptied the safety deposit box quickly, not wanting to sit in the sterile space to relive my mother's life.

I'd held tight to my bag on the subway ride back to my building before I explained to Carla that I had a headache and only needed the solace that my bed could offer. I'd seen the look of doubt on her face, but she didn't argue. She'd gone out for Italian food alone and hadn't checked in on me when she came home.

I spent most of the night looking at the two pieces of jewelry that were kept in a small velvet bag in the box. There was a simple gold chain and a small bracelet made from colored rope. I'd cupped them in my palm and imagined my mother's face when she took them to the bank. Neither would hold any real value to anyone but her and it breaks my heart that I'll never understand their true significance.

I'd tucked them back into the bag before I closed my eyes, not wanting to focus on the old, weathered spiral notebook that was hidden beneath insurance documents and savings bonds at the bottom of the box.

I showered this morning, crying into the steam before I'd called Ben to tell him that I didn't feel well enough to cover my shift. He was understanding and compassionate. I know that he senses that there's something gnawing at me. I saw the concern in his eyes, yesterday, before I went to the bank.

The moment I opened the notebook and read the first page, I felt as though I was drowning within my own sorrow. I'd tucked the notebook into my purse and had gone to sit in Central Park, hoping that the joyous cries of children playing and the visions of mothers cradling their babies in their arms would wash away the blue inked confessions of my mother in that book.

Now, hours later, I'm sitting at a table, the notebook resting in my lap, as I stare into the street beyond the glass of the pub's windows.

"Vanessa?"

I almost audibly sigh when I hear his voice. It's what I craved all day. I could have called Zoe and let her read what I read. I could have called Carla to tell her to rush home after work but I hadn't. I'd come here with the hope that he'd sense my need.

"Garrett." I look up into his eyes. I see concern and confusion within them.

"Ben told me you called in sick." He lowers himself onto the stool next to me. "I went to your apartment, but your roommate said you were out."

I rub my index finger over the bridge of my nose. "I needed some air."

"How did it go yesterday?" He motions towards the server. "Do you want another drink?"

"No." I tap the bottom of the untouched glass of wine in front of me. "I'm fine."

"A beer," he says in a hushed tone to the woman who approaches our table. "Domestic. I'll have whatever is on tap."

I glance down at the notebook. I hadn't made it past the first few pages before I'd slammed the thin paper cover closed. "I found a key in the safety deposit box."

"An extra key to the box?" His eyes float to my lap. "What's that?"

I look down slowly, my fingers clinging tightly to the edge of the book. "It's nothing. It's just a notebook."

"Where's the key?" He nods as the waitress sets his glass of beer down on a paper napkin. "Can I see it?"

I reach to the table to pull my purse towards me. I fish within, searching for the cool metal of the key. "It's here."

He holds out his large palm and I place it carefully within it.

"This looks like it belongs to a storage locker." He turns it over twice before handing it back to me. "Does your mother have a storage locker?"

She has secrets. My mother has horribly painful secrets that she's kept hidden within her mind for years.

"I don't know," I answer honestly. "She might have had one."

"If she did, it's likely it was close to somewhere you two lived." He brings the bottle to his lips and swallows a large mouthful. "Most people rent a unit from the facility closest to their home."

"That would be in Maine," I begin. "Or it could be in Brooklyn. She lived there for a few years before I moved her to the place she lives now."

"She'd be paying a monthly or yearly fee for that unit." He gestures towards the key, which is still in my palm. "If you have access to her bank account or credit card statements, that might help you find it."

"That's helpful." I manage a small smile with the words. "I'll check on that tomorrow."

"I can do it for you," he offers with a tilt of his chin. "I'd like to help."

"You've already helped me more than you know, Garrett." I inch closer to him on my stool, my hand resting against the edge of the table for balance. "Thank you for that."

"I like you, Vanessa." He leans towards me his fingers brushing against my cheek. "Just tell me what you need, and I'll do it for you."

I don't respond. I part my lips only slightly as I watch him close his eyes before I feel his lush, moist lips slide over mine.

THIRTEEN

His lips are on my neck the moment the elevator doors close behind us in the lobby of his building. "Christ, Vanessa. I could come just from the taste of your lips."

I almost fell of my stool when I felt his hand on my thigh in the pub. He'd kissed me deeply, moaning into my mouth as he pulled me closer to him. I didn't resist. I couldn't. I wanted him in that moment, and now, that we're on our way up to his apartment, I want him even more.

The doors of the lift fly open when we reach the eighth floor. He kisses me briefly, his tongue darting over my bottom lip before he steps out into the corridor. "Come," he commands as he holds his hand out to me.

I take it silently following a quarter of a step behind him as he walks towards a door to the left. I watch as he pushes a key into the lock before he turns it and I sigh the moment I hear the door slam shut behind us.

"Jesus." He grumbles into the air. "I've wanted this for weeks. I feel like I'm going to blow my load already."

I smile at the thought. He's so imposing and in control. I felt the outline of his cock when he pressed himself into me as we stood on the street in front of the pub waiting for a cab. I saw the outline of it when he pulled me close to him on the short ride to his place. I want it. I want to feel it inside of me. I want him to pull every ounce of pleasure he can from within me to deafen everything else that I feel. All I want right now is his body, his lips and his obvious desire for me.

"I need to calm down." He scratches his finger along the side of his nose. "I feel like a teenager about to fuck for the first time."

I'm tempted to drop to my knees and blow him off right now. I've never been this greedy for a man's body before. I'm aware enough to realize that it's not just about the fact that he's gorgeous and kisses in a way that suggests he'll own my entire body by the end of the night. I know that part of my desperate need to crawl into bed with him is about the river of uncertainty that I'm floating in right now. I don't know who I am. I have no idea where I belong but I know that right now, for at least the next few hours, I'm going to belong to him.

"Can I have something to drink?" I ask breathlessly as I walk into the open concept space.

I feel him turn behind me, his hand brushing against the curve of my ass through my jeans. "I have some wine. I might have a beer."

"Water." I soak in the dark browns and neutral tones of his apartment. It's comfortable and suits him to a tee.

"I'll get you a bottle." He walks towards the kitchen as he slides his suit jacket from his shoulders, tossing it onto the back of a brown oversized sofa. "I need something stronger."

I take the bottle he offers and swallow half in one long, leisurely gulp. I feel his eyes glued to me. The beer bottle in his hand is dangling loosely between his index finger and thumb.

"Did you know I'd come looking for you at the pub?" he asks it without any real curiosity in his tone.

"Yes," I say calmly.

"Did you come there hoping we'd end up here?" His hand glides through the air. "Were you hoping I'd fuck you tonight?"

"Yes," I repeat as I talk a step closer to him. "That's what I want. I want you to fuck me tonight, just this one time."

His eyes rake slowly over my body. "You're aching for it now, aren't you?"

Any semblance of self-control I had left me when I grazed my hand across his crotch before I exited the cab. "I am."

"Everything between us will change once I take you to my bed."

I carefully place the half full bottle of water on the counter before I reach for his hand. "Lead the way."

***

"You're so wet, Vanessa." The words fill the room as he glides his fingers through my folds. "Come for me like this and then I'll eat you."

The mere promise of his skilled lips on my core makes my legs twitch. I've been on my back, in the middle of his bed since he stripped me nude. He'd pulled off my clothes slowly, his eyes taking in every inch of my skin, his hand stopping to run over my ass.

"The light is so bright," I whisper into his neck. "I want you to turn it off."

"No." His voice is a low growl. "I want to see you. I want to see your face when I taste this beautiful cunt."

I moan loudly from the sensation of him sliding his index finger into my channel. He's still fully dressed. He crawled onto the bed next to me and kissed my nipples greedily. I'd writhed beneath him, wanting him to touch my clit.

"Take off your clothes." I pull at the collar of his blue button down shirt. "I want to touch your skin."

"No." His hand catches mine before he brings it to his lips. "Right now it's all about you."

I almost gasp aloud when I feel him pull away from me. I close my eyes knowing that soon I'm going to feel his tongue on my core. I'm not sure I can last beyond one lick before I'll come all over his face.

"The first day I saw you in the ER, I thought about this." He pulls his tongue over the length of my smooth cleft. "I thought about what you must look like under those scrubs."

I don't respond with anything that even remotely sounds like a word. I can't control the low, soft moans that are coming out of my body.

"Then I saw you at the pub and I thought about your taste." He licks my clit hard.

"Oh, no." I reach down to pull my fingers through his brown hair. "That's the spot. Lick that spot."

His tongue moves quickly, diving shallowly into my channel. He moans into my wetness, his hands sliding beneath me to cup my ass in his palms.

"Garrett." His name escapes me with a heady cry. "I'm close."

"We're going to slow it down." He pulls back and looks up at me. "I'm going to make you ache for me, Vanessa. I want to hear you whimper my name because you need it so badly."

The promise only draws me closer to the edge. "Don't. I need it now."

He rests back on his knees, his breath coursing hot over my engorged clit. "You're so snug. Your body is so tight. You're going to feel it so deep when I fuck you hard."

I groan loudly. "I need to come."

With a moan he dives into me, pulling my body into his. His head moves quickly as he lashes my clit over and over again. I brace as I feel the orgasm bearing down on me. I grind myself into his face shamelessly with each one of his growls and I cry into the silence of the room as I come hard.

FOURTEEN

I'd closed my eyes when I felt my breathing finally level off. He didn't move. His face was nestled next to my pussy, his breath blowing hot over it with every heave of his chest.

I feel movement and I open my eyes. He's there, standing by the bed, unbuttoning his shirt. "I have to be inside of you."

I nod as I watch the shirt slide off his body, revealing a perfectly toned chest and stomach.

"You're going to scream my name, Vanessa." His hand deftly pulls the black belt free from his pants. "I know that you think you can fuck me once and it will be enough."

I cover my eyes with my hands, wanting to block out his words as much as the image of him driving his dick into me. "It will be."

"You've been fighting yourself." He unzips his pants. "I've seen it in your face. I see the want that's there."

The flush that takes over my body is too much. I feel more exposed than I've ever felt in my life before. "I just want to fuck once."

"Once will never be enough." The sound of him ripping open a condom wrapper fills the air. "I know it already."

I feel the bed shift and my eyes pop open. He's there, above me. His eyelids are heavy as he stares down at me.

There's nothing but heated silence between us as he runs the wide crest of his cock over my core. I arch my back when it touches my clit and I grab tightly to his shoulders as he pushes himself into me with a loud growl.

"Garrett." My lips move to say his name but the only sound in the entire room are his moans as he plunges his cock into me over and over again.

I look down, wanting to see it as it slides into my core. It's so deep, much deeper than any man I've ever been with before. He shifts back on his heels, pulling my hips into his hands. I almost scream when I see the lush head between my lips before he drives it with force back into my body.

I throw my hands over my head into the soft linens of his bed as I come, my core gripping onto the thick root.

He grunts loudly, pushes forward and fucks me hard until he screams my name into his own release.

***

"I told you." His breath is on my cheek. I can't open my eyes. I can't move. He'd fucked me again after he'd flipped me onto my stomach and licked my pussy until I collapsed on the bed. When he entered me from behind, the bite of pain was that much more intense and with each driving thrust of his cock, I'd cried out from the sheer mix of sensations.

"Told me what?" I whisper.

I feel the coarseness of his jaw along my chin as evening stubble takes root on his face. I want to look at him. I want to see the same satisfaction in his expression that I know is in mine.

"I told you that you wouldn't be able to fuck me just once."

"Don't be an asshole," I say through a smile. "Don't be that guy that thinks he's the best lover any woman has ever had."

"I'm the best lover you've ever had, Vanessa." His hand is on my hip. "You've never come that hard with a man before."

I pull my hand over my face to hide the blush I know is there. He's right. I've been with men who were skilled in how to bring me to the edge, but it's never been this intense. I got lost in the pleasure with him. I couldn't stop coming when he was eating me.

"You're so arrogant." I rub my hand over his cheek. "I don't like it."

"You like it." He kisses my nose. "Open your eyes."

I nuzzle my nose into his neck as I slowly pull my eyes open, grateful that he's dimmed the lights in the room. "I need to go home."

"You don't need to go anywhere." He traces the pad of his thumb over my bottom lip. "You're going to sleep here."

It's too intimate. It's too much. I didn't come here to spend the night. "No. I can't do that."

Before I have time to react he's on top of me again, his knees on either side of my waist. "I'm not done with you yet."

I smile up at him. He's different in the soft light of this room, without the suit and with his hair out of place. He's boyish, and charming and irresistible in a way that isn't about how he owns any space he walks into. This man is about pleasing and desire. He wants me to stay. I want it too.

"I can stay," I offer as I reach up to cup his cheek. "I need to be able to walk tomorrow though."

A ghost of a grin flashes over his lips. "I'll keep that in mind."

FIFTEEN

"You slept with Garrett?" Zoe can't contain the shock, and maybe awe, in her voice. It wouldn't be so uncomfortable if we were standing anywhere other than in the middle of a baby store on the Upper East Side.

"No." I shake my head as I pick up a tiny blue pair of socks. "We didn't sleep. That man is a machine."

Her hand leaps to her chest. "He's not my type. I love Beck but you can tell when you look at him. I don't know how but it's just there. Do you know what I mean?"

I know exactly what she means. When I slid out of his bed yesterday morning shortly after four to get home to shower before my shift, he'd pulled me onto his face. I'd cried from the depth of the pleasure as I held tightly to his headboard as he coaxed two orgasms from me. When I finally got dressed to leave, he'd kissed me with a tenderness I've never felt from any man before. It left me feeling as though I was in a daze the entire day.

"Van?" She shakes my shoulder lightly. "Do you know what I mean?"

I nod even though I can't remember the question.

"Will you see him again tonight?" She rubs her hand over her ever growing belly. "Or do you have to work?"

"Neither," I answer honestly. I look past her to where a crib is set up complete with bedding and stuffed toys. "Did you and Beck pick out a crib?"

"We ordered one last week." She glances briefly in the direction I'm looking. "My mom wanted to ship my old crib here from Philadelphia."

"The crib you slept in when you were a baby?" I touch her shoulder. "Your mom kept that?"

"She kept everything. She still has all the clothes she bought for me back then."

I feel a pang of envy. She says the words as though the only meaning they hold is the fact that her mother has been hoarding things for a quarter of a century. That crib and those clothes in Philadelphia are rich with history and memories.

"Have I ever told you that your mom sounds amazing?" I ask with a sigh. "She sounds like she's going to be the most amazing grandmother ever."

"I already know that she will be." She picks up a package of newborn diapers. "She's going to come to New York a week before my due date to stay for a month."

"I can't wait to meet her." I shake a small rattle shaped in the head of a lion. "I'll get this for baby Beck."

"He'll love it." She pats my hand. "He's going to love his Auntie Van too."

***

"Have you thought more about finding out where that storage locker is?" Garrett nods across the table in the crowded diner. "I told you I can look into it for you."

He did tell me that. In fact, he told me that when I was talking to him on the phone this afternoon during my coffee break. "I'm going to do the detective work myself."

I had started. Yesterday, after Zoe and I had gone back to her place, I'd had dinner with her and her husband and then had boarded the subway to take me into Brooklyn. I had sat by my mother's side for close to an hour while she stared at the wall just past my shoulder. I'd read to her from the notebook I found in the safety deposit box, crying as I felt the desperation in her words as she wrote about wanting a child and not being able to conceive. She'd drifted from lover to lover in her thirties hoping each would be the source of the miracle she wanted, before she realized that giving birth to her own baby would never be part of her story.

I wept as I read the passages about her wanting to adopt but being turned down by an agency because of her limited finances. I'd stopped at that page, unable, or maybe more unwilling, to learn more about how I came to be her daughter.

After I'd kissed her lightly on the cheek, I'd shoved the gold chain and rope bracelet back into my purse along with the notebook and I went to the storage locker facility seven blocks from the apartment where she'd lived. They had no record of my mother's name. The key didn't magically open anything there.

He looks up from his smartphone. "Have you contacted her bank? You have access to her funds, right?"

I do and so far I haven't found any trail of payments that lead to a locker that fits the key. "If the rent on it stopped being paid, they would have auctioned everything in it off, right?"

"Not without contacting her first." He slides his phone back into the inner pocket of his suit jacket. "Where is her mail being sent?"

"To my apartment." I look down at my hands. They're twisted together in my lap. "I had the post office forward everything to me when she started living at the facility."

"If you give me the key, it won't take me more than a day or two to find the locker." His palm rests against the table, turned upwards tempting me to trust in him again.

"I'm going to fly to Maine to see if I can find it on my own. I need to do that."

"I get it." His head tilts to the left as he runs his hand over his jaw. "You want to uncover her secrets on your own terms."

"It's something like that," I try to brush off the comment. "I'm tracing her past. I need to do it alone."

SIXTEEN

"I don't think I've seen a body more beautiful than yours." He rests his chin on my shoulder. "There's not one thing about it I would change."

I pull his arms around my waist as I lean back into him. "I wouldn't change anything about your body either."

The sigh that escapes him reverberates through me. I knew I'd end up back in his apartment. I couldn't have known that after he'd fucked me slowly in his bed, that he'd draw a warm bath for me while I closed my eyes. I'd awoken to him scooping me up into his arms and carrying me into the bathroom. The candles that surround the large tub were the only light as he helped me step in before he slid his body behind me, water flowing over the edge and hitting the dark tiled floor.

"Tell me how old you are, Vanessa."

"You don't know how old I am?" I push my head back so I can catch a glimpse of his face. His hair is wet and pushed off his forehead. A fine mist of moisture has beaded on his upper lip.

"I think I know how old you are." His hands edge down my body until one is resting against my core. "I think you're twenty-seven."

"I'm not twenty-seven." I push my legs apart wanting him to circle my clit with his skilled fingers.

"You're twenty-six." It's a statement, not a question.

I graze my hands over his knees. "No. I'm not twenty-six."

"Tell me," he whispers into my neck. "Tell me how old."

"I'm twenty-four." I lean back against him. "You're thirty-two. I saw it on your chart."

"You're so young." He chuckles in a low tone. "How the hell did I end up wanting you?"

"I'm not that young." I slap his thigh playfully. "I'm very mature for my age."

"You're perfect for your age. You're perfect for me."

***

"Take it down your throat." He's leaning against the counter in his kitchen, his hands on the back of my head. "Fuck it, Vanessa. Fuck it all with your mouth."

I feel my eyes watering at the sheer girth of it. When I first dropped to my knees, and I took the spongy head of his cock in my mouth, his desire for release had taken over. He'd held my hair in his hands as he slid between my lips. He'd started fucking my mouth leisurely, curse words rolling off his tongue slowly and sensuously.

I moan as I feel it swell even more when I cup his heavy balls in my hand. I push back to pop it out of my mouth, wanting to flick my tongue over the tip.

"You know how to suck me." He looks down, his gaze meeting mine. "Christ, look at you. Look at your tits and your mouth."

I smile around his cock, knowing that the slight pressure of my tongue on the underside will bring out a low groan. It does. He throws his head back as his hands grip tightly to my hair.

"I have to fuck it, Vanessa." He suddenly reaches back to grab the edge of the counter. His fingers splayed out across the marble. "I want to come all over your tits."

I feel my core ache at the image of that. I move my body slightly, grab hold of the base of the thick root and slide my mouth slowly over it as he chants my name.

I don't pull back when I feel the first burst of his release hit the back of my throat. I want to taste him. I need to have this.

He pushes back hard, grabs hold of his cock and pumps everything he has onto my face and my breasts.

I stare up at him as he levels his breathing, his cock still resting in his palm.

"That was fucking amazing." He looks down at me. "You're fucking amazing."

I push myself forward, open my mouth and run my tongue over the semi-erect tip of his cock, collecting the last drop onto my tongue.

"That right there," he stops to pull in a deep breath. "That right there makes me want to keep you here forever."

SEVENTEEN

He's fallen asleep. I didn't think it was possible but Garrett Ryan has finally run out of steam. He's next to me, his breathing deep and controlled. I've stared at him for at least the last thirty minutes, debating whether I should pull my jeans and sweater back on and go home. I know if I do, I'll wake up to a bounty of messages from him asking me why I bailed. He wants me to stay. He said it before he drifted off to sleep when he was telling me about his childhood in Boston.

I've avoided talking about myself. He hasn't asked any direct questions and I haven't offered anything. I can't yet. I won't share who I am until I have a clear picture of that myself.

I slide out from under his arm and pull on the white dress shirt he threw on the floor when we first walked into his bedroom. It's large, so large that I have to roll up the sleeves. It smells like him. It's the scent of his skin and his cologne.

I pad quietly out of the bedroom and into the living room. I reach for my purse, retrieving the notebook before I sit in an oversized brown chair. I pull my knees up to my chest and open the tattered pages to where I last read.

The words flow together, each more painful than the one before as my mother writes about entering her forties and the deep ache within her heart to be a parent. She wishes she had worked harder and saved more so she could travel to a place in the world where children are given to foreign families who have meager means but a lot of love to give.

She writes about her friends who are mothers and how they ignore their children even though they've been given the greatest gift a woman can have. The names that she's written aren't familiar to me. I don't remember any of them. I don't recall the descriptive details of the park by her home where she sat for hours at a time watching the children playing in the grass and swinging on the swings.

I watch my tears fall onto the paper as I turn the last page to read the pain she's in. Her loneliness is evident in the cursive handwriting, each letter so structured and woven into the next, even when her heart was breaking apart.

"Vanessa?" His voice is filled with sleep.

I twist in the chair to look at him. He's wearing pajama bottoms and a slight grin on his face. "I was worried that you left without waking me."

I want to run across the room and into his arms. I want him to hold me and I want him to know me.

"What are you reading?" He takes long strides towards me. "Is it that notebook you had at the pub?"

I close the cover carefully not wanting to disturb the bindings that are almost falling apart. "It belonged to my mother. I found it in the safety deposit box."

He pulls on the fabric of the pants before he lowers himself to the table in front of me. "Is it a diary?"

"It's something like that." I hold it close to my chest wanting to keep its secrets buried within the pages.

"Is reading it helping you?" He reaches for my left foot, massaging it in his hands. "Are you learning anything about her?"

"I am," I say hoarsely. "There's a lot about her I didn't know until now."

"It's a treasure then." He leans down to kiss my ankle. "You're lucky you have it."

I don't answer because I don't consider myself lucky at all. I won't until I understand who I am and how I came to belong to Rowena Meyer.

***

"What time does your flight from Maine get in?" He straightens the lapels of his navy blue suit jacket.

"I'm on a morning flight." I glance down at my smartphone. "I'll be at La Guardia before noon and then I have to work the night shift."

He exhales quickly. "You're leaving to go to Maine today; you're coming back tomorrow morning and then working?"

"That's my entire itinerary," I tease.

"When do I get to see you?"

I pull my hair into a high ponytail as I study his reflection in the large mirror in his bathroom. "I can come by your office tomorrow afternoon. I've never been there."

He pulls me into his chest, his broad arms enveloping me. "I'd love that, Vanessa. Shit, I'd love to have you there but I have to be somewhere else tomorrow afternoon."

I shouldn't feel as disappointed as I do. I have no idea what's waiting for me in Maine. I don't even know if I'm going to find a match to the storage locker key but I do know that the promise of coming back to New York to see Garrett's face will make the entire ordeal bearable for me.

"I'll stop by the hospital tomorrow night." He brushes his lips across my forehead. "You'll text me and tell me when you're break is and I'll be there."

"My break is usually at two in the morning when I'm on the night shift."

"I'll be waiting in the cafeteria for you."

"You'd get up in the middle of the night to come down to the hospital to sit with me for thirty minutes?" I cock my brow at his reflection.

"I would go anywhere at any time to see this beautiful face."

EIGHTEEN

"You better believe I remember her." He claps his plump hands together. "Your mother is a looker."

She is. She was. My mother was beautiful for as long as I can remember. Even now, that her hair has grayed and wrinkles have overtaken the landscape of her face, she's still one of the most breathtaking women I'll ever know.

"You look nothing like her." He points out. "How do I know you're really her daughter?"

I yank open my purse and fish frantically for my wallet. I open it quickly, pulling open a zippered compartment before I feel the edges of a small, rectangular photograph. I scoop it into my palm.

"My mother and I took this when I was fifteen. We were at Coney Island." I hold the picture towards him, mindful of the fact that it's one of the few of the two of us together. We'd sat in a photo booth and had made ridiculous faces as the flash blinded us. This photograph is the only one where we're both smiling brightly. It's the last picture I have of my mother and me together, where her gaze is actually focused on the camera.

"That's the woman I remember." He pulls the picture closer to his nose, his head diving down to look below the line of his bifocals. "You look good in this too."

I accept the compliment with a smile. "I'm glad you remember her."

"She rented 7A." He gestures down a long hallway of lockers. "It's one of the inside units."

"I have the key." I reach into the front pocket of my jeans to pull it free. "I wasn't sure if you'd still have her things. I thought you might have auctioned them off."

"No way." He chuckles as he leans against his desk. "Your mother and I were friends. She gave me a watch in exchange for keeping her stuff here. I always hoped she'd come back to get it."

I don't question the watch or its worth. It's inconsequential now. What matters is that when I walked through the doors of this building, the third I've been in today, I finally found the missing piece of the puzzle I've been searching for. I'm ten feet, and one lock away, from knowing all of my mother's secrets.

***

Zoe rubs her hand over her brow. I can tell that she's on the verge of tears. I am too. I have been since I arrived back in New York this morning.

After I'd rummaged through the boxes of old clothes and holiday decorations in my mother's storage locker, I'd felt numb. I'd sat in the corner, holding tight to a toy doll she'd packed in a cardboard box with all the Mother's Day cards I'd given to her. I'd picked up two before the pain of knowing that she'd never smile at me the same way she did when I was a child overtook me. I'd wept in the tiny space all alone, convinced that I'd never know where I came from and who gave me away.

I reached to pick up the small pink suitcase my mother had given me on my tenth birthday when we took a weekend trip to Disneyland. She'd worked two jobs to save for the trip and I'd spent months at Aunt Nora's after school and in the evenings while my mother waited tables for meager tips so she could take me to see the place where dreams are made of.

I remember the trip's every rich detail. We'd stayed at a cheap motel in Anaheim and shared breakfast sandwiches bought from a local fast food place. There wasn't enough money for the rides, so we'd sat on benches, and closed our eyes, imagining what it would feel like to raise high in the air on a rollercoaster, or splash through the water as we raced down a mountain. It was the perfect three day trip. The pink hard shell suitcase that sat on the floor in the storage locker was proof of that.

When I reached to pick it up, the latch fell open. It had rusted over time and as I bent down to scoop up the papers that had fallen onto the concrete floor, my entire life had shifted on its axis.

I'd left the space with the broken suitcase in my hands, calling back to the man at the desk to donate everything else.

I'd fallen asleep feeling nothing and woke the same way. I don't remember boarding the plane or getting into the taxi that brought me to Zoe.

I'm here now and as she clings to me and sobs, I stare at the yellowed newspaper clippings and the grieving face of the woman with blonde hair and the same blue eyes as me. She'd turned her back in Central Park for not more than a brief moment and when she turned back, her little baby girl was gone.

NINETEEN

"Are we still on for tonight?" Garrett growls into the phone.

I pull in a deep breath. "I need to work tonight. I'll be at the hospital at eleven."

He's preoccupied. I can hear voices in the background and movement. "I'm looking forward to seeing you. I miss you, Vanessa."

I can tell that it's shifting to something more than two people who crave each other. He'd called me several times yesterday but I couldn't talk. I couldn't bring myself to even utter a word to myself, let alone him. I'd explained it away with bad cell service in Maine when I finally answered just now.

"I miss you too," I say it softly wanting to know how it feels on my lips. I do miss him. I want to tell him what's happening. I want him to tell me what to do but I can't. I won't. I have to find my way out of this maze by myself.

"I have a confession." He chuckles. "I can't believe I'm about to tell you this."

I close my eyes. "Tell me what it is."

"I took a picture of you that night you were reading your mother's diary," he pauses before he continues. "You looked so perfect sitting in the chair in my apartment, wearing my shirt."

My voice is thick as I try to hold in everything I'm feeling. "I don't have a picture of you. Can I take one when I see you tonight?"

"You can take as many as you want. I need to go." His voice shifts slightly. "I have a busy day but I'll be at the hospital at two. I'll kiss you in the middle of the cafeteria for as long as I can."

I cradle the phone against my ear, wishing he could talk for just a moment longer. "I'll be there."

The line goes dead and I close my eyes as I lean back into the seat and stare out the window of the dark sedan Zoe had called for us. The driver is taking us through the crowded streets of mid-town Manhattan as we make our way to the Upper East Side and the townhouse where Francesca Tomlin lives.

***

"I'm scared," I whisper as I hold tightly to Zoe's hand. "What if I'm not her daughter?"

"We don't have to do this today." She rests her tablet in her lap. "We can go back to my place and research it more."

I know that she sees the panic in my expression. After she'd read all the clippings in the suitcase about the missing child from twenty-four years ago, Zoe had opened her tablet and typed in the name of the mother. We were flooded with images of her as she aged. There were pictures of her stunning home where she hosts charity fundraisers and dinner parties for some of the city's theatre greats. She is beautiful and giving and when I'd scrolled through the image results, I saw the shape of my nose, and the curve of my brow. I saw a familiarity in another's face that I've never seen before.

"I think I should just go to the door and talk to her." My heart leaps with the idea of seeing her face right in front of me. "I won't say who I am. I'll just talk to her for a minute."

She nods as if she thinks my plan holds any merit at all. "If she's your mother, she'll know Vanessa. She'll feel it inside."

I know she will. I sense it already. I know it's not wishful thinking that has brought me to the woman's doorstep. It's the words my mother wrote within her notebook, it's the newspaper clippings, but most of all it's the thin brightly colored rope bracelet I saw wrapped around her wrist in some of the photographs. It's the same colors as the bracelet I'm holding in my hands.

"Do you want me to go to the door with you?" Zoe nods towards the shuttered windows of the townhouse. "It would be easier if I was next to you, holding your hand."

She's right. It would be easier to have her support right next to me but this is a moment I've longed for since I was old enough to understand that there was a woman on the earth who had carried me within her body and had endured the pain of giving birth to me.

"I think I need to go by myself." I point towards the concrete steps. "Can you wait here for me though?"

"I'll be right here with the driver until you come back." She pats the seat between us. "I promise I won't go anywhere."

I lean towards her to pull her into an embrace. I need her strength. I need the belief that she carries within her that everything is supposed to turn out a certain way because of fate. It's how she lives her life since she met her husband and it's only given her the gifts that she's always wanted.

I want this to be the end of my journey. I want Francesca to open the door and pull me into her arms and cry because I've finally found her. I want that but I know that when I knock on the door, the woman who answers may not feel anything for me. She may view me as one of the many solicitors who roam the city's streets trying to sell magazine subscriptions or calendars for charity.

I push open the door of the car, dart my head back to look at Zoe one last time and step onto the sidewalk.

TWENTY

"I'm here to see Mrs. Tomlin," I say with every ounce of strength I can pull from within me. I'd knocked softly on the door twice before ringing the bell.

"Mrs. Tomlin?" The shorthaired woman scratches her chin as she stares down at my face. "Francesca Tomlin?"

"Yes," I nod as I try to peek around her body to the interior of the townhouse. "My mother was a friend of hers many years ago and I was hoping she could spare a moment to see me."

"What's your name, dear?" she asks as she peers past my head to where the town car is idling on the street. "I'll need to know your name."

"It's Vanessa," I answer in a muted tone. It may be Charlotte Tomlin. That was the name of the child who was taken from her mother's clutches when she briefly turned her back.

"Come inside and I'll be right back." She pulls open the door and moves to the side.

I don't hesitate at all as I step over the threshold into the elegant space.

"I'm going to go down that hallway." She rests one of her hands on my shoulder as she points down a narrow hallway with her other hand. "I won't be more than a minute."

I nod, knowing that my voice won't serve any useful purpose right now. I pull my gaze around the foyer, noticing all of the small details. There is a tall, slender vase filled with flowers sitting atop an antique table. A pair of high chairs offers a respite for anyone who first enters the space. The walls are lined with paintings in ornate frames.

I reach into the front pocket of my jeans, seeking the comfort that the rope bracelet offers me. I've held onto it without thinking when I've felt overwhelmed the past few weeks. I'm never without it now and even though I couldn't have understood its significance before today, I'd known instinctively that it held importance in my life. I knew it when I saw it in my mother's safety deposit box.

My head pops up as I hear the sound of heels moving across the floor. I sigh when I see a woman, not much older than me round the corner and walk towards me. She's not Francesca.

"Vanessa?" She holds out her hand as she nears me. "How can I help you?"

I reach for her delicate hand and shake it briskly before I pull mine back. "I was hoping to speak with Mrs. Tomlin."

"May I ask how you know her?"

I can't exactly launch into the twisted tale of my journey of self-discovery these past few weeks. My hand twitches next to me and I suddenly wish I'd have taken Zoe up on her offer to come with me. I feel isolated and shut off from everything I know and now I'm staring at the face of an unfamiliar woman who wants details I'm not sure I can share with anyone yet.

"My mother actually knew her many years ago," I lie with ease. "They used to meet in the park sometimes."

"Really?" Her hands leap to her chest in excitement. Her shoulder length brown hair bounces with the movement. "Was your mom one of the ladies she had tea with on Thursdays?"

I nod without thinking. "Yes. It was a long time ago."

"You wouldn't happen to have any pictures of them together, would you?" Her brow jumps up. "I'm trying to find more pictures for the memorial."

I feel all of the air rush from my lungs. "The memorial?"

"Yes." She nods with the assurance that I have every understanding of what she's talking about. "We've scheduled it for next week. If you have any pictures I'd love to see them."

"She's gone?" I feel the crack in my voice before I hear it. "Is Francesca gone?"

Her hand moves to my forearm. "I thought that's why you were here. I assumed you came to share your condolences."

"When did she die?" I can't control the rush of tears. I don't even try to.

"I'm sorry." She motions towards the high back chairs. "Do you want to sit?"

"No." I swallow hard. "When was it?"

"My mother died two weeks ago." Her voice trembles slightly. "She passed in her sleep."

I almost sob aloud not just for the loss that I feel but also for the realization that I have a sister. I stare at her face, seeing my own blue eyes reflected back in hers. "What's your name?"

"My name?" Her hand moves to her chin. "Who are you?"

"I'm Vanessa," I say because it's the only name I've ever carried. It's who I am regardless of where my life began.

I watch her lips quiver as her head darts behind her quickly. "My name is Connie."

"Connie," I repeat holding my hand out towards her. "I'm really happy to meet you."

Her eyes lower slowly and before her hand can touch mine she stumbles back on her feet. "No. It can't be. You can't be."

I look down to where her eyes are focused and I see my open hand with the small rope bracelet resting in my palm.

"You're not her." Her finger waves in the air at me. "You can't be her. What kind of sick game do you think you're playing?"

I reach behind me looking for any leverage I can find. "I don't know who I am."

"What's that supposed to mean?" She points at me with the precision of a dagger. "Why are you here? You tell me why you're here."

I glance back at the door, wondering if I should pull it open and run down the steps to the car. I can leave now. I can take the promise of what could have been and keep that close to me.

"Tell me why you're here." Her tone is insistent. "I need to know why you came here now."

"I wanted to talk to her." I look down at the bracelet. "I just wanted to talk to her."

"You waited until she was dead." She tucks her face into her hands. "You actually waited until she was dead before you came here."

"No," I say quietly. "I came to talk to her."

"Do you know that she never stopped looking for you?" She pushes her hands onto her hips. "She searched for you everywhere. She died crying because she never got to hold you again."

The gravity of the words hits me full force and I pull my hands to my stomach. "I would have come sooner. I didn't know."

"You waited until she was dead to get your hands on her money." She pushes against my shoulder. "That's why you're here, isn't it? You think you're entitled to our things?"

I brush my hand over my cheek, pushing aside all the tears. "I don't want anything. I just wanted to see her."

"You won't get away with this." She raises her hands in the air. "I won't let you get away with this."

I reach behind me to grab hold of the doorknob, wanting the reprieve that the world outside these walls will give me. I shouldn't have come. I should have read all the news stories that popped up in the search results instead of just gazing at the pictures of her face. I would have known she had died. I would have known that my birth mother was gone.

"I need to go." I fumble with the doorknob, "I can't stay here."

"You're not going anywhere." She yanks hard on my hand. "You're not leaving until we settle this."

"There's nothing to settle." I hold tight to the bracelet. "I shouldn't have come."

"You're right." She stares down at my hand. "You never should have come here. You don't belong here anymore. You're too late."

She's right. I am too late. I'm too late to hear my mother's voice and I'm too late to see any love that she may have had for me in her eyes. I'm too late to hold her hand when I tell her that I missed her every day and would have fought my way back to her if I'd have known. I'm too late for it all.

"My husband will make sure you don't get your hands on any of our things." She waves her hand down the hallway. "He won't let you near our family."

"I don't want your things," I sob. "I just wanted to see her."

"Darling," she calls into the quiet apartment. "You won't believe who finally decided to show her face after all these years."

I listen to the spite in her words. I stare at the eyes that look like mine and I see nothing but an angry, bitter stranger looking back at me.

"What's going on?" A man's voice calls from the hallway.

"Charlotte finally decided to come home." She waves her hand over my head.

"What?" His voice is husky as his footsteps near. "Charlotte is here?"

"She's right here." She steps to the left and I look towards the voice.

He stops in his tracks.

I stare into his face.

It's him.

Garrett Ryan is standing next to my sister.

TRACE

Part Two

ONE

"Charlotte?" Garrett repeats the name for the third time. "This isn't Charlotte. This is Vanessa. She's a friend of mine."

"A friend?" Connie's gaze slides over me. "What do you mean a friend?"

I should be the one to respond but my voice left me the moment Garrett Ryan walked into my field of view. The man is married to my long lost sister? He's the husband who isn't going to let me get away with whatever sinister plot Connie thinks I'm here to hatch? I've never lived on the Upper East Side of Manhattan. Maybe when you step over the threshold of one of these ridiculously over-priced townhomes, you walk into an alternate universe. It wasn't even two nights ago that Garrett was buried deep inside of me pushing me from one orgasm into another in a plush bed in an apartment he claimed was his. Now, he's the spouse of a woman I once shared a mother and father with? I didn't sleep a wink last night. Maybe this is my mind playing tricks on me.

"We spend time together," he offers in a smooth and controlled tone.

I haven't known my sister for all of five minutes and I already know that's the wrong answer. The moment she realized I was Charlotte, she almost tore my arm off. I presume that was so she could beat me over the head with it. I can't even fathom what she's about to do now that she knows that her husband has been fucking me. I take two heavy steps back towards the door hopeful that when she lunges at me, I'll be able to slide out of the townhouse and make a mad dash for it.

"Spend time together?" Her index finger waves past my nose. "What does that mean?"

I scrub my hand over my face. I knew when I walked into this space that my life would change. It was inevitable. I had visions of my birth mother pulling me into her warm embrace and telling me how she always knew that I'd find my way back to her one day. That dream shattered and has now been replaced with the cold, and unexpected, reality that the man I'm sleeping with married into the family I lost so long ago.

"Vanessa." His hand reaches out to me as he steps in my direction. "Did my office tell you I'd be here? Is something wrong?"

I shake my head meekly not able to draw any words to the surface that could begin to explain the path that brought me to this house.

"She's Charlotte." Connie steps between us. "She has the bracelet."

"What bracelet?" Garrett's eyes dart down to my wrist as he loosens his navy blue necktie. "I've never seen her wearing a bracelet."

"It's in her hand." Her hands leap to my right hand, which I've pulled, into a tight fist. "She showed it to me."

"She showed you what?" he shoots back. "You're obviously upset right now, Connie. I think you should go back to the study and wait for me."

"I'm not going anywhere." She straightens her back. "You're going to tell me right now what is going on between you and Charlotte."

"Connie? What are you screaming about?"

I jump at the sound of a man's voice in the approaching distance. I follow Garrett's head as he turns towards the hallway to where an average height, gray haired man is walking. He's old enough to be my father and the fact that he's holding his index finger to the bridge of his nose to keep his glasses in place, adds an unusual charm to his otherwise unexceptional face. I didn't take the time to read far enough into any of the newspaper articles to gather details about my dad. I stare at his face, trying to pull any resemblance to myself from it.

"My friend Vanessa is here." Garrett signals towards me. "Connie thinks she's Charlotte."

The knowing glance that the gray haired man throws Garrett suggests that there's a hidden meaning within the words that I can't quite grasp.

"I'm Leif," he says softly as he extends his hand towards me. "I'm sorry for this. We just suffered a tremendous loss. We're all on edge."

"Don't touch her." Connie's hand darts out to slap Leif's in mid-air. "Why would you touch her?"

I clear my throat. I doubt that there's ever going to be an opportune time to jump into the madness of this conversation, but I'm not about to let my sister treat me like I have the plague. "I'm Vanessa."

"She's not," Connie hisses. "She's Charlotte."

Leif nods towards me. I catch a glimpse of what looks like veiled compassion in his expression. "Charlotte is gone, Connie. We have been over this dozens of times. She's never coming back."

"Don't treat me like this," she protests. "I'm telling you both that this is Charlotte. She has Charlotte's bracelet."

His eyes fall to my hands and I know he's surveying my wrists for the bracelet, just as Garrett did. "We should leave Garrett and Vanessa alone. He'll come back to the study when he's done."

Garrett nods in agreement. "I need a few minutes here and then the three of us can finish up."

A few minutes aren't going to be nearly enough time for me to adequately explain to Garrett how I really feel about men who cheat on their wives. If you add the fact that I'm his missing sister-in-law, the impending discussion is going to take at the very least a couple of hours. A few minutes won't even be enough to lightly scratch the surface of this twisted mess.

"You both know that Charlotte had a bracelet when she disappeared." Connie stands firmly in place. "This woman has it."

Leif rubs both sides of his head with his index fingers. "You don't know what you're talking about. A month ago you thought the woman who worked at the bakery was Charlotte. Last year it was that woman who you passed in Central Park. You can't keep doing this to yourself."

I know that I should step in and correct this man. My mind realizes that the right thing to do is to tell him who I really am. I'm still gripping tightly to the bracelet and to the knowledge that I once lived in this beautiful home and that Connie and I shared a mother and a father. I glance at Leif again studying the curve of his nose and the plane of his forehead trying to find any hint of similarity to my own face.

"Garrett, you believe me don't you?" She turns abruptly towards Garrett. "You went out and found her, didn't you? Why would you do that and not tell me?"

I don't know Garrett Ryan well enough to gauge anything from his demeanor. His arms are crossed over his chest. There are small pellets of perspiration on his forehead. If he's panicked because I'm standing in the doorway of his home within inches of his wife, he's not giving any of that away. If anything, he looks, at most, slightly uneasy.

"Connie." He leans forward so his face is hovering close to her. "Vanessa is my friend. She came here to see me. Give me five minutes with her and I'll be back in the study and we can talk about this."

"What do you need to talk to her about?" Her head tilts to the left in my direction, even though her eyes never leave his face. "Just do it now. Say what you need to say to her in front of me."

"Let's give them a minute." Leif rests both of his hands on Connie's shoulders. "We'll go back to the study."

"I'm not going anywhere." She tries to pull free of his hands, but he only firms his grasp. "I want to hear what he says to her. I have a right to hear it."

I've heard of the concept of open marriage but I've never been witness to one in the reality of my life. This woman may think she has a right to listen in on our conversation, and maybe she does. I, for one, just want out of this madhouse.

"I need to go," I say because it's the only rational thought running through my mind.

"You think you can just leave?" Connie pulls on the arm of my sweater. "You can't just walk out of here."

"I'm sorry I bothered you and your wife." I ignore the incessant yanking on my arm and look directly at Garrett. "I won't bother you again."

Garrett's brows pop up just as he opens his mouth to speak.

"You're not bothering us at all, Vanessa," Leif says quietly. "I apologize for my wife's behavior. Please stay and talk to Garrett. Connie and I will give you some space."

TWO

I scratch the back of my neck as I watch Leif try and guide Connie down the long hallway back to wherever they came from when I first arrived. That moment was only mere minutes ago in tangible time, but it feels as though I stepped over the threshold and into a den of confusion. I knocked on the door to this townhouse with a hope filled heart and now I'm standing alone with Garrett Ryan, unsure of why he's here or what he actually knows about my past.

"You thought I was married to Connie?" he asks quietly. "Why would you think I was married?"

I knew he'd bring it up. I can't look at him. I feel like I'm breaking apart inside.

"Vanessa." He traces his index finger over my jaw line before bringing it up to settle on my bottom lip. "Do you think I'm the kind of man that would cheat on a woman?"

It's an unfair question since I don't really know the man. I know that he's an accomplished lawyer judging by what I found online after he essentially dared me to confirm his claim that he's the best probate attorney in the state. He's left little doubt in my mind, or within the now ever present ache deep in my body, that he's a skilled and generous lover. I have no idea, beyond that limited knowledge, of who he is or what he's capable of.

"She called to her husband." I motion down the empty hallway. "You came around the corner."

His green eyes float over my face and I wonder, for a brief moment, if he's going to see Connie within my features. "I heard her yelling. Leif was on a call so I came to see what was going on. I don't cheat on women. I would never marry a woman and then be unfaithful to her."

The sincerity in his words would be immensely reassuring if the entire scope of what I'm feeling was directed towards his supposed infidelity. It's not. I'm still reeling from Connie's reaction to my showing up on our mother's doorstep. There wasn't a single

74

note of joy in her voice. My sister doesn't want me here and right now, I don't want to be here either.

"I think I should go." I nod towards the door and the solace that I know is waiting for me in the car within Zoe's arms. "Zoe is waiting for me outside."

He brushes past me to gaze out one of the curtained, rectangular windows that run parallel to the heavy wooden door. "Why did you come with Zoe? Has something happened?"

"It's my mother, "I half-lie as I twist my hands together. "I came about my mother."

"Is she okay?" He turns quickly on his heel. "Did something happen to her?"

Yes, I want to say. She died before I had a chance to tell her that I thought about her every day and wondered what she was like.

"I shouldn't have come here." I push my hair behind my ear, my eye catching on my watch. "I need to get to work."

"Vanessa." He doesn't move from his place directly in front of the door. "I need you to tell me why you came here to see me."

"Why are you here?" I ignore his question in favor of one of my own. I admit I'm relieved that he's not married to my sister, but I'm still confused as to why he's standing in my birth family's home.

"Here?" He points at the polished marble floor. "Are you asking me why I'm here?"

He's a lawyer. He's trained to twist words around into a knot of confusion but I'm skilled with people who dance around the truth. I lived with one my entire life.

"Why aren't you at your office?" I push because I want a clear understanding of his connection to my sister and her family. "It's the middle of the day."

A small smile tugs at the corner of his mouth. "I'm working. The woman you just met, Connie, her mother died recently. I'm handling her estate."

Of course he is. It's so obvious that I feel foolish for thinking his presence was tied to anything but the legalities of Francesca's death. It's expected that he'd be taking on the task of steering her will through probate given the fact that he's so in demand in high profile cases like this.

"I'm sorry I bothered you here," I say quietly, wishing I had taken a deep breath and counted to ten before I'd left Zoe's apartment. I hadn't given myself any time to process what I'd read in the newspaper clippings I found in my Rowena's storage locker. I'd just jumped, head and heart first, without a safety net, into that car to come here to see my mother.

"I got to look at this beautiful face in the middle of my day." He leans down and brushes his soft lips across mine. "Never apologize for that."

I reach up to touch his face before I stop myself. I need to tell him. I should confess that I didn't end up inside this space because I was desperate to see him.

"I'm coming to see you late tonight at work." He kisses the tip of my nose before pulling back. "Will you tell me then what's going on with your mother?"

I nod, not because I have any intention of telling him that my mother took me from Francesca when I was too young to remember. I nod because I know that if I don't offer him the promise of an explanation for why I'm standing in the townhouse of one of his clients, he'll never let me walk out of here.

"I'm glad you tracked me down here." He grazes his hand over my hair. "It reminds me why I can't stop thinking about you."

I close my eyes briefly before I pull them open to look directly at his face. This is a man who could mean everything to me. I see it in his eyes. I feel it when he kisses me and touches my body. I should feel my heart volleying with the promise in his words but all I feel is emptiness. The emptiness of knowing that the secret I carry in my heart, and in my hand in the form of the small rope bracelet, is enough to change everything that is happening between us.

THREE

"You're actually telling me that Garrett was inside that house?" Zoe motions behind us as the car speeds up the street.

"He was there," I say softly as I stare down at my lap. "My mother wasn't there."

I hear the heavy sigh that escapes Zoe's lips as she reaches to cover my hands with one of hers. I haven't been able to look directly at her since I got in the car and blurted out that Francesca had died. I've seen Zoe carry other people's emotions as if they were her own. I know it broke her heart when I told her the news. I know that if I look into her face, I'll see the same sorrow I feel.

"I'm sorry that she's gone." Her voice cracks slightly. "I can't believe she died just a few weeks ago."

It's irony at its cruel best. If I had taken Zoe's advice and forged ahead with my plan to find my birth mother months ago, I may have had the chance to see her before fate took her away. I might have heard the joy in her voice and saw the love in her eyes when she realized that I had built a life for myself. I wanted to know that she was proud of me for becoming a nurse. I needed the validation that only a mother can provide.

"I can't believe it either," I offer back sullenly. I truly can't. Francesca Tomlin wasn't the type of woman to openly advertise her age. Last night, when Zoe and I had frantically searched online for any fragments of information we could find about her, the pictures all spoke of a youthful woman. If I had to wager a guess based on a trio of images I saw of her from last spring at a benefit dinner, I would have pegged her to be in her late fifties or early sixties. My medical training has taught me that nothing is impossible, but when a person that age dies in their sleep, there are definite questions that need to be answered. I'm just not in a position to ask anyone in the family for any explanations.

"You said you have a sister?" The delight woven into the question is grossly misplaced. I know that she's trying to find the silver lining to this depressing cloud, but from where I'm sitting, there isn't one.

"Connie," I say her name with little emotion. "She wasn't happy to see me."

"Why not?" She pulls softly on my hands. "Did you tell her who you were?"

I finally look up at her face. I can see the hope that is there, within her expression. She wants this to be like those reunions that you see on daytime television when the host of a show surprises their guest with a long lost relative. They awkwardly embrace with the promise that they'll forge ahead with a relationship. No one ever bothers to ask any of them if having their past come barreling into their present, is actually what they wanted.

"She saw the bracelet." I motion down to where my hands are still tightly curled around the rope bracelet. "When she saw it, she knew who I was."

"What did she say?"

Replaying my sister's cruel reaction to my showing up on the doorstep isn't going to offer anything beneficial to either Zoe or me. She'll try to explain it away based on my sister's shock at seeing me, but I know it runs deeper than that. Connie didn't want me there and judging by the words she was spitting out at me, most of her refusal to welcome me back into the family with open arms has to do with money.

Her eyes widen as I scan her face while I think about how to respond. I have to trust someone. I know that anything I tell Zoe will only go as far as her husband, Beck. She won't run off and share the news that I'm the baby that was stolen from one of Manhattan's most affluent families decades ago. She'll help me. She'll steer me in the direction I need to move. She'll offer me an anchor in this sea of uncertainty that I've fallen into.

"Can you tell me what she said, Van?" She pushes my hair behind my shoulder. "Tell me."

I pull in a deep breath, hoping that it will contain some of the courage I need. "She was angry. She immediately started talking about money and how I came back for part of the estate."

"Really?" She can't mask the surprise in either her voice or on her face. "Why would she think you came back for money?"

I shrug. "I have no idea. She accused me of waiting to come back until Francesca had died."

Zoe's hand leaps to her chest. "Wow. She actually said that?"

I turn to look out the car's window. "She thinks I'm after whatever Francesca left when she died."

"Van?" She pats my shoulder lightly. "What are you going to do now?"

I breathe a small sigh of relief as we turn into the hospital's parking lot. "I'm going to work. It's the only thing I can do."

***

"I went to see your mother yesterday," Ben doesn't look up from the tablet in his hand. "Her nurse told me that you hadn't been to see her in a few days."

I swallow hard. "I've been really busy."

"It's more than that." He closes the cover of the tablet before he finally pulls his gaze to my face. "I can tell something is wrong, Vanessa."

He can't really tell that. Ben and I aren't close friends. We're acquaintances who are working on developing a closer friendship. I'm aware enough to realize that anything I share with him will likely work its way back to Garrett in short order. Ben has to know that Garrett and I are seeing each other.

"I've had a lot going on, Ben." I say dryly. "I'll go see her soon."

"Soon?" he repeats back. "It's not like you to avoid seeing her."

"I'm not avoiding her." I laugh half-heartedly. "I've just been very busy."

"You went out of your way earlier today to find Garrett when he was at a client's house." He rests his hand on my shoulder. "You told him it was because of your mother."

Shit. Why didn't I see that coming? I should have known that Garrett would confide in Ben.

I pull back. I feel exposed even though there's no possible way that Ben can know what I've been dealing with during the past twenty-four hours.

"I'm here if you need a friend, Vanessa." He pulls his smartphone from his pants pocket. "I'll always be around if you need me."

FOUR

"Didn't you get my message?" I try to ask without sounding as aggravated as I feel. It's late. It's actually well past midnight and my shift, up to this point, has been one angry patient after another. I'm exhausted and I don't have a firm grasp on my emotions. I'd texted Garrett almost an hour ago to tell him that meeting during my break tonight, wouldn't work. I hadn't heard back and now I know why. The man is sitting at one of the tables in the almost vacant cafeteria with a wide grin on his face and a bouquet of flowers in his hand.

"I got it." He bolts to his feet. "I got these for you."

I don't resist as he pushes the large arrangement of flowers into my chest. I wrap my arms around them, inhaling their beautiful scent. It's a thoughtful gesture and since it's the second time he's given me flowers, it's obvious that he's naturally chivalrous. I can't think of another man who would stay up half the night to bring someone flowers during a coffee break.

"They're beautiful." I smile up at him. "I didn't expect this."

"You need them." He leans forward to brush his soft lips over my forehead. "I can tell that you've had a bad day."

It's a gross understatement. My entire life has changed dramatically in the past few days. "It's been a rough day."

"Sit." He points to one of the plastic chairs next to the table. "Can I get you a coffee or something?"

I glance briefly towards the corner of the cafeteria to where two women are serving beverages and food. Normally, I'd order a juice and some fruit or oatmeal to fuel me for the remainder of my shift, but I can't stomach the thought of anything stronger than water. "I'm fine."

He lowers himself into the seat next to me. "How has work been tonight?"

It's an easy out and I latch onto it without any thought at all. "Brutal. The ER is crazy busy tonight."

"You must see some wild things working there." He takes a large gulp from the paper coffee cup in front of him. "There has to be things that are crazier than guys that ram their bikes into trees."

I smile at the reminder of how we met. "You recovered from that quickly."

He rubs his forehead. "I still can't believe I did that. I don't remember most of what happened in the park that day."

I need a reprieve from everything that I've had to face the past day-and-a-half. I want to laugh. "You were chasing a woman with perfect tits."

His chin dips down as he cocks a dark brow. "What?"

"It's true." I reach across the table to pick up his coffee cup. I inhale the rich aroma before I bring it to my lips. "You told me in the ER that you hit the tree because you were chasing the most perfect pair of tits you'd ever seen."

He leans back in his chair before he pulls his hand across his stubble covered chin. "You have the most perfect pair of tits I've ever seen."

"I don't." I nod towards my chest. "According to you I have the most perfect looking ass you've ever seen."

"You do." He taps his index finger on the table. "I'm not going to argue that point with you. We've already talked about that."

"You were such a jerk when they brought you into the ER." I push the coffee cup back towards him but he motions for me to stop.

"You keep that. It's already my third cup."

"Your third cup?" My gaze moves to his eyes. "How long have you been here?"

He looks up at the clock on the wall opposite me. "Almost two hours."

"What?" I search his face, realizing that when I texted him telling him not to come, he was already sitting here waiting for me. "Why have you been here so long?"

He stands with effortless ease, rests one hand against the table as he leans down so his lips are hovering next to mine. "I just needed to be in the same place as you. I had to be close to you."

***

"You've slept with him, haven't you?"

It's Carla. I can tell by the giddiness in her voice. It's always there when she's talking about sex.

"Vanessa?" She taps me on the shoulder. "You fucked him, didn't you?"

"No." I turn quickly on my heel to where she's standing behind me. Thankfully we're the only two people waiting for the elevator. "He fucked me."

"How the hell did that happen?" She scoops her arm around my shoulder. "Tell me everything."

That's not happening. I don't kiss and tell or fuck and tell. I may have shared a few juicy details with Zoe, but that's where my confessions about making love with Garrett Ryan stop. "I'm not telling you anything."

"I saw him kissing you in the cafeteria. I think he had a boner."

"A boner?" I pull my hand over my mouth as I giggle. "Seriously, Carla? A boner?"

"Is that why you're never home anymore?" She guides me into the elevator once the doors pop open. "Is it because you're in bed with him?"

I push the button to the ground floor where the ER is located before I tap the button for the third floor. "My life consists of more than work and that."

We both grip tightly to the chrome bar that stretches around the entire perimeter of the lift. I can feel her eyes honed in on my face, but I stare at the doors wishing we'd get to her floor.

"If I was sleeping with him, I'd never get out of bed."

I shake my head slightly, trying to hold back a smile. "You're one a kind, Carla."

"He is, Vanessa." She brushes past me as the doors open on the third floor. "Hold onto him. Men like that only come along once in a lifetime."

FIVE

"Are you going to go to the police?" Zoe reaches past me to grab another handful of newborn diapers from a package. "I can go with you."

I step to the left. "I hadn't thought about it."

She pulls the rest of the diapers free before tucking them into the top drawer of the change table that was delivered not more than an hour ago.

"I don't know what it would accomplish at this point," I say under my breath. "It was so long ago. My birth mother is gone and from what I read online last night, my father died ten years ago."

"It's probably still an open case." She runs her hand across the top of the diapers before she carefully closes the drawer. "I think it's the right thing to do, Van."

I have no grasp on what the right thing to do is anymore. Since I said goodbye to Garrett at the hospital early this morning, my mind has been on overdrive. I was finally able to get a few hours of sleep in after my shift, but I was jarred awake by the image of Connie's face. If she's the only family I have left, there's no reason to pursue anything related to my birth as a Tomlin. I'm Vanessa Meyer now and I have to accept that and all the tangled emotions that go with that.

"My mother will get in trouble." I look past Zoe to one of the nursery walls. Beck has started to paint a mural. It's vibrant, colorful and full of life. "I don't think any of it matters anymore."

She rubs her hand over her swollen stomach. "If someone took my baby away from me, I don't know what I'd do."

I knew when I first showed her the newspaper clippings that it would hit a chord deep within her. Zoe's entire life has been focused on the impending arrival of her son for months now. She's juggled her schedule at law school so she can have the time she wants and needs at home after the baby arrives. He's her life and I can only hold onto the hope that I was just as wanted and loved by Francesca in the months and days leading up to my birth.

"Are you at least going to tell Garrett?"

I know that she doesn't mean for the words to sound as challenging as they do. I'm absorbing them that way because I've been struggling with whether or not to tell Garrett that I just discovered that I'm the daughter of Francesca Tomlin.

"I haven't had time to think about everything," I say truthfully. "I need time to adjust first before I make any decisions."

She nods. "You're right. I know it has to be hard, Van. Just know that Beck and I are here if you need us."

I take as much comfort from the words as she's offering. More than ever, I've come to view Zoe as my family. She's the one person I can depend on and right now, I know that even though she's pushing me to do the things she views as right and expected, that she'll stand by me regardless of what I finally decide to do.

"Do you think it might be worthwhile to talk to a lawyer?" She scratches her brow. "I know someone who I think could help you figure this all out from a legal perspective."

"I don't know. It would have to be off the record." I look down at my fingernails. "I can't afford anyone expensive."

"I know someone." She reaches to where she tossed her purse on the rocking chair. "She's kind of my mentor. I think she'd be happy to help."

***

"I'd like to talk about something." Garrett refills my wine glass. "We haven't had a chance to talk about why you came to find me at my client's townhouse the other day."

We haven't talked about it because I don't have any feasible explanation for why I was there. I've been holding my breath waiting for Garrett to tell me that he asked around his office to find out who gave me that information. I bring the wine glass to my lips and take a leisurely swallow, hopeful that the silence will spur him to carry on the conversation on his own.

"I wish you'd stop by the office again." He taps the top of the table with his hand. "I'd love to have a surprise visit from you in the middle of the day."

I need to stop this runaway train of assumptions before it falls right off the tracks. I've never stepped foot in the man's office.

Until this afternoon, when I did a quick search online, I had no idea where it was even located. I admit I'm impressed that he works for one of the most influential firms in the city, but I'm not surprised. He obviously knows what he's doing as a lawyer. The list of notable clients he's handled probate for speaks of that.

"You'd take time out of your busy day for me?" I tilt my wine glass towards him. "Would I get a personal tour of your office?"

"Can I get either of you anything else?" The soft voice of the waitress breaks into our conversation. "We have a delicious dessert menu."

I promised myself, when I agreed to have dinner with Garrett, that I'd at least tell him that I'm adopted even though I'm technically a missing person who was raised by a desperate woman. I'm not sure I'll need to tell him anything beyond that. He doesn't strike me as the type of man who dates a woman for more than a few weeks. Maybe by the time this thing between us finds its end, I'll have a firmer grasp on whether I'll share with anyone that I'm Charlotte Tomlin.

"We're not interested," Garrett answers as he looks directly at me. "We're ready to go."

She whispers something under her breath as she quickly takes her leave and disappears into the bustling crowd of this mid-town Italian eatery.

"We're ready to go?" I repeat back as I smooth my hands over my black pants. "What's the rush?"

"It's been four days since I've been inside of you, Vanessa." He rests his palms against the edge of the table as he pushes back the chair he's sitting in. "I can't wait another minute. We're leaving now."

SIX

I almost scream the moment I feel his mouth on me. He'd kissed me, in the taxi on the way back to his apartment, like a man who was starved for my touch. My mind has been telling me to stop him so I can explain that I'm holding tightly to something that he deserves to know. I can't or more precisely, I won't. I want this and I need it. I want to feel desired, and adored by this man.

I hear the snap of the material of my panties as he rips them from me. It had taken all the strength I had to hold him back as I'd quickly pulled off my pants and sweater when we came through the door. He'd scooped me into his arms and carried me into his bedroom before throwing his own clothes onto the floor.

"I've been craving you, Vanessa," he says quietly as his tongue circles around my swollen clit. "I've thought about nothing but you for days."

I reach down to pull my hands through his lush, dark hair. I want to take as much pleasure as I can from this. He knows exactly how to bring me to the edge of an orgasm with his tongue and fingers. "It feels so good, Garrett."

"I was so hard in the restaurant." His breath glides over my core. "I thought about taking you into the hallway near the back entrance so I could fuck you against the wall."

The crude image of him taking me within earshot of the other restaurant patrons only adds to my arousal. "You wouldn't do that."

"Don't dare me, Vanessa." He reaches for my hands, pulling them into one of his. "Never dare me."

I arch my ass off the bed, wanting him to lick me. "I'm so ready. Please."

He looks down to where I'm completely exposed. I'm wet. I'm so wet from my own arousal and from the lashes of his tongue over my folds. "Your body craves mine. It's the same for you, isn't it? You ache when you think about us together."

I press my cheek into the soft reprieve that the pillow offers. "It feels so good when we're together."

He licks a long, slow path over my cleft. The deep moan that escapes from him runs right through me and I arch my back even more.

My hands fall back into his hair, tilting his head slightly to the left. "My clit, Garrett. Please."

He doesn't say anything as his tongue circles my throbbing clit. He slides one of his long, elegant fingers into my channel as he licks me harder and faster until I come in a heated rush.

***

"You've been asleep for more than four hours." His breath flows over my shoulder. "I could watch you sleep every night forever, Vanessa. You're so beautiful."

I try to sit up but his strong arms are around me, my back pressed into his chest. The last thing I remember is him licking me to a second intense orgasm. I had screamed aloud, unable to control the depth of what I felt.

"I need to go home."

"We've talked about this before." He pulls me even closer. I can feel his erection pressing against my ass cheek. "You're going to stay here with me. I'm going to fuck you nice and slow as soon as you wake up more."

My body involuntarily moves at the promise of him inside of me. I press against him, wanting him to slide his cock into me now.

"You're going to come again for me like this first," he whispers into my neck.

I whimper when I feel him press his hand between my legs. I'm wet again already. I reach down to cover his hand with my own. "It's too much. Please just fuck me."

"Not yet," he growls as his teeth graze my shoulder. "You're so tight. I'll hurt you if you're not ready for me."

I'm ready. I'm so ready that my core is aching for him to be inside of me. I want him more than I've wanted any man in my life. I don't have to tell him. My body has already told him that over and over again tonight.

I moan when he glides his fingers over my clit. I gasp when he pushes two fingers into my depth and I grab tightly to the bed covers as I come.

I whimper the moment I feel him pushing me onto my stomach. I groan when I feel his large body curving over mine and I hold my breath as he slides his long, thick, sheathed cock into me.

"You're everything I've ever wanted," he says hoarsely. "I've never wanted anyone like this. It's never been like this."

I push back with my hips. "Fuck me, Garrett. Just fuck me."

He rocks his hard body into mine, each thrust deeper than the last. I grip the sheets in my hands, tensing with each small burst of pain that comes when he pushes hard. "Your body is incredible. You're perfect."

"You are…" I murmur into the pillow as I try to control my breathing.

He fucks me slowly, his grunts taking over the silence in the room. "I'm going to come so hard."

I cry out when I feel his hand slide from my hip to my core. I fall into my own climax the moment his finger touches my clit.

"Goddammit," he says gruffly as he pulls on my hips, pushing my body onto his cock with each deep thrust.

I hold tightly to the sheets as he skillfully grinds his body into mine. I feel the lush head as it pushes deeper and deeper and I know the moment he tenses that he's about to find his own release.

"Jesus, Vanessa," he says softly as he holds onto my waist before his body shakes as he comes in a series of deep, powerful thrusts.

I push back, wanting to feel every tremor from his body within my own.

"I need you." He leans forward to brush his lips over the back of my neck.

I shove my face into the pillow, not wanting to show him that I'm starting to need him to. It's more than what he can draw from my body in moments like this. I'm getting attached to him. Garrett Ryan is starting to feel like home to me, and I can't let that happen.

SEVEN

"Ben told me that you haven't been to visit your mother in a few days." He clasps the cufflink he just put on into place. "Do you want me to go with you to see her?"

It's much too personal an offer. At any other moment in my life, I'd jump at the chance to take a man I'm feeling so many things for, to see my mother. I'm not ready for that yet. I can't do it. "Thank you for offering but I'll probably just stop by there today. I have the day off."

He studies my expression in the mirror. I've just pulled my hair into a messy bun on my head. I'm wearing the same clothes that I was last night when he took me for dinner. The only difference is that my ripped panties are somewhere caught within the linens of his bed.

"What else are you doing today?" He picks up the other cufflink from where he rested it on the bathroom counter. "Do you have any fun plans?"

If meeting with Zoe's friend, the lawyer, falls into the category of fun plans, I'm going to have an amazing day. "No fun plans."

"You can meet me for lunch." He tips his chin towards my reflection in the mirror. "We can even meet back here."

I can't contain the smile I feel. "If we meet back here, we'll end up back in your bed."

"You wouldn't mind that one bit, Vanessa."

I blush. I don't want to, but I can't control it. He's right. I wouldn't mind it at all. When I'm with him I feel more wanted than I ever have in my life. He woke me up this morning with a few soft licks of his tongue over my cleft. Before I could react, he scooped my ass into his palms and ate me to another climax.

"You're being arrogant again." I point my finger at him in the mirror. "You know I don't like that."

"It's one of the reasons you're so crazy about me." He moves forward, his arms circling my shoulders. "You like me exactly the way I am."

I do. I dip my chin toward the floor to hide my reaction to his words. "I don't think I can make lunch. I have a meeting today."

"A meeting?" He reaches forward to cup his hand around my chin, pulling my face back up. "Who do you have a meeting with?"

"No one you know," I throw back with a smile. "It's just about some loose ends I need to tie up."

"Loose ends?" His brow furrows. "Why do I get the feeling you have secrets?"

The question catches me off guard enough that I reach for the counter for stability. "We all have secrets, don't we?"

His head tilts to the side as he studies my face in the mirror. "I guess we all do. I hope one day we can share them with each other."

I don't respond. I drop my gaze again as I realize that the closer I get to Garrett Ryan, the harder it's going to be to tell him my secrets.

***

"Tell me how you know Zoe." Imogen Ford motions towards a leather chair in her office. "She's an amazing person, isn't she?"

I nod as I take in the surroundings. When I'd arrived in the financial district to the offices of Corteck, I never imagined that the woman I'd be meeting would be as striking as she is. She's sophisticated, charismatic and from the nameplate on her door, she's the head legal counsel at one of the biggest tech firms in the country.

"We're friends," I offer as I take a seat. "We met when Zoe was volunteering at the extended care center my mother lives in."

"I'm not surprised to hear that." She reaches to hold her tailored skirt in place as she sits across from me. "She has a good heart."

I like that she sees Zoe through the same eyes that I do. "Zoe said that you're an attorney."

"I am. This isn't exactly where I thought I'd end up when I went to law school." She laughs as she looks around her office. "I started off as junior attorney here and now I'm primary legal counsel for the company and its owner."

The owner she's referring to is Clive Parker. He's not only one of the most gifted minds in tech development; he's also the cousin of Zoe's husband, Beck. When my best friend explained to me that she'd been coming down to Corteck once a week to meet with Imogen, I felt an immediate connection to her. She's been offering her time and mentorship to Zoe for months, all the while expecting nothing in return.

"Zoe told me all about how much you've been helping her." I feel the need to thank her myself. I know how much it means to Zoe to pursue her lifelong dream of being a criminal defense attorney. The passion in her voice is palpable when she talks about how she'll do the very best work she can for her future clients.

"I admire her." She glides her hand over the arm of her chair. "She is going to be a great lawyer."

I scratch my finger over my eyebrow. I had rehearsed in my mind everything I wanted to ask this woman and now that I'm sitting in the same room with her, I suddenly feel as though I can't find a place to start that will make any sense.

"Vanessa." She taps me lightly on my knee. "Zoe explained to me that you're dealing with a delicate situation."

I nod as I look at her face. "It's very complicated. I don't know that I need a lawyer though. Zoe just thought it might be good for me to ask your advice."

"I'm here to help." She swings both her arms into the air in front of her. "You're Zoe's best friend, which means I want to do what I can."

I bite my bottom lip. "Can we keep this between the two of us?"

"You have my word." Her mouth thins. "Whatever you tell me won't leave this office."

I draw in a heavy breath, look directly at her face and take the plunge. "My birth name is Charlotte Tomlin. I was kidnapped when I was an infant."

EIGHT

It's true what they say about lawyers. Apparently, it's even true when the lawyer in question has just heard a dramatic confession. Imogen didn't have any discernable reaction when I confessed that I was abducted almost a quarter of a century ago.

"I just found out," I continue. "It was just a few days ago when I found out."

Her eyes scan my face. Her lips part slightly before they close again. I watch her shoulders move as she swallows hard. "How did you find that out?"

I heave a sigh once I hear her speak. "I found some newspaper clippings in some of my mother's things…I mean, the woman who raised me. I went to a storage locker that she kept and found the clippings."

"They were newspaper articles related to the abduction?" She reaches towards her desk, scooping a notepad and pen into her hand. "You don't mind if I take a few notes, do you?"

"Notes? What for?" I blurt out without any thought.

"Solely for my own reference," she says quietly. "I'll admit this wasn't what I expected when Zoe asked me to meet with you."

It wasn't what I expected either when I went to the storage locker in Maine. "You won't show the notes to anyone?"

"Vanessa." I hear the faint sound of a crack in her voice. "I want to keep everything clear. That's why I'm taking notes."

I rub my hand over my forehead. I need to trust in Zoe's judgment. She's the one studying to be a lawyer. If she thinks that this woman can help me, I need to believe that she will too. "I understand."

"You found newspaper clippings of the abduction in your mother's storage locker," she starts before she pauses. "Is that all that you're basing your assumption on?"

I'm not offended by the question, even though I might have been if I knew Imogen better than I do. It's natural for her to ask me something like that. She only knows me through a shared connection with Zoe. "No, there's more to it than that."

"What else is there?"

"I always knew that I was adopted." I tap my foot against the carpeted floor. "I mean, my mother, Rowena, never hid the fact that I wasn't her child at birth."

"Did she tell you that you were adopted?" She jots something down on the notepad without looking up.

"She did," I confirm. "I'd ask her about my birth parents, but she was reluctant to share anything."

Her head darts up along with her brow. "Did you wonder why she was like that?"

I'm not an idiot. I don't want this woman, or anyone for that matter, to think that I am. There's no possible way I could have known the lengths that my mother went to all those years ago. I can't begin to comprehend the desperation that a person has to feel to do what she did. I know that she did it because there was a frantic yearning inside of her that she couldn't quiet. She took me from my stroller in the park that day to fill an empty hole within her. It was wrong, there's no denying that.

"My mother has always been secretive," I say quietly. "I understand more now why she was that way."

She stares at me for a moment before she pulls her gaze back down to the notepad. "Have you confronted your mother with the clippings? Have you shown them to her and demanded an answer?"

It's the one thing I've been wishing I could do since I found the tattered suitcase in her storage locker. I want my mother to have a brief moment of lucidity so she can explain to me what happened. I know that's not going to happen. I have to find my way through the maze of my past alone.

"My mother has advanced Alzheimer's. She's not in a position to offer any explanations."

The pity is there in her expression almost instantaneously. I'm accustomed to it even if I don't welcome it. "I'm sorry to hear that, Vanessa."

"My mother also had a safety deposit box." I want the conversation to move forward. Getting caught up in a lengthy discussion about my mother's prognosis won't help me at this point. She's lost to me. I accepted that fact a long time ago.

"Was there something in there?" She moves the pen across the paper, writing something in handwriting.

"Her journal was in there and some jewelry."

"Does she make an admission in the journal?" She stops writing to look at me directly. "Did she confess, in writing, to the abduction?"

"No." I shake my head from side-to-side slowly. "It's mostly just thoughts she shared about wanting to be a mother."

I can't judge from her expression whether she believes me or not. "What about the jewelry? Does it have any significance?"

I rest my hand over the front pocket of my jeans where I'd pushed the bracelet before I came to Imogen's office. "One of the pieces of jewelry was a bracelet. It's the bracelet that the Tomlin baby had when she was taken."

"You mean the bracelet that you had when you were stolen from your mother?"

I absorb each of the words, realizing for the first time, how heavy they feel. "Yes. I had it when Rowena Meyer took me away from my mother."

NINE

"I thought you'd come by my office today."

I smile the moment I hear his voice behind me. I had texted him to meet me at Easton Pub for a drink once he was done for the day. I'm still feeling shaky after my discussion with Imogen, and although I know Garrett would love it if I invited myself back to his apartment, tonight I just want to sit and talk, even if I'm not sure what I'll say to him.

"My meeting took longer than I thought it would." It's not completely untrue. I had been in Imogen's office for more than two hours while we scanned the Internet together looking at archived articles surrounding the events of that day in the park when I was taken from the stroller. She had explained the possible ramifications of going to the police. She wanted me to weigh the pros and the cons and she assured me, that given my mother's current state, there was virtually no chance that she'd be carted off to federal prison.

Once I left Corteck, I'd taken the subway into Brooklyn before I sat on a bench outside the extended care center. I didn't have the strength to go inside to face my mother. I haven't been able to do that since I discovered what she'd done. After sitting there for what felt like hours, I got back on the subway and made my way here.

I watch him as he sits next to me. The end of his patterned tie is sticking out of his jacket pocket and his hair is a disheveled mess. He looks as rumpled on the outside as I feel on the inside.

"You look like hell." I lean forward to run my hand through his hair. "Did you have a bad day?"

"Tell me about your day first." He pulls my hand into his, running his lips against my palm. "What did you do today? How did your meeting go?"

He asks the questions with the same comfortable ease of any man who cares for a woman. I know that he's feeling things for me that reach beyond the scope of what happens when we're wrapped around one another in his bed. The way he holds my hand and looks at me tells me that.

"I didn't do a lot." I stumble with what to add. "I met with one of Zoe's friends and then I went to Brooklyn."

"You saw your mother." It's not a question, it's an assumption. "I keep forgetting to ask you about the day you came by the townhouse. You never did tell me what that was about."

I take a long sip of the club soda I'd ordered when I first arrived thirty minutes ago. I have to work tomorrow, so anything stronger is off limits for me tonight. As much as I want to break the promise I made to myself not to drink when I have a shift the next day, I honor it, because I know that in the state I'm in, one drink may turn to two or more.

Garrett asks the server about her day before he orders a beer. I don't interrupt, grateful that her presence is giving me a momentary escape from the looming discussion we're going to have to inevitably have about why I was at Francesca's house. I take another heavy swallow of the club soda as she walks away.

"I know it can't be easy dealing with a parent who has Alzheimer's." He inches the stool he's sitting on closer to me. "You came to my client's house because you found something in that storage locker in Maine, didn't you?"

I study his face. His features are strong and chiseled. He's handsome, but there's more to his appearance than that. He's confident and magnetic. I'm drawn to him more and more each time I see him.

"Was there something in the locker that would give you more power over your mother's affairs?" He looks directly into my eyes. "If you found anything like that, I just need to see it and we can move forward from there."

I know all of my mother's secrets now and ironically I feel as though she's stripped any power I've had away from me. She stole my chance to see my birth mother before her death. She took away my opportunity to have a sustainable and loving relationship with my sister. There's no power left for me to have at this point.

The server stops by with Garrett's beer and a question about whether he comes in often. I give the woman props for trying to pick him up right in front of me. I should interject so she's clear that I'm with him, but as I watch him try to disengage from the conversation with her, I glance down at my smartphone to an incoming text message from Imogen Ford. They are four short words that complicate my life even more than it already is.

TEN

"I thought you'd spend the night with me." Garrett brings the beer glass to his lips before he finishes what's left. "I want you to come home with me."

If I hadn't gotten that text message from Imogen, I may have taken him up on his offer, but I feel as though I'm floating in a sea of nothing right now. I can't crawl back into bed with him tonight. I have to talk to Imogen. I need to understand the gravity of the can of worms I opened up when I went to talk to her today. She promised me, when I left her office, that she wouldn't share what I'd confessed to her with anyone. Now, I'm not certain whether I should have trusted her in the first place.

I lean forward to kiss him deeply, relishing in the taste of his breath mixed with the beer still lingering on his lips. "I would love to, but I have an early morning shift."

"So you'll come with me, we'll make love and then you'll fall asleep in my arms." He kisses me again, his tongue running over my bottom lip. "I'll get up when you do and ride with you in a taxi to the hospital before I go back home to get ready for work."

I touch his lips with my fingers. It's so tempting. I want the world to fall away so that I can enjoy everything that he's offering to me. I wish he had walked into my life a year ago. I would have fallen into his bed and into his arms and I would never have let go. "I should go home. I need to go home."

"You're sure?" He kisses my neck. "You don't want me to rip your clothes off so I can devour your body?"

My breath catches in my chest. It's not the words that stall my heart. It's the touch of his lips against my skin and his hands on my thighs.

"I would hold you all night, Vanessa." I can sense the smile on his lips as he whispers into my ear. "I'll chase all the bad things away."

He can't possibly know how much I wish that were true. I want everything that is clouding my life to dissipate so I can breathe again and live. I want to go back to being Vanessa Meyer, the young woman who doesn't have all the answers but is okay with that. My life was so much simpler before I started on my own self-initiated path to find the truth out about my adoption. Looking back now, I realize that not knowing offered a sense of peace that I can't find now.

"Tell me what time your break is tomorrow." He leans back so he can look at my face. "I want to bring flowers to the hospital."

"No," I say breathlessly. "You just gave me flowers the other day."

"I'd give you flowers every day if I thought you'd accept them," he went on, "I know that you wouldn't. You sometimes like to play hard to get with me."

I like that he sees my reluctance to give in to everything I'm feeling as playing hard to get. "Is that what I'm doing?"

His brow arches. "I know all your tricks, Nurse Meyer. Soon I'll have you all figured out."

I lean forward and glide my lips against his knowing that he's very far from figuring me out.

***

"I didn't expect you to come down here, Imogen." I reach across the table to hand her a paper cup filled with hot coffee. "I would have come to your office after work."

"I feel very badly about the way I handled the news." She shakes a small pink package of artificial sweetener between her fingers before she rips open the edge to pour the white crystals into her cup. "I shouldn't have sent that information in a text. I should have asked if you could meet me today."

I watch as she twirls a plain, brown stir stick in the coffee. "I was very surprised when I got your message."

"I could tell that talking about Francesca's death was hard for you." She runs her hand through her long, brown hair as her gaze takes in the faces in the cafeteria around us. "I wanted to look into her estate after you left. I thought it was the prudent thing to do."

It feels intrusive but I'm the one who went to her in the first place asking for advice. I don't know why I expected her to do nothing given that she's gone out of her way to help Zoe for the past few months. She may have gone snooping into Francesca's financial affairs out of the goodness of her heart, but it's opened a door that I have no intention of walking through.

"I was shocked that you found out so much so quickly," I admit. "I thought wills were private. I've never had one but I didn't know that just anyone could look at a person's will after they die."

If she takes any offense at my offhanded remark calling her 'just anyone' she doesn't show it in her expression or in her words. "They can't. Unless a will has entered probate, it's not public record."

"Her will is in probate?" I should know more about the process given the fact that I'm sleeping with a probate attorney.

"It's fast, isn't it?" She asks as if I have a firm grasp on what she's talking about. I don't want to delve into my limited knowledge of probate law so I ignore the comment. She doesn't miss a beat as she continues. "You understood the message I sent to you last night, didn't you?"

"I do understand. Your message said that I'm included in Francesca's will."

"You are." She blows softly on the coffee before taking a small sip. "This is actually not bad for cafeteria coffee."

I cock a brow. I try to limit my intake of coffee brewed in the hospital to one cup a day. It's not bad, but it's strong and if I'm not careful, the caffeine boost makes me feel like I'm bouncing off the walls.

"How is it that I'm included? Aren't most people declared...I mean...well, it's just that I've always heard that after seven years a person who is missing is presumed..." I stammer.

"Dead?" she interrupts. "Are you asking if Charlotte was presumed dead?"

Charlotte is dead in my eyes. Connie wishes she were dead so if that legal step has been taken, it would clear up a lot of the confusion I'm currently feeling.

"Generally that's a step that the courts will take in the case of a missing adult." She sighs heavily. "In the case of missing children, it's rarely done unless there is a life insurance policy or if there's a suspicion of homicide. Neither of those applied in your case."

I don't know how to react. I can't connect with the persona of Charlotte Tomlin. I've tried but the feeling of being that baby who was abducted is just as foreign to me as the idea of carrying her name. "What does that mean for me?"

"It means that if you make it known that you believe that you're Charlotte that will set the wheels in motion for you to collect the portion of Francesca's estate that was left in Charlotte's name."

"What wheels?" I ask hesitantly.

"This isn't my area of expertise, but I'd imagine that the first step would be a court ordered DNA test to prove your claim."

I'm not surprised. It's a natural and expected part of the process. "What would happen after that?"

"I suspect the police would begin an investigation into your disappearance. Ultimately your mother would be charged. As I already explained, I believe they'd be lenient given her condition."

"Everyone would know what she did?" I narrow my gaze at her. "I wouldn't be able to keep it a secret, would I?"

"You're the stolen Tomlin baby, Vanessa. If you claim your part of Francesca's estate, every paper in the state will have that story on their front page."

ELEVEN

"Do you remember when I was seven and I asked for a dog for my birthday?" I stare out the window towards the brick building next door. There hadn't been any choice of available rooms when my mother first began living in the extended care center. I wanted a room that faced the park across the street, so she could sit by the window and watch the children play but that wasn't possible. She had been assigned this small room at the end of a long corridor. It was acceptable, comfortable and private.

I hold tightly to the notebook and bracelet as I turn to look at her. I've been in her room for the past twenty minutes. I walked right past where she was sitting in her wheelchair by a small table. The staff put her there each morning before they hand feed her breakfast. She whimpers softly, as she often does, as I move towards her.

"You told me that the manager of the building wouldn't let us have a pet." I pull out one of the wooden chairs by the table before I sit down. "I was heartbroken over that."

Her eyes float aimlessly through the air, never settling on anything for more than a few seconds. I don't expect her to look at me. She hasn't in months. Her doctors have told me that it's part of her condition. They've also explained that deep within her mind there may be crevices that can still hold some shallow understanding of what I'm saying to her. That's why I'm here.

"Do you remember what you did for me?" I push my hand across the table to cover her small, weathered one. She doesn't pull back and I'm grateful for that. "You took me to the animal shelter that was three blocks from our place. You took me there once a week for more than two years so I could play with the dogs, and feed them and brush them."

A low sound escapes her chapped lips. I stare at her face. Her eyes are vacant and sunken. The once vibrant woman, who would pull me into her arms and twirl me around every day after she came home from work, isn't there anymore. This woman is a tortured and lost soul. She's been carrying a burden too heavy for one person for more than twenty years. Now, she's confined to her own type of prison.

"I always thought that when I grew up and got my own place that I'd want a dog." I smile softly. "I don't right now. Maybe one day if I have a child I will."

Her eyes dart quickly around the space. I pull mine down knowing that I need to do what I came here for. I've been avoiding her for almost a week and today I need to put to rest the nagging anxiety that has kept me away.

"You taught me so much about making the best with what we had." I study her profile. It's changed so much since I was a young girl. "You helped me understand things no one else could have."

I push the notebook and bracelet towards her. I feel awash with so many emotions that pinpointing any of them is impossible. I weep even before I speak another word to her. I take a heavy swallow and look directly at her face. "I know, mom. I know what you did."

The only movement she makes is a slight tilt of her chin. She doesn't make a sound. The air is filled with a deafening silence.

"I went to see her," I say the words quietly and slowly, hoping that she'll absorb even a fragment of what I'm sharing with her. "I went to see Francesca, the woman who gave birth to me."

I reach inside my purse for a tissue to help stop the flood of tears. "She died, mom. She died just a few weeks before I found her."

I pat the top of the notebook where the bracelet is sitting. "I have a sister. She's all that's left. She doesn't want anything to do with me."

"I know you took me because you wanted a baby to love." I pull the bracelet into my palm. "You gave me a beautiful life. You really did."

Her gaze falls briefly to my face before it slides off into the distance again. I move forward to adjust the collar of the simple, pink, housedress she's wearing.

"I love you, mom." I brush my lips softly over her cheek. "I forgive you."

I sob heavily the moment I see a single tear fall from her eye.

TWELVE

"Was Imogen able to offer you any advice?" Zoe leans back on one of the uncomfortable chairs in the staff lounge. "My back is really starting to hurt. I think the baby is going to be fifteen pounds."

I laugh at the notion of that. "I'm guessing he'll be somewhere in the seven or eight pound range."

She cocks a brow. "I can't wait to meet him. It's not much longer now."

"It'll be soon. Is that why you're at the hospital? Is everything okay with the baby?"

"I'm here to see my best friend." She tosses me a bright smile. "I also had to fill out some paperwork for when I go into labor."

"You should have told me you were coming by." I motion towards my watch. "I would have planned to have a break so we could have something to eat."

"I've already had two breakfasts today." She pats her stomach. "My huge baby has an insatiable appetite."

"Two breakfasts?" I hold up two fingers. "How many lunches are you planning? I have a break in about ninety minutes."

"I can come back for that." She inches forward on the chair. I can tell it's not doing her posture any favors. I'm not pregnant, and I always feel like I've pulled a muscle in my back when I sit in these chairs. Investing in comfort for the staff isn't a priority in this hospital.

"Do you want to meet in the cafeteria at one?" I jump to my feet, extending a hand to help her up. "Lunch is my treat today so bring both your appetites."

"Did Imogen help you, Van?" She holds my hand tightly as she pulls herself up. "I hope it wasn't too upsetting talking about everything with her."

"I guess she helped." I shrug my shoulders. "She checked out Francesca's will. Apparently I'm a part of that."

"What?" Her hand leaps to her chest. "You're actually in her will?"

"Charlotte is," I clarify. "It really doesn't matter. I'm not pursuing anything to do with that family. Connie is the only one left and the woman made it very clear, that she wants no part of me."

"I don't think it matters what Connie wants." Zoe reaches behind her to pick up her oversized purse. "I think it's important what Francesca wanted."

"She's gone. I've accepted the fact that she's gone."

"She wanted you to have something that belonged to her." Zoe fumbles in her purse for a few seconds before pulling out her smartphone.

"Money?" I shoot back. "I don't want her money."

"Is it money?" She glides her finger over the screen of her phone. "What if there's more? What if your mother left you something that's more valuable than money?"

"What do you mean?"

"My mother showed me her will." She shakes her head as if to ward off the thought of anything happening to her own mom. "When something happens to her, I inherit photos, some of the books she loves to read, the pieces of art that she saved up to buy. Those are the things that matter."

"I would love to have something like that." My eyes close briefly. "It would mean a lot to me to have anything that Francesca treasured."

"You can ask Imogen exactly what the will says." She rests her hands on my shoulders. "It can't hurt to ask."

***

"What made you want to be a probate attorney?" I push my foot against Garrett's under the table in the cafeteria.

"What made you want to be a nurse?" He pushes back with his shoe more forcefully. "I've wanted to ask you that since I saw you in the ER."

"Is that a lawyer thing?" I shoot back. "Do you ask a question to avoid answering a question?"

"It's a Garrett thing," he says, leaning back in his chair. "Being a probate attorney is just a job. It's an area of the law I find interesting. It's nothing like being a nurse."

"How would you know that? When's the last time you were a nurse?" I tease. "I think what you do is fascinating."

"Fascinating?" I hear a playful lilt in his voice. "Is that why you can't get enough of me? You think I'm fascinating?"

"No." I try to contain the smile I know is floating over my lips. "I said that I think your job is fascinating. I didn't say anything about you."

"You're the fascinating one." He grins. "You're very mysterious. There's something about you that I can't quite put my finger on."

"You've put your finger, and a lot more, on every part of me."

"You're making me hard, Vanessa."

"Zoe is going to be here any minute." I glance towards the entrance of the cafeteria. "There's no time for you to push me up against a wall in a deserted hallway so you can have your way with me."

"I was thinking more of taking you to a supply closet and sliding my cock down your throat, but I'm game either way."

I feel the flush that overtakes my face before he sees it. I reach to cover my face with my hand, not wanting him to see the impact that his brazen words have on me.

"I just stopped by to say hello to the most beautiful woman I know." He pushes the chair back from the table and stands in one fluid motion. "Tonight I'm going to fuck your gorgeous mouth and then," he pauses as he leans down to kiss my cheek. "After that, I'm going to spend the rest of the night making you forget everything but my name."

THIRTEEN

"I couldn't work at all this afternoon." His voice is raspy, hoarse and rushed. "All I could think about was this. I was so hard thinking about your mouth."

I'd respond but I can't. I'm flat on my back, Garrett's large frame above me. He's hovering over my chest, his wide thighs on either side of me, as he tangles his fist in my hair and pumps his thick cock into my mouth over and over again.

"You must be so wet." His head darts quickly to the left as he steals a glance at my nude body.

I moan around the swollen root. I want to tell him to reach back and touch me. I want to come too but I know that he's chasing his own release. It's been the only thing on his agenda since I arrived at his apartment. My scrubs are on the floor just inside the door. My bra and panties were lost somewhere in the hallway. When he threw me on the bed and held me still while he straddled me, I almost came on the spot. He's so commanding and desirous.

"Suck it, Vanessa," he growls into the air. "Suck it hard."

I do. I arch my neck up to take more into my mouth. My eyes are already burning, my throat is on fire. He's pushed himself farther into me than any man has ever been.

"Fuck, yes," he calls out as I twirl my tongue along the thick vein on the side. "You're so good. You know how to suck cock."

I move my legs slightly, wanting to create enough friction that I can come too. I'm aching. I need to touch my clit. I pull my hands off his thighs but that only brings forth a loud groan and more tension on my hair.

"Get me off," he commands. "Suck it. I want to come down your throat."

I let him guide me. His other hand jumps to my hair and he pumps my mouth in even, long strokes. With each one, his grunts only become louder and deeper.

I wrap my hands around his thighs again, needing the leverage it offers. My head is bouncing quickly, his cock plunging deeper with each stroke. I feel the moment his body begins to tense.

"Jesus," he hisses out between clenched teeth. "I'm going to come. I'm coming."

I brace my head wanting to take it all but the first stream is so much I choke when I feel it.

"Vanessa," he whispers my name as his eyes lock on mine. "Swallow. Slowly. Take it."

I nod as I feel another thick stream hit the back of my throat. I keep my gaze on his as I take every last drop his body gifts me with.

***

"It was too much, wasn't it?" He's still nude, his semi-erect cock bobbing between his thighs as he walks. "Vanessa, I was too rough. Fuck, please. Please don't go."

I rub my hand over my face. I had rushed from the room the moment he slid off of me. I had put on my panties before he had gotten off the bed, and now I'm standing in the kitchen of his apartment, dressed in my scrubs, while my bra still lies where he threw it when he was taking me into his bedroom.

I mumble something that neither of us can decipher. I'm not even sure of what I'm trying to say.

"I got caught up in how good it felt." His hand drifts over his cock. "It was so good. I hurt you, didn't I? Did I scare you?"

My bottom lip trembles so I bite it, hoping the rush of pain will ward off the visible anxiety I'm feeling. "No. I'm not scared."

"I should have stopped." He stomps his foot hard against the floor. "Fuck. I wasn't thinking straight. I won't do that again."

"I liked it," I admit softly. "I really liked it."

"You liked it?" I hear the relief in his voice just as I see it in his expression. "It wasn't too much?"

I shake my head from side-to-side. "I liked it all. It wasn't too much."

His gaze narrows. "What's wrong? Why are you leaving?"

I'm leaving because I'm a coward. I'm running away because I'm falling for this beautiful man who makes me feel things I've never felt before. I have secrets that I've waited too long to tell him.

"There are things about me you don't know." I point my finger at his chest. "Things I can't tell you about me."

I see the veil of compassion that blankets his eyes the moment the words leave my lips. "You can tell me anything, Vanessa. I want you to tell me everything."

"I can't." I cover my bottom lip with my fingers. "You won't understand."

"Try me," he challenges as he crosses his arms over his broad chest. "Just try me."

"I'm adopted," I blurt out because it's been resting at the tip of my tongue since I showed him Rowena's will weeks ago. "My mother isn't my birth mother."

"You're adopted?" He backs up slightly.

"I've known for years," I offer. "My mother and I don't look alike."

"My sister and I look nothing alike." He takes long strides across the room to scoop a framed picture into his hand.

I look down at the photograph as he holds it out for me. He's younger. The picture must have been taken more than a decade ago. His hair is longer, his face thinner but the exuberance in his smile is there. It's unmistakable. His arm is draped around a woman, probably the same age as him. She's stunning and the graduation gown and cap she's wearing only adds to her beauty.

"My parents adopted Lynn from China when I was a baby." He nods towards the picture. "She's beautiful, isn't she?"

"Yes. She's so beautiful."

"I understand about adoption. It's part of who I am too."

I look up into his face. I need to tell him more. I have to tell him that I'm Charlotte. "There's more to it than the adoption."

"It's your mother's condition, isn't it?" He bows his head so his chin is resting against my forehead. "Ben told me that she doesn't have a lot of time left."

"I'll miss her when she's gone," I say as I stare at the picture of Garrett and his sister. "She gave me an amazing life."

"You'll always have your memories of her." He brushes his lips over my forehead. "It takes a very special person to adopt a child. It takes a remarkable person to adopt a child and then raise them on their own. Your mother is a saint, Vanessa."

I stop myself before I disagree. She may have given me a life that was filled with love and all of the necessities, but what she took from me is irreplaceable.

FOURTEEN

"I have a copy of it here." She holds tightly to a stack of papers in her hands. "I've read through it myself, but if want to take a look at it, I can give you a few minutes alone."

I should take her up on her offer, but since she called me at work this morning, I've been a bundle of nerves. Imogen was willing to help the moment I asked her if she could find out exactly what Francesca had left to her infant daughter who had been abducted. I had texted her about it last night, after I got home from Garrett's apartment. He had tried to get me back into bed with him, but I told him I was tired and he hadn't argued the point beyond that.

"Do you just want the abbreviated version of what she left you, Vanessa?" I feel her hand rest on my shoulder. "I can share that with you and then you don't have to read through all the legal jargon."

"Okay," I say quietly. "I guess that would be best."

She sits across from me, resting the document in her lap. "Francesca updated her will late last year. The executor is a close family friend."

I study her face for any clue about what she's about to say next, but there's nothing. I grip the armrest of the chair. I came here for this, yet I'm not prepared to hear it. It shouldn't matter what she left me but it does.

"She left a large portion of her estate to charity." She glances down briefly at the papers. "She was a philanthropist. I'm not sure if you're aware of that. She generated a large amount of donations for many organizations, hospitals, children's charities, things like that."

"I read about that online." I cross my legs at the ankles. "She was very generous."

"There was a separate sizable donation to a charity that provides hospice care for cancer patients." She rubs her hand along the side of her face. "Your mother had a hand in establishing that two years ago."

"I didn't know about that."

"She kept her name out of it." She smiles softly. "It seems like a great organization. The people there do good work."

"Will you write down the name of it for me?"

"Of course." She reaches towards her desk to retrieve the notepad she was writing on the first time we met here. "I'll jot that down for you now."

I wait in silence as she scribbles out a few lines on a sheet of the paper, before ripping it off and handing it to me.

"The remainder of her estate is left to her two daughters," she begins before she stops to swallow. "Constance and Charlotte."

"Connie and me," I say under my breath.

"It's a generous amount." Her jaw tightens. "There are provisions for Charlotte's inheritance if she's never found."

"What provisions?" I ask out of nothing but a deep sense of curiosity. I'm actually grateful that she hasn't offered a specific dollar amount. It's not that it would sway my decision to come out of the shadows and declare myself Charlotte. It's not about the money for me. I just want a piece of the woman that Francesca Tomlin was.

"Charlotte's portion of the estate will be placed in a trust that is to be overseen by the executor of the estate." She flips through a few pages, her finger running along the lines of typed text. "If Charlotte isn't located by the date of her twenty-fifth birthday, her portion of the estate will go to her sister."

"I'll be twenty-five in seven months," I offer without thinking.

"You can't wait too long to make a decision then."

"Was there anything else?" I lean forward to try and catch a glimpse of the papers. "Did she leave me anything other than money?"

She studies me briefly before a small smile pulls at the corner of her lips. "I've never seen anyone less interested in millions of dollars."

The number doesn't surprise me. I knew that wealth was part of my birth family's life when I walked into the townhouse. "I'm just wondering if she left me anything personal. Is there anything that might have had sentimental value that she wanted Charlotte to have?"

"There's a necklace that belonged to her grandmother," she pauses before she continues. "That would be your great-grandmother."

"A necklace?" My hand leaps to my neck.

"There is a silver collection." She studies the papers more carefully. "It doesn't indicate what the significance of that is."

"Okay." I heave a heavy sigh. "Anything else?"

"Vanessa." She inches forward on her chair. "I think you need to carefully consider what you want to do. I can set you up with a great probate attorney who can help guide you through the process. She's very good."

"I'm not sure I want to pursue it." I glance at her. "I still need to think about it."

"Francesca left a sealed envelope for Charlotte." She taps her finger on the edge of the notepad. "If you're not located by your twenty-fifth birthday, that envelope will be destroyed."

"An envelope?" My breath leaves me in a hurried rush. "Does it say what's inside?"

She flips the pages over in her lap. "It says, in no uncertain terms, that no one but Charlotte Tomlin is permitted to open the envelope."

That envelope may hold all the things I need and want to hear from my birth mother. It may hold nothing, but that one envelope changes everything.

FIFTEEN

"Beck donates a lot to different charities, doesn't he?" I stare down at the piece of paper that Imogen gave me when I was in her office yesterday.

"He's very generous." Zoe's gaze is fastened past my head to the counter at the ice cream shop we just walked into.

"Do you know much about them?"

"I know the strawberry is really good." She points to the menu. "I might have something more daring today though."

"Live a little." I pat the top of her stomach. "I was asking about whether you knew much about the charities that Beck donates to."

"Oops." She pulls her hand up to her mouth to stifle a loud laugh. "My mind is on one track right now. Food."

"I'll go order for us both and then we can talk about the charity thing, okay?" I motion towards an empty table in the corner. "Go rest your swollen feet."

"You'll get me a double scoop?" Her eyes brighten. "Maybe some whipped cream on top?"

I giggle at how excited she is over the prospect of ice cream. Her joy is infectious. I don't think I could have chosen a more perfect best friend. "A cherry too."

"This was such a good idea," she mumbles as she walks away. "You're the best, Van."

She is. Zoe Beck may be the most amazing woman I've ever met.

***

"You're crazy, Zoe," I call out to her as she exits the taxi before me. "I don't think this is a good idea."

"It's the best idea I've had in weeks," she says as she tucks her wallet back into her bag after paying the driver. "We should go inside and get some answers."

We should get back in the cab and rethink this spur-of-the-moment decision. This is oddly similar to when we jumped into a car and headed over to Francesca's townhouse. That ended in the worst way possible and now we're standing on the street in front of Ravel Hospice Center. This is the place that Imogen gave me the address for. It's the organization that Francesca helped establish before her death.

"Zoe," I try to catch my breath as I chase her through the crowded pedestrian traffic of this busy Tuesday afternoon. "Please stop for a minute."

She does. She turns towards me. "What's wrong?"

"We need to think about what we're doing." I pull on the arm of her sweater. "We can't just walk in there."

She motions towards the glass door with her chin. "There's a sign on the door that says they're open, Van. Let's just go inside."

I twist my hands together in a knotted fist. I can feel a pit in the bottom of my stomach. "We're intruding. This is a care center. The people in here don't need us barging in."

"We're going to talk to the person at the front desk." She cocks both her brows. "I'm going to ask about making a donation."

"You are?" I feel a sense of relief flood through me.

"This place mattered to your mom, Van. You matter to me. Let's just go inside."

I don't stop here as she turns, puts her hand on the door handle and pulls it open.

SIXTEEN

"This is incredibly generous of you, Mrs. Beck." The young woman holds the check Zoe just wrote to the center in her hands. "I know your husband's work. He's very gifted."

"I'll tell him you said that." She glances around the barren waiting room near the entrance. "I'm going to talk to Beck about donating a few small pieces to brighten up this space."

I swear the woman holding the check in her hands is near tears now. "You would do that? You would ask Brighton Beck to donate paintings?"

"I will tell him to do it," Zoe teases. "He loves helping. He knows how much a calm and beautiful place can help people who are ill."

"I wish Mrs. Tomlin was here." She blinks innocently as she stares at the check. "She would be so thankful for all of this. She felt the same way about a calm place."

"Mrs. Tomlin?" Zoe steps into the opening with effortless ease. "Is she a patient here?"

"No." She leans closer to us. "Mrs. Tomlin isn't with us anymore."

I open my mouth to speak but Zoe's hand on my forearm halts me.

"She died?" Zoe asks softly. "Was she a patient who passed away?"

"She wasn't a patient." The woman's eyes float over Zoe's face. "She funded all of this. She helped set everything up."

"She must have been a special person." Zoe rests her hand on her stomach.

"The best person I ever met. It's so sad that they couldn't help her."

"Who couldn't help her?" I can't veil my curiosity any longer.

I feel Zoe's eyes lock on my face just as the woman's gaze falls to the floor. "There wasn't a doctor who could help her. She had terminal liver cancer. There was nothing anyone could do."

***

"Is it painful to die from cancer?"

"What?" Ben's head pops up. "Are you sick?"

"No." I realize that it might not have been the best thing to say when I first approached his office door. "I'm just wondering what the final stages are like for someone who has terminal cancer."

"Is this about a patient?"

It's an easy lie that he's actually leading me into. This is my mother we're talking about though and I don't want to tarnish what she suffered with because I'm too fearful to share. "It's not about a patient. It's someone I'm related to."

"Oh," he says the single word with absolutely no emotion. "I didn't realize you had family beyond Rowena."

"I was adopted," I point out. I don't elaborate because right now I just want to understand the depth of the discomfort that Francesca would have had to endure.

"What type of cancer?"

I'm grateful that he doesn't probe me for more details about the person in question. "It's liver cancer."

He closes the cover of his tablet and motions towards a chair opposite his desk. "You should sit down, Vanessa."

I know Ben well enough to know that the suggestion isn't based on anything other than compassion. I lower myself into the chair.

"Advanced liver cancer is brutal." He clasps his hands together on his desk. "The most we can offer the patient is some relief from the pain."

"What exactly will the person experience?" I ask nervously. "I don't know much about it."

"Each case is different," he points out. "Some patients are cognizant until their last breath. Others aren't lucid because of the degree of pain they're in."

"They suffer though?"

"Some patients experience difficulty breathing. Many lose their sight."

"Is it a slow death?" I can't control the emotion in my voice.

"It's a horrible way to die, Vanessa." He motions towards me with his hand. "I'm sorry that someone you care about is that ill."

"Thank you, Ben." I slouch back in the chair, suddenly feeling very weak. "I need to get back to the ER."

"There's one more thing." He looks up as I pull myself to my feet. "Liver cancer itself isn't hereditary. Some of the conditions that weaken the liver and make it susceptible to disease are. You might want to get tested for those if we're talking about a blood relative."

"That's good to know." I look towards the open door of his office. "Can you keep this between us?"

"Between us?" He flips open the cover of his tablet.

"I'd prefer if you didn't tell Garrett that we talked about this."

"I won't." He smiles gently. "You have my word."

SEVENTEEN

"You've been working a lot lately." He butters one of the warm pieces of bread the waiter dropped off for us just moments ago. "It feels like weeks since I've seen you."

"It's been three days," I point out. "Lawyers like to exaggerate."

"That's not true." He takes a hearty bite of the bread. "What's going on with you?"

I tense for a moment as I consider his question. I trust Ben but I also know that he's a close friend of Garrett's and given the choice of who to uphold a promise to, I doubt I'd win out. I knew when Garrett asked me to dinner that there was a chance that I'd be bombarded with questions about my ill relative.

"What's going on with you?" I counter.

"You're learning." He rests the remaining bread in his hand onto a small plate in front of him. "I've got nothing going on."

"You have nothing going on?" I ask with a grin. "You're the best probate attorney in the state. You must have some exciting stories to tell."

"There's that pesky client, lawyer privilege thing I have to keep my eye on." He winks at me. "I can't spill the beans or my clients will drag my ass into court."

"They can actually do that?"

"I don't think any of them would." He scans the interior of Axel NY. It's one of my favorite restaurants in the entire city. I haven't told Garrett that, so I can only assume, he's a fan of the food here too. "I'm working on a case right now that's really complicated. The woman...my client...she's a piece of work."

I'm tempted to ask if he's referring to my sister, but I know he won't answer. Beyond that, I also realize that my showing any interest in the woman will only peak his curiosity.

"It must be really hard to deal with loved ones right after someone dies." My grip on my water glass tightens as I think about Francesca's death.

"You do the same thing, don't you?" He takes a heavy swallow of wine. "People must die in the ER every day."

He says it so callously but that's to be expected. People who don't face death that directly on a daily basis have no idea about the toll it takes on the medical professionals who are witness to it. I've gone home in tears after watching one of the doctors explain to a newlywed that his wife died in a car accident. I've also been in the room with a family when their small child took his last breath because he fell down a flight of stairs. It's the very worst part of working at the hospital.

"It's never easy." I exhale softly. "I still get upset when we lose a patient."

"That's because you have a good heart." He looks at me. "I knew it when you helped me that day I had my accident."

"You wouldn't let me help you," I correct him. "You wouldn't cooperate at all."

"At first," he concedes. "Ben told me how you stepped up to the plate when I fell and smashed my face in the ER."

I wince physically at the reminder of that. "I don't like thinking about that."

"Me either," he pauses. "I'm just grateful that you were there to help."

***

"How's your mom been?" He rests his fork against his now empty dessert plate.

I glance down at the untouched chocolate cake on mine. I'd barely eaten any of my dinner and when he insisted I order dessert, I hadn't argued the point. I need and want to talk to him about what I'm dealing with, but now that I'm sitting across from him, I'm not sure I can.

"She's still the same." I shrug. "I went to see her the other day."

"I'd still like to go with you one day so I can meet her."

"Garrett, it's not…"

"You're going to tell me that it's not necessary." He swipes the linen napkin across his mouth as he interrupts me. "Your mother may not be fully aware of who comes to meet her, but I'll be fully aware of meeting her. I'd love to meet her."

I've never dated a man who offered something that genuinely kind before. "Maybe at some point we can do that."

"You're playing hard to get again, Vanessa."

"No," I pull my hand through my hair. "I'm not doing that."

"Next you're going to tell me that you can't come home with me."

I was going to say that. "I can't. I have an early day tomorrow."

"That excuse is as lame tonight as it was the last time you used it." He tosses the napkin onto the table. "Do you have a secret boyfriend you haven't told me about?"

I sigh overly dramatically, enjoying how playful he is. "Is that what you think is going on? You think I have a secret boyfriend that I'm keeping hidden from you?"

He leans forward slowly, his eyes never leaving my face. "It might be a boyfriend. Maybe it's an entire family. You're hiding something from me and it's big."

EIGHTEEN

I'm back in the exact same spot I was weeks ago. I'm in a chair in the living room of Garrett's apartment. I couldn't catch my breath after he blurted out that he knew I was holding onto a secret. I let him guide me into a taxi and I clung to him as he kissed my neck and told me how much he wanted me.

I'd twisted my hands in his hair as he ate me to one exquisite orgasm after another. Then I kissed him deeply when he pulled me onto his body so I could ride his big, beautiful cock. He'd screamed my name when he came and held me close to him as he drifted off to sleep. I'd rested there, with my eyes wide open until I felt his breathing level. Then I carefully pulled myself free of his strong embrace, pushed my arms through the white dress shirt he'd been wearing all day and came out here, to sit and think.

I reach into my purse and pull Rowena's notebook into my lap. I open the pages, scanning the messily written words. I wonder if her confessions will mean more to me now that I know the true depth of her desperation. I read through one page before I see the shadow of his large frame cast darkness over my lap.

"That's your mother's journal, isn't it?" He reaches out with his hand. "Stand up, Vanessa."

I do without any thought. He looks different in the pale light of the room with sleep still in his eyes. IIis hair is a touslcd mcss from where I gripped tightly to the strands as I ground myself into his face chasing my own release. His body is nude, his toned frame on full display. I doubt I'll ever know anyone like him again. I don't want to know another man the way I know him.

"Sit on my lap." He lowers himself into the chair and pats his legs. "Let me hold you."

I sit down carefully, mindful of where his cock is.

"You can't hurt it." He nuzzles his face into my neck. "It's going to be hard again in about ten seconds."

I laugh loudly, throwing my head back with abandon. "You're…"

"I'm what." He doesn't let me finish. "Handsome? Sexy? You think I'm the best looking man you've ever met, don't you?"

I wrap my arm over his shoulder, my hand resting on his neck. "You are the most incredible man I've ever met."

"I've never met anyone like you." His voice is deep and raspy. "I never imagined I could meet a woman like you."

"A nurse?" I tease as I kiss his cheek softly.

"No." He grabs my chin, tilting my face towards his. "A beautiful, sexy, smart woman who sees things in me that no one else can."

I swallow hard. "I'm not that special."

"You're a fucking angel." He brushes his lips over mine. "You're the best person I know."

"No." I lick my upper lip. "I'm not a good person. You're wrong."

He studies my face carefully. "Why would you say that? Something is eating you up, Vanessa. Tell me what it is."

I pull on the edge of my hair. This can never move forward if I'm not honest with him. "My mother did something… it was unforgiveable."

"That's on your mother." His tone is controlled. "You're not responsible for anything she's done."

"That's true," I agree. "I have to live with the consequences of it though."

"It hurt you, didn't it?" he asks quietly. "The thing she did, it's still hurting you."

"It will always hurt." I lift my chin. "It's complicated my life."

"Complicated in what way?" He wraps his arm around my legs, adjusting my body slightly on his lap.

"Legally, emotionally." I push against the back of the chair to level myself. "My life is always going to be fucked up because of what she did."

"Legally?" he ignores everything after that word. "In what way? Did your mother do something illegal?"

"A long time ago she did." I know timing doesn't matter, but it lessens the severity of her actions in my mind, if I'm able to put tangible distance between that day in the park and now.

"If the statute of limitations has passed, it's not relevant in the eyes of the law, Vanessa. When did this happen?"

"Almost twenty-five years ago."

He doesn't mask the surprise in his expression at all. His mouth even falls open briefly. "That's so long ago. It was before you were born?"

"No, it happened shortly after I was born."

"Unless it was a federal crime, it's likely not on the books anymore. I doubt that anyone would even remember what it was."

"It was a federal crime." I know that because I'd asked Imogen about it. She explained that in the case of child abductions, charges could be brought decades later. It's happened in many cases in the past.

"Have you talked to a lawyer about this?" he pauses briefly. "I'm talking about a criminal defense attorney. Has your mother ever consulted with one?"

"I don't think so," I say genuinely. "I don't think anyone but me knows what she did."

"Do you want to tell me what it is?" He taps my knee with his hand. "I can draw up a contract that says I'm representing you and that will invoke client, attorney privilege."

"We have to take that step?"

"We're lovers." His hand sweeps across my thigh." We're dating. It's prudent. It would be best to have something in place before you confess your mother's crimes to me."

The playful lilt in his voice irritates me. He can't possibly know the gravity of what I'm dealing with, but I still feel annoyed that he's finding humor in something that is tearing me apart.

"Actually." He reaches to clasp my hand in his. "Maybe you should talk to a criminal defense attorney I know. It might be the best thing to do for your mother and for you."

NINETEEN

I can't scramble to my feet fast enough. "I have to get her a lawyer? I can't just tell you?"

"No. Well, yes." He's on his feet now too. He rakes his hand through his hair. "I'm not your lawyer right now. You can't tell me."

"You're a lawyer. Let's sign a contract." I push my index finger into his chest. "If I tell you anything then, you can't tell the police."

He scratches the bridge of his nose. "It may not be that simple. I don't have a thorough grasp on criminal law, Vanessa. I want you to have the best advice you can."

"I told Zoe's friend, Imogen, about it." I don't think before I start throwing out names. "She's been helping me."

"Imogen?" He takes a heavy step towards me. "Are you talking about Imogen Ford?"

I nod briskly. "Zoe arranged it. I needed some legal advice."

"About this?" He waves his large arms in the air. "You went to Imogen Ford to talk about a federal crime? The woman works for a tech company. She's an expert in corporate law. Not this."

"She is helping me understand things."

"What things?"

"I didn't have anywhere else to go." I grab the front of the shirt I'm wearing. "I needed someone to help me."

"Why didn't you ask me, Vanessa?" he scowls. "I have friends who are skilled in this area of the law. I could have arranged a meeting for you with any of them."

It's a half-hearted, late, attempt to offer me some assistance. Judging by what happened just now, when I was set to confess my mother's crime to him, he would have treated me with even less compassion if I would have asked for his help weeks ago.

"It doesn't matter, Garrett." I circle my fingers around one of the buttons on the front of the shirt. "I'm handling it myself."

"You can't tell anyone about this." His gaze narrows on me. "The law is very complicated when it comes to serious crimes. If you have knowledge of a federal crime and you don't report it, you are an accessory after the fact."

"I haven't done anything wrong." I wring my hands together. "My mother did something to me. She is the one who broke the law."

"How long have you known about it?" He crosses his arms over his chest. "Have you told anyone besides Imogen?"

"It hasn't been that long." I pull on the hem of the shirt. "Zoe knows. She probably told her husband."

"Vanessa." He throws his head back in a huff. "You have to stop telling people. You can't go around just telling anyone about a federal crime. You're going to get yourself into serious trouble."

"I trust the people I told." I bark back. "I trust all of them."

"That's just being foolish." He points his finger at me. "People can turn on you in the blink of an eye. You can't trust anyone in a situation like this."

"I'm leaving," I announce before I turn on my heel. "I can't do this right now."

"You can't ignore this." He's right behind me as I walk down the hallway. "Whatever this is, you have to deal with it."

"I am." I turn to face him. "I am trying to do that."

"Please." His hands fly to my shoulders. "I care so much about you. Christ, just so much, Vanessa."

I don't react. I want to find faith in those words but the man was quick to shut me down the moment I started to open my mouth about what my mother did. "I can't do this, Garrett. I can't stay here."

"I am going to have one of my friends call you." He reaches past me to where his smartphone is sitting on a nightstand. "He's the best there is. I'll cover his fees. Please, Vanessa. Please talk to him."

TWENTY

"Vanessa?"

I dart my hand into the air between us. "You must be Mr. Tiller."

He gives my hand a firm shake. "It's Jonah."

"Jonah," I repeat quietly.

"Garrett didn't have a lot to share." He opens a tablet on his desk. "He paid my retainer so we're good to go."

We're not good to go. It's been more than a week since I walked out of Garrett's apartment unsure of what I should do. I went to visit my mother twice and cried with my head in her lap, looking for answers that she couldn't offer to me. I'd spoken to Imogen once, who assured me that it wouldn't hurt to talk to someone skilled in the area of criminal law and I had held Zoe's hands as she confessed that she wanted me to protect myself and if this was the way to do it, I should.

"I don't know much about the law."

"That's why you're here and I'm ready to help." He smiles genuinely. He's older. His face is kind. "Garrett told me that you have knowledge of a crime that your mother committed."

"You can't tell him about this conversation, can you?" I lean forward to rest my hand against the edge of his desk. "I know he's paying your fees, but you can't share what I'm about to tell you with him, can you?"

"I can't," he assures me. "Although I was under the impression, from what Garrett told me, that you were just about to share details of the crime with him before he stopped you."

I was. I wanted to. My heart was aching to but when he jumped into full legal mode, any desire I had to share my deepest, darkest secrets with him vanished. We've barely spoken since that day. We shared a strained visit in the hospital cafeteria along with a few brief phone calls.

"I'd like to pay the retainer myself." I reach to pick up my purse from where I rested it on the floor next to the chair I'm sitting in. "I don't want to be in debt to Garrett."

"I can have my assistant take care of that after our meeting." He punches a few keys on the tablet. "I'd like to record our meeting if you're comfortable with that."

I'm not but I've come this far. "It's not something that can be used against me, can it?"

He smiles broadly. "It's for my reference."

"I'm fine with it." I survey the room, taking in all the certificates hanging on the walls.

"Let's start at the beginning, Vanessa." He leans back in his chair. "Tell me about your mother. Is she aware that we're meeting today? Did you ask her to attend with you?"

"My mother has advanced Alzheimer's disease. She lives in an extended care center in Brooklyn."

"I'm sorry." His expression gives nothing away. "I wasn't aware of that."

He's not aware of anything. I'm sitting in a room with a stranger about to confess my mother's worst sins all because I wanted to feel closer to Garrett. It's irony at its best.

"Let's cut to the chase." I take a deep breath. "My mother kidnapped me when I was an infant. I only discovered it recently."

He sits straight up in his chair. His eyes dart from me to the tablet on the desk. "Your mother kidnapped you?"

"Yes. That's what I said."

"When was this?"

I blow out a puff of air, knowing that I've gotten past the worst part. "It was almost twenty-five years ago."

"Where did this happen?" He rests his elbows on his desk.

"Here. It happened in New York." I gesture toward the bank of windows overlooking the city's skyline behind him. "It was in a park. She took me from a stroller."

He leans closer, his eyes studying my face. "You're not the Tomlin girl, are you? You can't be her."

"That's exactly who I am." I smile briefly. "I'm Charlotte Tomlin."

"Charlotte," he says the name slowly and with extra effort. "I know you, Charlotte. I was one of your father's best friends."

TWENTY-ONE

"This is my father?" I stare down at the framed picture of Jonah and another man. "He was so handsome."

"Oh, he was a looker, little one." He stops himself. "We called you that. Your dad did, before you disappeared."

"Little one," I repeat it back.

"You were named after him, you know." He points to my father's handsome, rugged face in the faded photograph. "Charlie Tomlin. Charles. That's what your mom called him."

"I knew his name was Charles. I read that online."

"He loved you bunches." He touches my shoulder briefly. "He would have been so proud of you. Look at you. You're all grown up."

"I wish I could have known him before he died." I push the picture back into his hands.

"That's your picture now if you want it." He rests it on my lap. "I have a lot more at home. I can make you copies if you want them."

"I would love that." I don't try to hide the excitement in my voice. This is the first person I've spoken with who knew my parents. "It would mean a lot to me to have them."

"You'll give me your address, and I'll send them over this week."

I know I should pull the conversation back to that day in the park, but I can't. I'm still amazed by the fact that Garrett steered me right into the office of one of my birth father's closest friends. "Tell me what he was like."

"Charlie?" He settles back into his chair. "He was funny as hell. The man could make everyone in the room laugh."

I smile as I imagine the man in the picture laughing. I can't recall his voice. I was too young to remember anything about my birth family.

"Your mom passed a few weeks ago," he says grimly. "She was strong as an ox. She got sick and couldn't beat it."

"I know," I mutter. "I went to her townhouse to see her, but…"

"You were at the house?" His lips thin. "Did you talk to Connie?"

"Briefly." I nod. "I haven't seen her since."

An alarm on his smartphone jars us both from the conversation.

"Dammit." He looks down at the screen. "I have another meeting in ten minutes. We have to wrap this up."

"I'm not sure what I should be doing next."

"We need to talk to the police." He flips through the calendar on his phone. "I have a detective friend downtown. I'll talk to him and then we can go in together next week."

"I'm not sure…I don't know…" I stammer. "What will happen to my mother? The woman who raised me is a good person. I don't want her to get in trouble."

"I understand." His lips twitch slightly. "You can't sit on this. It's an open case. We have to go to the police."

"She's too frail to face any of this. She won't understand what's going on." I hold in a sob. "I'm all that she has."

"All of that will be taken into consideration," he assures me. "If we don't go to the police now, and this comes to the surface in the future, it will be much more serious."

I twist my hands together, suddenly aware of the gravity of everything that's happening. I wish I had brought Zoe with me for moral support. "I need to talk to my friend about this."

"Garrett?" he asks while he studies his phone. "He's handling Franny's estate, isn't he?"

Franny? My mother had a nickname. A fun, playful name that the people who cared for her called her.

"He is, yes."

"You haven't told him, have you?" He rubs his hand over the back of his neck. "He doesn't know who you are, does he?"

"No," I confess. "I haven't told Garrett."

"Tell him." He stands up from his chair. "You have to do that. He needs to know you're Charlotte."

"Why?" It's a question I put absolutely no thought into.

"You are Charlotte Tomlin." He moves around the desk until he's stranding right in front of me. "You may have been taken away from that family, but you are still part of it. Your sister isn't fit to carry on the family name. You are. Make your mother proud."

TWENTY-TWO

"She's always been so proud of you, Vanessa." Zoe taps me on the back. "I remember when you told me about your perfect report card in the third grade and how she took you to buy a jump rope."

I rest my forehead on the coarse blanket that covers the hospital bed. I can't lift my head to respond to her. I've been sitting in this wooden chair for the past five hours holding tightly to my mother's hand.

After I'd met with Jonah yesterday afternoon, I'd come to the hospital for my shift. I had taken the vital signs of a boy they had pulled out of the Hudson River who was going to be fine. I'd helped stitch up the forehead of a young man who had decided it would be a good idea to jump off the roof of a house in Queens onto a pile of worn mattresses he found in a dumpster. I had laughed with a couple who passed through the ER on their way home with their newborn baby wrapped snuggly in a car seat, and I had held onto Ben's arm for support when an ambulance brought my mother in just as I was walking out the entrance to go home.

"You should go home," I say quietly into the air. "You shouldn't be here, Zoe. You should be resting."

"I'm not leaving." Her voice is firm and unyielding. "I won't go."

"I'll be fine." I twist my neck to the left to look up at her. "I have so many friends here. I'm not going to be alone."

"Do you want me to call Garrett?" She reaches towards me. "Give me your phone and I'll call him to tell him what's going on."

"No." I reach down to my pocket. "I don't want him to come here."

"He would want to be here, Van." She pulls on my ponytail. "He'll be upset that you didn't tell him."

I haven't told Zoe about Garrett's response when I tried to tell him about what my mother did. "You don't understand, Zoe. Things aren't great between us right now."

"Why not?" Her voice is barely more than a whisper. I have to strain to hear her. It's as if she thinks that we're going to wake my mother even though I've already explained to her that Ben sedated her so she could rest.

"I don't want to get into it right now." I rub my hand across my forehead. "I only have the energy to deal with my mom right now."

She nods. I can tell she's not completely agreeing with my decision, but she's not arguing against it, so I take that as a small victory.

"Go home, Zoe. You've been here most of the night" I reach for her hand. "I'll text you in a few hours."

"You promise me that if anything changes, you'll call." She pats her purse. "I'll have my phone with me all day. I can be back here in fifteen minutes."

"I promise." I squeeze her hand. "Go get some sleep."

She leans as far forward as her stomach allows before she kisses me softly on my cheek. "She's going to be okay, Van. She's a fighter."

She is. I watch her walk out of the room before I turn back to look at my mother. "Don't leave me yet, mom. Please, please don't leave me."

***

"There's an available bed on the fifth floor." Ben touches my mother's arm softly. "I'm going to admit her. She needs to stay for at least a few days. We have to clear that congestion out of her lungs."

"It's pneumonia again?" I already know the answer to the question. It's the very same ailment that landed her in this same hospital nine months ago. It's not uncommon for someone with my mother's condition to face this.

"It's not nearly as bad as it was last time, Vanessa." Ben punches a button on her heart monitor. "She'll bounce back from this in a few days."

"You always take the best care of her." I look up at him. "Thank you for sticking around to watch over her."

"There was no way I was going to leave when one of my favorite patients was on her way in to see me." He smiles. "I'll handle the admitting and then I'll take off. You should too."

I glance down at my watch. It's now past noon. I've been here almost twenty-four hours. "I start another shift at three. I'm going to sleep for a couple of hours in the staff lounge and have a shower. It's easier than going home."

"I got another nurse to switch with you. Your next shift isn't until eleven tonight."

"You're kidding?" I'm relieved and I know it shows. "I'll go home then. I'll be back before tonight to check on her though."

"Can I offer a suggestion?" He falls in step beside me as we walk out into the corridor.

"What kind of a suggestion?" I pull my hair free from the messy ponytail I shoved it into when I started my shift. "About my mom?"

"About Garrett." His chest expands as he pulls in a deep breath. "I told him about your mom. He's been texting me non-stop for hours about it. Give him a call. Tell him she's okay. Tell him you're okay too, Vanessa."

I can't chide him for sharing with one of his closest friends. "He hasn't texted me at all."

"He said that he's trying to give you some space to work through some stuff," he explains. "He also said that it's killing him to do that. He misses you. I've never seen him this crazy about a woman before."

TWENTY-THREE

"Well, hello." A blonde haired man extends his hand towards me as I step off the elevator. "What can I do for you?"

"You can take your hands off of her." Garrett rounds the corner, a stack of file folders in his hand. "Get away from her. Now, Bruce."

I laugh at the voracity of his tone. I look back at Bruce. "Bruce, is it?"

"You're Vanessa, aren't you?" He holds out his hand again. "I've heard a lot about you."

I shake his hand lightly as Garrett steps closer. "Vanessa, you look beautiful. Wow."

I look down at the simple t-shirt and jeans I'm wearing. I'd wrapped a colorful scarf around my neck and had left my hair down after I showered. After listening to Ben talk about Garrett's concern, I decided that a visit to his office was in order. Talking things over on the phone was too impersonal. I wanted to see his face.

"You're busy." I touch the edge of the folders he's holding. "I didn't come at a good time."

"I have a short meeting." He turns to look at Bruce. "Take these and go up. Tell them I'll be five minutes."

Five minutes isn't long enough to begin to explain things to him. On my way home from the hospital, Jonah had called. He wanted to reassure me that things were in place for my meeting with the detective. The police want to see me as soon as possible so Jonah and I are going in tomorrow morning as soon as my shift is over. Jonah had given them the broad details of my situation, and they'd assured him that they'd consider everything in carefully.

"Come to my office." Garrett holds out his hand. "We can talk in there."

I wind my fingers through his as we walk past countless people all sitting next to desks. Some are speaking on the phone, other are typing away on the keyboards of their laptops. Not one of them looks up as we pass.

"In here, Vanessa." He guides me into a large office with a breathtaking view of the city. "I'm so glad you came."

"I wanted to see you in person." I look down to where my smartphone is in my hand. "I didn't want to call. I need to tell you some things."

"How's your mother?" He leans down slightly so we're at eye level. "Ben said that she was brought to the hospital."

"She'll be fine," I say through a sigh. "She'll stay a few days but Ben says she'll be okay."

"I'm so glad." He wraps his arms around me. "I was worried."

"I spoke to your friend. I talked to Jonah."

"Yes." His gaze narrows as he pulls back to look at me. "He told me you were there. He said it went well."

"It did. I want to tell you about it. I need to tell you."

"I want that." He glides his lush lips across my forehead. "I'm going to go do this meeting and I'll be back down here in fifteen minutes. Can you wait for me?"

I glance at my watch. I have time. I'll go to the hospital after I'm done here to check on my mom and then back home to sleep until I need to leave for my shift. "I'll wait. I want to talk."

"It killed me inside to not be the one to help you, Vanessa." He cups my face in his palms. "I need you to understand something before I go to my meeting."

"What is it?"

"I only want to protect you." He takes a heavy breath. "I want you to have the best legal advice money can buy. Jonah is the best. He will help you and your mom, regardless of what's happened."

"He's helping." I pat him on the shoulder. "I'm going to talk to the police tomorrow."

"I can come with you." He traces a line over my eyebrow with the pad of his thumb. "I'll come with you. I can wait outside the interview room if you want. I just want to be there."

It's an offer that touches me deeply. "I'd like that. I want that."

"We'll talk about it when I get back." He leans down to rest his forehead against mine. "I'll go do this meeting, and then I'll be back. You won't move from this spot."

"I'll stay. I'll be right here waiting for you."

***

"Can you tell me where Garrett Ryan is?" I ask a middle-aged woman who is sitting at a desk outside of Garrett's office. "I need to tell him something."

"You're Vanessa, aren't you?" She stands quickly. "Garrett talks about you all the time. You're as pretty as he says you are. I'm Donna. I'm his assistant."

"Thank you." I pull my hands together to stop them from shaking. "I need to talk to him. My mother…she's in the hospital, and I just got a call that I need to go back there."

"Oh no." Her hand leaps to her chin. "Is it serious?"

"I'm supposed to wait for Garrett in his office, but I need to go."

"I can tell him that you had to leave." Her eyes dart around her desk. "Or do you want to leave him a note?"

"I can text him." I look down at my smartphone. "I'll text him to explain."

I type out a simple message, explaining to him that the nurse in charge on my mother's ward called to tell me to hurry back. I press send.

"Dammit." Donna points towards his office when the sound of a smartphone chime fills the air. "That's his phone. Let me call up to the conference room to see if he can come back down."

I don't have time to wait. I want to get back. I didn't get any concrete details from the charge nurse on the phone but I know enough to read between the lines. We don't call family back to the hospital, unless things are grave.

"I'm just going to go." I point towards the elevator. "Please tell him to call me when he's done."

She nods as she speaks into the phone. I hear her say something about Garrett as I race past her desk towards the bank of elevators at the end of the hall.

TWENTY-FOUR

"Why the hell are you here?" Connie grabs onto my scarf the moment I step out of the lift. "You tell me what you're doing in this building."

I try to push her off of me, but her grip is too firm. "Let me go. I have to go."

"Were you here to see Garrett?" She pulls on my elbow with her free hand. "Did you finally tell him who you are?"

"I'm not telling you anything." I push against her chest. "What I tell Garrett is none of your business."

"You haven't told him because of that woman who raised you. That's the reason, isn't it? You're trying to protect her."

I stare at the faces of the people passing by us in the lobby. Some turn briefly to look at the two of us, but most continue on their way, oblivious to the scuffle that is taking place right in front of them.

"No," I counter. "I'm not talking to you about this."

"I wish you would have stayed away," she hisses the words at me. "Everything was better when you were gone."

"I wouldn't have stayed away if I knew then who I was." I pull on her fingers, trying in vain to dislodge her grip on my arm. "I wish I could have seen her before she died."

"I took care of her before she died." Her eyes float over my head. "I was the one who helped her get into bed because she was too weak. I was the one who rubbed her back after she vomited half the night. That was me."

"It should have been me." The words leave me before I have time to consider them. "I'm a nurse. I could have taken care of her better than anyone else."

"That's not fair." She finally drops my arm. "I did everything I could for her. I sat there for months watching her slip away."

"I'm sorry." I don't know what type of education she has, but I doubt that it's in medicine. She lacks a basic sense of compassion I can instantly spot in my co-workers. "I know it couldn't have been easy."

"My life hasn't been easy since that day in the park." Her mouth thins. "Everything changed that day. It never was the same again."

"A lot changed for all of us that day." I try not to sound completely annoyed by her inference that her life was somehow impacted as deeply as mine when I was taken from my family.

"I was at the park with my mother that day." She finally drops my arm. "I was sitting on a bench. I saw the entire thing happen."

"You were too young to remember any of that." I study her face. I doubt that she's more than a few years older than me. Her memory of that day can't be rooted in fact. It has to be born mostly of fiction. She's likely listened to our mother retelling the story time and time again and her young mind picked out the parts she felt were most substantial.

"I was eight that day, Charlotte. I can tell you every detail of that day. I'll tell you exactly what you were wearing. I'll tell you how much mother cried for weeks after that day."

"Don't." I put my hand out to stop the words, as much as to ward off her vindictiveness. "I don't want to hear about it."

"Do you want to read about it?" She pulls an envelope from the bag that is slung over her shoulder. "My mother wrote you a letter. Do you want to read that?"

My eyes scan the plain business sized envelope. It's sealed and thin. It can't contain more than a single piece of paper. "Is that the letter from her will?"

"I knew you'd come sniffing around the estate." She waves the envelope in the air. "You heard about this? I was bringing it up to Garrett's office for safe keeping."

"I don't believe you." I try to sound as sincere as I can. "Why would you have that envelope?"

"It was in mother's desk. She locked it away in a drawer." She holds it in front of her. "Leif found it when he was cleaning it out. He insisted I bring it to Garrett."

I stare at the elegant handwriting. It's Charlotte's name. "You could have written that."

"Why the hell would I write a letter to you? I wish you had stayed missing."

"Give it to me." I hold out my hands. "I have to go. I want you to give it to me."

"It doesn't belong to you yet." She dangles it between her fingers. "You have to jump over a bunch of legal hurdles before Garrett will give it to you."

"You can give it to me. You know that I'm Charlotte." I'm almost sobbing. I need to go to the hospital but I can't tear myself away from this spot.

"I don't know if I should."

"I want to have it." I reach towards her.

"If I give you the letter, will you stay away from us?"

"What?" I try to grab hold of the envelope but she's too quick. She hides it behind her back. "Give it to me."

"You're going to be twenty-five on the 26th of January. I'll inherit everything the day after that."

"My birthday is the 4th of February," I push back. "I won't be twenty-five until then."

"No, Charlotte." She takes a step closer to me. "You were born on the 26th of January."

I feel my bottom lip tremble. Even my birth date has been a lie. "I promise. Please. I'll stay away forever. You can have everything. I just want the letter."

"I'll make your life a living hell if you try and claim a dime." She pushes on my shoulder. "I will make you regret it."

"Give me the letter," I spit out. "Just give it to me."

"Here." She laughs as she tosses the envelope into the air between us.

I scramble to catch it but the crowds of people heading toward the elevators get in my way. I fall to my knees, wanting to scoop it into my hands before anyone steps on it.

I hear the faint sound of my smartphone ringing as I rip open the seam of the envelope. I feel people pushing against my thighs as I rest on my knees in the crowded lobby of the building, there's a hand on my shoulder but I ignore everything.

I carefully unfold the paper. I see the name Charlotte written in beautiful handwriting at the top of the note and I read each word carefully and slowly until I reach the last line.

I hear Garrett's angry voice calling Connie's name. I look up.

"She can't be Charlotte." His arms are flying through the air over her head. "She would have told me. She wouldn't keep something like that from me."

"She's Charlotte. Get a DNA test if you want. You'll see that I'm right." Connie points down at me. "I gave her the letter our mother wrote to her. She doesn't want anything else."

"I told you weeks ago that she's not Charlotte." His voice cracks as he turns to face me. "Tell her, Vanessa. Tell her that you're not Charlotte."

I don't answer. I can't find any words that will satiate his frantic need to understand why I've hidden this from him.

"Vanessa," he repeats my name. "Say something. Please, just say something."

I stare back down at the letter as I dart my tongue over my bottom lip.

"My mother gave me away that day. She dressed me in a pretty dress when I was a baby, put her rope bracelet on my arm and handed me to a stranger in the park because she didn't want me anymore. She just didn't want me anymore."

TRACE

Part Three

ONE

Garrett pulls on the edge of the paper so hard that the corner tears away in his fingers. I won't let him have it. The letter, written by Francesca Tomlin, may contain her tortured thoughts about what she did in the park twenty-five years ago but it's my letter. She wrote it for me. I'm not handing it over to anyone.

"No," I say quietly as I scramble to my feet with the letter still clutched tightly in my hand. "This is mine. You can't have it."

"Vanessa." He reaches for my elbow to help steady me. "Connie shouldn't have given that to you. You can't have it. You're not Charlotte."

I stare into his face. The composure that is normally there has shifted into something else. I can't tell if it's panic or just confusion. He's lost. I can see that. When he exited the elevator, into the lobby, he walked into something that he shouldn't have. This wasn't how I wanted him to find out who I am.

"You're a liar," Connie interjects. "Mother wouldn't have written that to you. She wouldn't do that."

I glance down at the perfect handwriting on the paper. For a brief moment, when I was reading the words, I wanted within my heart, to believe that it was Connie who had written them. I wanted it to be a cruel joke that she was playing on me, but the sentiment that each word contains couldn't have been fabricated with just a pen brought to a paper. There is real emotion woven into each sentence. The letter is the bittersweet confession of a mother who had become overwhelmed with a baby she wasn't expecting. The guilt that she expressed is real and heartbreaking. Francesca had made a decision, based within the depths of her depression, to give me to someone else.

The piercing bite of my smartphone's ring yanks me back to the moment. "The hospital," I mumble under my breath as I fish the phone from my purse. "I need to go there."

"You think you can just walk away now?" Connie lunges towards me. "You're going with me up to Garrett's office. I want you to sign something. You can't have anything else that belonged to my mother."

I scan the screen of my phone. It's another missed call from the charge nurse who is assigned to the ward where my mother was taken when Ben admitted her. "My mother needs me. I need to leave now."

"I'll go with you." Garrett exhales roughly. "We can talk about all of this later."

It's a kind gesture even if it's grossly misplaced in the moment. His head has to be swirling with a million questions about what he just witnessed. If he hasn't pieced together all of the fragmented slivers of my connection to Connie and her family, he will the moment I look him straight in the eyes to confess that I've been hiding my identity from him for weeks. I can't do that now though. I need to get to the hospital, to see my mother. She's the one person who needs me more than anything right now.

"No." I shake my head. "I want to go alone. Stay here. Deal with her."

His eyes dart quickly to where Connie is standing behind me. "Vanessa, I want to go with you. I want to help."

"You're going to let her walk out of here with that letter?" Connie reaches over my shoulder, her hands flailing wildly in the air. "What if she tells someone about what my mother did? What if the press finds out?"

If someone were to lock me and my sister in a room together, I'm certain she would tear me to unrecognizable shreds before the door closed. I pull away harshly, folding the letter up quickly and pushing it into my purse.

"Go, Vanessa." Garrett's hands leap into the air between us but he pulls them down to his sides before he touches me. "Just go. I'll call you later."

I don't respond. I have no words that could fill the empty space that is now there, hanging between us. I brush past him, walk as quickly as I can through the lobby of his building and take a huge mouthful of air the moment my feet hit the sidewalk.

***

"What is it?" I tap Ben on his shoulder to pull him out of a conversation he's having with several nurses. "What's wrong with her?"

"Vanessa?" He turns and his hand instantly springs to my arm. "Are you okay? Garrett called me. He said you were upset."

Upset? The one small word can't begin to hold the weight of everything I'm feeling. I want to bark the word back at him but Ben only means well. Judging by his anxious expression, I can tell that his concern is genuine.

"Your mom said your name, Vanessa." He gestures towards the door of her room. It's slightly ajar and from where I'm standing, I can tell that the blinds have been drawn. The dim light escaping the room is comforting and calming. "She said it twice."

My hand leaps to my mouth to quiet a sob. I've tried to recall at different times, within my own mind, the last time I heard my mother say my name. It has been months, maybe close to a year now. "She said my name?"

"Twice." Carla rounds the nurse's desk with two of her fingers flying in the air. "She was smiling, Vanessa. She looked really happy."

I close my eyes briefly to shutter all of the joy I feel. It may have been a momentary escape from the clutches of her disease but it's more than that to me. It means she remembers me. It means that the connection that I've always felt to her is still part of the innermost fabric of her mind.

"I'm going to go in to see her." I brush past Ben.

"She's asleep now." His fingers run through his dark hair. "She fell asleep about thirty minutes ago."

"I'll just sit next to her." I pull my purse closer to me, well aware of the secrets it holds. "There's something I want to read to her."

"I'm sure she'll like that." He glances at the clock on the wall. "You've got hours before you start your shift."

I'll need every second of that time to quiet everything I'm feeling. Now that I know exactly what happened in the park that day I need to go into the hospital room of the woman who gave me my life and hold her weathered hand in mine while I watch her sleep.

TWO

"You knew that day you showed up at the townhouse, didn't you, Vanessa?"

I knew he'd come looking for me. It was inevitable. I had ignored Garrett's calls and texts as I sat next to my mother's hospital bed and read the letter that Francesca had written to me. I had wept as I closed the door to my mother's room and lay next to her in the bed, clinging to her fragile frame as I talked about the moments in my childhood when she had told me that I was a gift given to her by a very special woman who couldn't care for me. She had raised me in a loving and supportive home even though each and every day she must have lived in fear of being discovered. She had held out her arms when a distraught and desperate woman wanted to give her child away. My mother had taken me and had never looked back.

"I did know then, yes." I turn to look at him. It's late. It's near three in the morning now. His hair is a tousled mess, his clothing disheveled and his breath is peppered with the heavy scent of beer. "I went there to see Francesca."

He swallows hard, his eyes darting over the unfamiliar faces of the staff that are waiting in line next to me in the barren hospital cafeteria. "You didn't think to tell me? Why didn't you tell me who you were?"

I hadn't given myself any time to even consider what I'd say to him. I've been so focused on myself the past few hours that any thoughts I may have had of Garrett and our blossoming relationship have been pushed to the back of my mind. I need to answer his questions. He deserves that.

"Vanessa," he hisses my name out through clenched teeth. "Why didn't you tell me?"

"I didn't know what to do," I say honestly. "I was scared about what would happen to my mother."

His eyes scan my face slowly. "When did you know? When did you find out you were Charlotte?"

I'm instantly grateful that we're not drawn back into the place we were in the lobby of his building when he was still holding onto some splinter of hope that Connie was delusional and that I was only Charlotte in her mind.

"I found out the day I went to Maine," I pause to pull my thoughts together. "It was the day before I came to the townhouse."

He takes a step back when a man in a lab coat rushes between us on his way to a table. "Did you tell Connie when you got there that you were her sister?"

I motion towards a vacant table. I need stability and standing in a spot where people are constantly walking past us is making me feel even more vulnerable and exposed than I already do. "Can we sit down?"

"How long is your break?" He asks as I walk in front of him.

"I have thirty minutes." I look down at my watch as I take a seat in one of the white plastic chairs. "Twenty minutes now."

He tugs at the bottom of his suit jacket as he sits across from me. "You told Connie when you got to her townhouse. That's why she was screaming at the top of her voice about you being Charlotte."

It sounds accusatory in an abstract way. I scrub my hands over my face. "She saw the bracelet in my hand and she made the connection."

"The bracelet," he begins before he leans back into the chair, pulling an audible pop from it. "You're talking about the bracelet that Francesca told the police she was wearing that day. She said it had gotten caught up in the baby's blankets when she was putting her into the stroller."

I reach into the pocket of my scrub pants to pull it free. "It's this bracelet."

He doesn't flinch at all. His eyes race over the rope bracelet before they meet mine again. "Connie talked about a bracelet that day when you were in the foyer. You didn't bother to show it to me then."

There's no masking the spite in his words. I know that I've put him in a precarious position. I don't have to have any lengthy understanding of the law to comprehend the fact that our personal relationship impacts his professional duty as Connie's attorney. "I was in shock, Garrett. I didn't know Francesca was dead until Connie told me that day. "

"You've been sharing my bed, Vanessa." He taps his hand against the edge of the table. "I thought we had something good going here."

The words bite. I fidget in my chair, scraping my heels against the tiled floor. "We do have something good going."

"We do?" His brow pops up. "What do we have? From where I'm sitting we have deceit, we have a conflict of interest and we have absolutely no trust."

I stare past his head. I don't want him to look into my eyes. If he does, he's going to see the pain that his words caused. "I'm sorry, Garrett. I was trying to protect my mother."

"I'm a lawyer." His hand fists before it hits the middle of his broad chest. "I could have helped you. I would have helped you."

I'm tempted to bring up the night in his apartment when he expertly dodged my legal confessions about my mother. I don't have time to dive into that discussion now. I have to be back in the ER in ten minutes.

"I'm going to need that letter you took, Vanessa." His eyes search my face. "I'm also going to need you to take a DNA test to prove you're Charlotte Tomlin."

"Should I get a lawyer?" I ask, not because it's a step I've been contemplating. I haven't considered it until now.

"That would be wise." He grazes his hand across his forearm as he stands. "You can ask Jonah for a recommendation. He'll know someone suitable."

I hang my head down. I stare at the bracelet in my palm as I listen to his heavy footsteps as he walks away.

THREE

"Garrett's assistant, Donna, called this morning." I tuck the letter into the plain, white envelope Zoe just handed me. "She said she can send someone to pick it up."

"No." She pulls it into her hands. "We're going to make a copy of it and then I'll go drop it off."

She's breathing heavy just from the short walk down the hallway of her apartment. Sending my very pregnant best friend on a mission to hand Francesca's letter back to Garrett is not only irresponsible, it's ludicrous.

"I'll take it." I start to reach for it. "I can drop it by his office on my way to the hospital this afternoon. I'm going to go visit my mom."

"Take a picture of it first." She pulls the letter back out of the envelope and places it on the table. "Give me your phone and I'll do it."

I had thought about doing the same thing this morning when I got back to my apartment after my shift and before I fell into a restless sleep for a few hours. I want to tell Zoe that I'm actually relieved, in some abstract way, that Garrett has demanded the letter back. I've read it so many times that I can almost recite it by heart but that hasn't lessened the pain I've been feeling. Seeing the bold letters that spell out Francesca's frank confession about handing me over to a stranger is etched in my memory forever. I don't need a reminder in the form of a photograph on my phone.

"I don't want a copy, Zoe." I hold tight to my phone, which is cradled, in my palm. "I already know what the letter says."

"Garrett told you to get a lawyer, Van." She tugs on the corner of my smartphone. "What if you never get this letter back?"

"It wouldn't matter. I've read it. It's not as though it's a sentimental keepsake."

"Do it for your mom then." She brushes her hand over mine. "That letter is proof that she didn't take you away. Francesca makes it clear, in her own handwriting, that your mom didn't kidnap you."

Arguing such a blatantly well thought out point is futile. "You're going to be a great lawyer, Zoe. You'll win every case."

"I just wish I was a lawyer now." She skims her fingers over the screen of my phone before she takes one picture of the front of the letter and another of the back. "If I could, I'd go to bat for you, Van, and I wouldn't rest until Connie gets everything she deserves."

***

"You don't deserve anything, Charlotte." She doesn't even try to conceal the anger in her tone. "Are you here because you think your lover boy is going to side with you?"

"Lover boy?" I cross my arms over my chest. "Are you sure you're older than me?"

"What?" She takes a step towards me. "What do you mean by that?"

"It was an insult, Connie. I always wanted a younger sister. You act like a spoiled four-year-old so I guess you'll have to do."

My eyes catch on the small grin on Garrett's face as I turn towards the doorway of his office.

"I brought… that thing that you… I brought what you asked me to bring," I stammer. "I was going to leave it with Donna but she's not at her desk right now."

"She's on a coffee break." He walks past Connie without acknowledging her at all. "I'm sorry I wasn't here when you arrived. I had to consult with another attorney."

I want to tell him that I wasn't expecting my sister to be sitting in his office when I stopped by to drop off the letter. I was almost able to escape without having to talk to her at all but when she turned around and starting yelling obscenities at me, I couldn't back down. It's becoming harder and harder to understand how the two of us are biologically connected. I seriously doubt that there's another person on the face of the earth who has as much vile contempt for me as Connie does.

"I hope like hell that the thing you're talking about is something you've signed that waives all rights you have to my mother's estate."

I turn to look at her, wondering for a fleeting moment what it would feel like to slap her across the face. She's never been denied a thing. Her posture and attitude are evidence of that. She believes she sits in a class above the rest of humanity, in particular, me.

"Were you always like this?" I turn to face her directly now. "Were you like this when we were children?"

"I, I guess I…" she starts before she looks towards Garrett. "Why is she even here? You're not still seeing her, are you?"

Listening to him try and explain what we are to each other isn't how I want to spend my time. I haven't seen my mother since I visited her after my shift ended very early this morning. I want to get back to the hospital now so I can sit with her for a few hours before I have to be on duty in the ER.

"Here's the letter." I reach into my purse to pull out the plain envelope. "I think I dropped the envelope that the letter was in. It must have fallen onto the floor in the lobby."

"I have it." His fingers brush over mine as he pulls the envelope into his grasp. "I'll get this back to you as soon as possible, Vanessa."

"It's Charlotte," Connie corrects him as she points at me. "You gave him back that letter, didn't you? It doesn't mean you get anything else that belonged to mother. We had an agreement."

"My name is Vanessa," I say hoarsely. "It will always be Vanessa."

"I don't care what you call yourself." Her gaze darkens. "You're not a Tomlin anyways. You never were."

"You're a Tomlin." I shove my hands into the front pockets of my jeans. "I never want to be like you. I'll stay a Meyer forever."

Her lips part and her nostrils flare and I steady myself to wait for the onslaught of insults that are about to leave her but there's nothing. She just stares at me as I glance at Garrett before I walk out of his office.

FOUR

"Why couldn't they do the testing here?" Ben's arm sweeps in the air past my head. "We have a great lab here."

I'd wondered the same thing until Jonah explained the simple facts to me. "My lawyer told me that it has to be a neutral testing facility. I work here, so if the DNA testing was done here, the results could be called into question."

"By your sister?"

I stare at his mouth. It sounds foreign to hear Ben talking about Connie in such an intimate way. I had confided in him yesterday during our dinner break. I knew it was only going to be a matter of time until he caught wind of what was going on. I doubt that Garrett would tell him directly, but Ben is intuitive. He knows I've been on a quest to find my birth parents. He also knows that Garrett and I haven't seen each other in more than a week.

"She's determined to keep me away from Francesca's things." I push the plastic fork I'm holding in my hand around the almost empty dish of spaghetti in front of me. "I don't want any of her things."

"You're sure?" He scratches the side of his neck. "Maybe you should take what she wanted you to have, Vanessa. It was her decision, after all."

"Francesca lost her right to make decisions for me when she handed me to a virtual stranger at the park that day." I tap the fork against the top of the table before dropping it into the dish. "She wasn't my mother anymore. I wasn't her daughter."

"Do you really feel that way?" He tilts his head to the side. "Do you think that your judgment is clouded with anger right now?"

I may be offended if I wasn't well aware of how compassionate and forgiving Ben is. I know his history. He has shared scattered details of his youth with me. His mother died while he was tending to her and he was blamed for her death by his twin brother. His life was sent into an immediate tailspin and his fractured connection with his brother has only been mended in the past few months. If anyone understands how bitter a family feud can become, it's Ben. He wants my life story to end with the same promise and renewed sibling love that his has. It's not possible for me.

"Francesca chose to give me to Rowena," I point out with a tap on my knee. "She didn't give Connie away. She gave me away."

I see the next question that is brewing behind his eyes. I know what he's going to ask me because I've asked myself the same thing since the confrontation with Connie in the lobby of Garrett's building.

"I don't resent Connie, Ben." I rest my elbows on the table. "It's not her fault that Francesca kept her and not me. She was a child back then."

"That's very adult of you, Vanessa." He smiles softly. "No one would blame you for resenting Connie or being envious of her."

"I guess." I half-shrug my shoulder. "The only thing Connie and I have in common is our DNA. We're very different people. I can't help but wonder if she's the way she is because of how she was raised."

"I hadn't thought of that," he says quietly. "Do you think you'd be like her if Francesca had raised you?"

"I'll never know." I reach inside my pocket to wrap the rope bracelet around my fingers. "All I do know is that Francesca gave me to a woman who loved me more than anything. My mom gave me a great life. I almost wish I could thank Francesca for that."

***

"Jonah says that you haven't called the lawyer he recommended yet." Garrett's deep voice carries over the low hum of the small crowd that has gathered in Easton Pub.

I look up at his face. I may not have admitted it to myself but I was hoping he'd stop by on his way home from work. Today was the first day shift I'd had in more than a week. I had hoped that I'd hear from him by now. I didn't care if he called to tell me the results of the DNA test or if he had a message to forward from my vengeful sister, I just wanted him to reach out. When he hadn't, I realized that I didn't have the nerve to call myself so I hopped in a taxi after work and came here for a glass of wine.

"I don't need a lawyer," I counter as I motion towards the two empty stools sitting next to the table. "Do you want to join me?"

He rocks back on his heels. "I'm meeting someone."

I knew, somewhere in the back recesses of my mind, that it was a possibility that he'd move on and find someone new to share his bed with. I haven't and it's not just because I've been so preoccupied with trying to sort through the tangled realities of my past. It's because I care about him, deeply. I've missed him and the ache that I've been feeling won't be quieted with the body of another man. I know that. I don't need to test my theory. I don't want anyone else.

"I didn't know." I drop my gaze to the almost full wine glass. "It was good seeing you."

It's awkward. What was once easy and breathtaking has become difficult and stunted. He shuffles briefly on his feet. He can feel the palpable tension between us just as much as I can. I had no right to sit here and expect him to show up and forgive me for not telling him I was Charlotte. It doesn't matter that I was fearful of the repercussions that my mother would face. The fact that I longed to confess everything each time he made love to me offers no peace now. I messed up. I let this gorgeous, kind and loving man walk out of my life because I was too scared to trust him.

"I'll call her and cancel." He pushes his hand into the inner pocket of his suit jacket.

Her? I knew it. It makes no sense that the confirmation that he was meeting another woman for a drink stings as much as it does. He doesn't owe me anything. We were two people who had fun for a time and that time has passed. My heart has to catch up to that.

"No." I'm on my feet before he pulls his phone free. "Don't cancel your date because of me, Garrett. I should get home."

"Date?" He scoops his phone into his palm. "You think I have a date?"

There's no right answer to that question. I know he's arrogant. It was the first impression I drew from him when he stood almost completely naked in the ER. He's shown his arrogance since. Confessing that I'm hurt by the knowledge that he's seeing someone new already will only feed into his own self-satisfaction. I don't want to see a smug grin on his lips right now. I don't want to look at his face anymore.

"Vanessa?" His hand is resting on my forearm now. "You think I'm meeting another woman?"

I nod. "It's none of my business, Garrett. You're free to do whatever you want. You can meet any woman you want."

He doesn't respond. His eyes flit between my face and the entrance to the pub. I don't want to keep standing here. I can't be here when the woman he's going to fuck tonight come waltzing through the door and into his arms. It will break me to see the desire on his face when he looks at her. I have to go. I pull my arm back from his grasp as I brush past him.

"Don't run away from me, Vanessa." His breath is on my neck as his hand circles my waist from behind. "I'm not letting you go yet."

I close my eyes briefly as my hand floats down to cover his on my stomach. "I don't want to stay. I don't want to see you with her."

"With who?" His lips press against my cheek. "Who do you think you're going to see walk through those doors?"

I feel the motion of his head as he nods towards the pub's entrance. He's pushing me. He's paying me back for the pain and embarrassment I caused him when he realized I was Charlotte. I let him stand, unaware in the lobby of his office building, while Connie told him, in no uncertain terms, that I was her long lost sister. I can't fathom how humiliated he must have felt.

"Just let me go home." I try to pull free of his grasp but he only pulls my tighter. I can sense he's aroused and as misplaced as it feels in the moment, it pulls on something deep within my core too. It's the same raw connection I felt for him the first night I saw him in this pub. It hasn't lessened at all. I still want him as much now as I did then, regardless of everything that has happened between us since that night.

"She's here, Vanessa." His hand leaps to my chin. "The woman I'm meeting just walked through those doors."

I close my eyes tightly. I don't want to see her face because if I do, I'll picture her lips parted just before he kisses her. I'll imagine the way she looks when she wakes up in his arms tomorrow morning. I'll see them together; their bodies tangled as he takes her to the edge of pleasure, just as he did with me.

"Garrett?" Her voice is sophisticated, rich and controlled. "What the hell are you doing?"

"You're late," he replies too calmly. "You said you'd be here before I got here."

"I'm here now." She sighs and it's in that instant that I feel a soft hand touch mine. "This is her, isn't it? This is Vanessa. This is the woman you're crazy about."

FIVE

"You met his sister?" Zoe tries to bend over to retrieve a small blue ribbon that she dropped on the floor of the nursery.

I stop her with a hand to her stomach before I reach down to pull it into my palm. "Lynn. She's in town from Boston. They were meeting at Easton's for a drink."

"What's she like?" Zoe jerks the ribbon back into her hand. "I need to tie the last few of these on the arms of the rocking chair. I think it looks cute."

That's the pregnant part of her brain talking. It's a tedious job that she's been trying to complete since I arrived at her apartment more than an hour ago. I know she's getting anxious. The baby is due soon and her lack of patience is starting to show. The nursery is complete and all that's missing is the new arrival. Zoe is finding new projects to take on to fill in her time, hence the reason that I've been cutting small strips of ribbon for her.

"I didn't stay to chat with her." I point to an empty spot on the wooden arm of the chair. "I can finish this for you, Zoe. Maybe you should rest."

"Not a chance." She lowers herself into the chair. I see relief wash over her expression. "It's hard to stand for too long."

I smile at the words. She's uncomfortable. I can tell by the way she's been hobbling around the room with her hand resting on the bottom of her back. I've been witness to dozens of women coming to the ER when they're near full-term. An unfamiliar pain, or sometimes just impatience, has brought them to the hospital. After a quick check, they're typically sent back home to wait until the baby is ready to be born. I see that same anticipation in Zoe's face now. She's ready to meet her son.

"I can sit with you in your bedroom." I nod towards the hallway. "We can play cards. I'll even let you win."

Her head roars back with animated laughter. She's beautiful and since she's been pregnant there's been an extra bright light in her eyes. This is what true joy looks like. I can only hope that one day, I'll be fortunate enough to experience it for myself.

"You know that I'd win." She leans back in the chair, her hands resting on her stomach. "I'm just going to sit here while you tell me what's going on between you and Garrett."

I rest my hip against the edge of the change table. "Nothing is going on between us anymore. Last night was the first time I've seen him in more than a week."

"You two haven't worked out anything yet?"

"I don't think we can," I push on knowing that she's about to argue the point with me. In Zoe's mind every problem has an easy solution. She doesn't understand how complicated things have become between Garrett and me. "I lied to him, Zoe. I didn't tell him I was Charlotte."

"You didn't tell him for a very good reason, Van," she counters. "You knew your mom would be in big trouble. Can't he understand that?"

Of course he can. Garrett is one of the most understanding and compassionate people I've ever met. He's a lot like Zoe in many ways but this isn't a simple and straightforward situation. I compromised him professionally and I did it knowingly.

"I can talk to him for you," she offers as she leans forward in the chair. "I don't know him that well but I think I might be able to get through to him."

It's a gracious gesture that would not only be misplaced; it would likely push an even wider gap between Garrett and me. "No, Zoe. It's nice of you to offer but I don't think it would help."

"Tell me what would help then."

"I need your honest advice." I shift my feet against the hardwood floor. "You're a soon-to-be-lawyer and I need some legal advice."

She smiles softly. "You know I'm years away from being a real lawyer, Van, but I'll do my best. Tell me what it is."

"Garrett thinks I need my own probate attorney," I pause as I adjust to the sound of the words. I've been pushing this to the side for weeks now, but I have to deal with it. The DNA results will be back soon and I'll be forced to face the legal ramifications of being Charlotte Tomlin whether I want to or not. "I don't want anything from her will. Do I still need an attorney?"

"You do." She glances towards the open door of the nursery. "Beck and I just updated our will. Beck really trusts the attorney we used. She's done a ton of stuff for Beck's dad too. Do you want her name?"

"Garrett suggested that I ask Jonah, the criminal defense lawyer he set me up with, for the name of a probate attorney, but if you know someone, I'd like to talk to her first."

"Beck will be here within the hour. You can get her number from him then. We can play cards until he gets here." She tosses me a wicked grin. "Unless you're scared you'll lose."

"I'll win." I pull on her hands to help her to her feet. "My mother taught me every trick in the book when it comes to playing cards. You won't stand a chance."

***

"Why the hell would you play cards with Zoe?" Beck laughs as he rifles through a pile of papers on his desk. "That woman is cut-throat when it comes to Go Fish."

I can't curb a giggle. "What is that about? It's like she morphed into someone else."

"She told me it was her favorite game when she was a kid." He opens one of the desk drawers. "She wants to practice so when the baby is old enough to play, she can teach him."

"I hope she shows him some mercy." I push my hair back behind my shoulders. "I thought I was good and I didn't stand a chance."

"It means a lot to her that you hang out here." He nods towards the floor of their home office. "You're the best friend she's ever had."

The words mean much more to me than he can ever know. Since I've started on my journey to discover my past, Zoe has been the only constant in my life. She's the person I know, without any reservation, I can count on. "She's my best friend too."

"I know." He leans forward and glances towards the door. "I know she hasn't told you this but she's naming the baby after you."

"She's not," I say without thinking. "You're not."

"Vane Beck." His lips curl into a smile. "I love the name. It's perfect."

160

"You're naming your son Vane?" I know he can see the tears. I can't control them. "After me?"

He rounds the desk and crouches in front of the chair I'm sitting in. "You're part of our family, Van. You're like a sister to Zoe. Our son couldn't have a better role model than you."

I lean forward as he wraps his arms around me. I rest my head on his shoulder and weep. I weep for everything I've lost the last twenty-four years and for everything that I've been given.

SIX

"I'm glad you came, Vanessa." Garrett greets me as I step off the elevator into the space that houses his offices. "I wasn't sure if you would."

If I'm being completely honest, I almost didn't come. Yesterday, I finally met with the attorney that Beck and Zoe had suggested. Her name is Bethany Cooper. She's older than me, polished and didn't bat an eyelash when I explained the circumstances of my past. She wants to help and before I'd left her office, I got a hug and a valuable piece of advice. She told me not to make any split second decisions based on emotion. I have to discuss everything with her. I need that. Her expertise and understanding is going to get me through the next few months until Francesca's estate is settled.

"It seemed important." My chest tightens as we walk side-by-side towards his office. "Connie isn't coming, is she? If she is, I should call my attorney."

A ghost of a smile pulls on the corner of his full lips. "You took my advice and got a recommendation from Jonah?"

"No." I shake my head. "I found an attorney on my own. Bethany Cooper is her name."

"Bethany?" He stops to look directly at me. "She's good. She's really good."

I hold back a grin. I don't need his approval but knowing that he's impressed with my choice gives me a sense of satisfaction I didn't realize I needed until this moment. "I like her."

He guides me through the open door of his office and motions towards one of the two leather chairs in front of his desk. "Have a seat."

I do. I sit on the edge of one of the chairs, trying to smooth away the wrinkles in my pants. I'd come to his office as soon as my shift ended. It's near four in the afternoon. I could have gone home to shower and change but it seemed as though it would be a wasted effort. I want to get this meeting over with and in my haste to do that, I hadn't even smoothed out my ponytail before I raced to the subway and hopped on a train to bring me here.

I sit in silence as he closes the office door behind us before he lowers himself into the chair next to me. I look directly at him for the first time since I stepped off the elevator. He's smiling at me, his green eyes soft and warm. His jaw is covered with the beginning of a beard. He hasn't shaved in at least a few days and I instantly wonder if that's on purpose or if the effort it takes is more than he can muster. I've been dragging my feet for days, going through the motions of my life.

"How's your mom?"

The question is unexpected and I know my expression reflects that. "My mom? She's stable."

"Stable?" he parrots back. "Can you tell me what that means in laymen terms?"

My tongue darts over my bottom lip. I'm thirsty. I should have known that my nerves would get the better of me. I've wanted to see Garrett every day, and now that I'm sitting less than two feet away from him, I feel my throat closing and my mouth drying out. Soon I'm going to lose my voice out of sheer anxiety.

"She's doing much better." I run my fingers along the arm of the chair. "Ben is going to release her tomorrow or Friday."

"Really?" He claps his hands together. "That's great news, Vanessa. I'm so glad to hear it."

His reaction is genuine. It's not one of those reactions that you expect people to offer when they're trying to be cordial. He seems sincerely happy that my mom is recovering. It's touching.

"Will she go back to the center in Brooklyn?"

I nod. "It's her home. She'll go back to her room there."

"She's comfortable there?" He rubs his right thumb over the palm of his left hand. "Are you comfortable having her there?"

I scrub my hand over the back of my neck. "It's the best choice right now. They take good care of her there."

"Good." His voice lowers. "I asked you to come see me because we need to discuss something."

I want the next words out of his mouth to be something related to the connection that we once shared. It's what I hoped for the moment I saw the text message he sent me two hours ago asking if I could stop by his office after work. My heart had jumped at the request until I realized that he could have asked me to meet him at the pub or at his place. This visit feels official.

"What is it?" I try to ask in an even tone.

"Vanessa." In one easy motion, he moves forward in his chair and scoops my hand into his. "The DNA results came back."

When Bethany asked me if there was a DNA test, I told her it was being processed. I hadn't thought to ask her to look into the results for me. I didn't think I needed to. I know what they're going to be. "I was expecting them anytime now."

He lifts my hand to his lips. I don't flinch as he brushes them against my palm. "I've missed you. God, I've missed the feeling of your hand in mine."

It's what I've wanted since I fell to my knees in the lobby of this building the day I read the letter. "I've missed you too, Garrett."

He swallows hard. "I've never dealt with a situation like this."

"I'm sorry I didn't tell you I was Charlotte," I spit the words out so quickly, they are almost inaudible. "I should have told you as soon as I knew."

"Charlotte," he repeats the name under his breath. "You're Vanessa to me."

"I'm Vanessa." I squeeze his hand. "It's who I've always been."

He lowers both of our hands to his knee. "I'm going to tell you something. I shouldn't be doing this but I didn't want you to hear it from anyone else but me."

"What?" My heart drops. "Just say it."

He inches forward until his knees brush against mine. "It's the DNA results."

If he thinks I'm going to melt into a puddle of tears when he actually tells me I'm Charlotte Tomlin, he's wrong. I've braced myself for this moment. I've known it was coming for weeks now. I got over any apprehension I may have felt at facing the truth when the lab tech at the testing facility in mid-town swabbed the inside of my cheek more than two weeks ago. I'm Charlotte Tomlin. It's my truth.

"You can tell me." I look directly into his eyes. "Just say it, Garrett."

"The lab took a sample from you and from Connie," he pauses to lick his lower lip. "She hasn't been notified of the results yet. I wanted you to know first."

"Know what?" I smile softly. "You're going to tell me that I'm Charlotte. I know that I am."

"You're Charlotte." He nods as he pushes a puff of air from his lungs. "There's something else you need to know."

"What?" I feel my jaw harden as anxiety builds within me. "What else is there?"

"The match between you and Connie," he begins before he cradles my face in his hands. "It's not a perfect match."

I'm a nurse and when I glance down at a patient's chart I can effortlessly understand their test results. This is different. I don't have enough of an understanding of DNA testing to know what he means. "I don't understand. Why would we be a perfect match? We're not twins."

He swallows so hard I can see the movement in his neck. "The match between you and Connie is only twenty-five percent, Vanessa."

"I...I'm sorry...I don't..." I stammer. "I don't know what that means."

"Francesca Tomlin was your mother." He rubs the pad of his thumb over my cheek. "You and Connie have the same mother."

"You're saying that..."

"I'm saying that," he interrupts. "You're not Charlie Tomlin's daughter."

SEVEN

I pull back from his grasp. My chest is heavy. I feel the weight of the past twenty-four years bearing down on it. I struggle to catch my breath. I can't think. I can't process what he just said.

"Vanessa?" He's crouching in front of the chair I'm sitting in now. "Are you okay?"

"Jonah said Charlie loved me." I hold my hands to my chest. "He told me that Charlie called me his little one."

"I'm sorry." His voice is kind and patient. "I don't know what to tell you. The results are very clear."

"Can we do the testing again?" I ask out of desperation. I had finally accepted the fact that my birth parents had both died. Now, I'm suddenly faced with the knowledge that at least one of them might still be alive. I can't open myself up to the possibility of hope. I won't do it. I just want this to be over.

"When I requested the initial test, I asked for them to run it twice." He moves back to sit in his chair again. "It's a step I always take. It helps to minimize any mistakes that may occur."

I can't be surprised that he did that. I've always known that he takes his job very seriously and he goes out of his way to make certain that his client's rights are taken care of. In this case, that's Connie. He probably had the DNA lab run the test twice because he wanted to make double sure that I wasn't some imposter trying to rip Connie's inheritance from her grasp.

"Vanessa." His tone is sober and low. "I want to help you in any way that I can."

I want to find faith within his words but I can't forget that he's representing my half-sister. "I don't think you can help me. You're Connie's lawyer."

He rakes his hand through his dark hair. "I would recuse myself from that if I could."

It's a weak excuse. I had asked Bethany, in a very roundabout way, if an attorney could step down from a case once it's entered the probate process. She was clear that if there's a conflict of interest, it can be done. If this triangle of confusion that is happening between Connie, Garrett and me isn't a conflict of interest, I have no clear idea of what one is.

"You're Connie's lawyer." I shuffle my feet against the carpeted floor. "We shouldn't even be talking about this."

"I'm your lover," he counters. "I was your lover. I want to be that again."

If I could have chosen a moment for the two of us to have this conversation, this wouldn't have been it. I don't want to associate my relationship with Connie with what happened with Garrett and me. It was nothing but unfortunate timing that brought me into his life when it did. I wish, almost every single moment, that I had met him months before I set out on my search for answers about my birth parents. I wish we would have known each other on an even deeper level when I realized that I was the sister of his client.

"We can't be that to each other anymore, Garrett," I spit back. "How can we be? You're representing my sister."

"I don't like your sister." He rubs his hand over his face. "Your sister is a bitch."

I smile even though I don't want to. It's a true statement. It's the same thing I think every time I end up in the same room with her. "Why are you still helping her then? Why haven't you quit?"

"You're not the only one with secrets, Vanessa." He hangs his head towards the floor. "There are things I haven't told you either."

I drop my purse into my lap, settle myself comfortably in the chair and look directly at him. "Let's just put everything on the table. It's time. We both need to be honest with each other."

"You're right," he says in a hushed tone. "You matter more to me than anything else, Vanessa. I know I haven't been clear about that in the past but I want you to know it."

I want to tell him that nothing matters more to me than him, but I'm not there yet. I can't let my heart jump into something like that when there's this much uncertainty circling us. I've shared some of the most amazing moments of my life with him. I've felt myself falling for him and yet, in tangible time, I barely know the man.

"I've told you everything," I start because I want him to understand. "I found out I was Charlotte when I went to Maine and found a suitcase filled with newspaper clippings. I looked at images of Francesca online and I came to the townhouse to see her. I should have told you then. I wish I had."

"I wish you had too," he blurts out. "I wish you had felt close to me then. I would have helped you, Vanessa."

I don't doubt that now as I look into his face. I see the meaning of his words in his expression. He cares for me. I know that. I knew it when I was spending the night in his arms and I feel it, even more deeply now.

"What about you?" I feel an urge to reach out and hold his hands, knowing that it will offer him the comfort he needs to share with me. I can't do it though. I'm wary of the next words that will leave his lips. "Tell me what secrets you have, Garrett."

"They're not sinister." A small smile tugs at the corners of his lips. "I've kept something from you that you deserved to know weeks ago."

"What?" I ask the question without any thought behind it. I'm anxious. I'm scared that he's going to tell me something that will shatter me in two.

He's quiet for what feels like endless moments. His eyes scan my face as if they're searching for something that isn't there. "I've known your mother a long time. Francesca. I've known her for many years."

This is the secret he's been holding tightly to for weeks? I'm not an expert in hiding the truth from others, but this is anticlimactic. It's not shocking to learn that he knew her for a time before her death. I've sensed that when people of wealth start to anticipate the end of their lives that they plan for that. They gather together a team of advisors and lawyers who guide and counsel them.

"I guessed that," I say tightly. "You seemed comfortable at the townhouse with Connie."

His green eyes change in an instant. "I've been there often. I visited your mother there frequently."

"To help her with legal advice?"

He turns his head to the left as he scratches his ear. "That's part of it. I made a promise to her that I'd handle things personally after she died. It wasn't just about legal advice though."

"What then?" I know my voice isn't calm. It's a direct reflection of what I'm feeling inside. "Why did you visit her so often?"

He slouches back in his chair. "My mother went to college with your mother, Vanessa. They were close friends for as long as I can remember."

I twist in my chair, feeling completely out of place. "How long have you known Connie then?"

"We were born just a few months apart." He taps his knee. "I'm only a few months older than her."

"Did you know me?" I feel my bottom lip tremble. "Did you know me when I was Charlotte?"

"I did." He nods slowly. "I was eight when you were taken in the park. I cried for weeks. It broke my heart."

EIGHT

"What are you going to do?" Zoe leans back on her bed. "Are you going to try and find out who your father is?"

I had come to her place right after I'd left Garrett's office. He wanted to explain more about his friendship with Francesca, but I'd heard enough. I had to have space to breathe and time to absorb what he told me. He knew me when I was an infant. He was devastated when I disappeared from my stroller in the park and he had remained close to my birth mother his entire life. He knew her. He knew things about her that I'd never know.

I didn't share any of that with Zoe. I only told her that I'd gotten the DNA results back and that Connie and I didn't share the same father. I held tightly to my emotions as I explained to my best friend that my birth father might still be alive.

"Vanessa?" Zoe taps my knee. "Do you want Beck and I to hire a private investigator? We can help you research who your father is."

It's an incredibly generous offer but that's not a road I want to travel down. "I have so much to deal with right now. I haven't thought about him. I don't know. Maybe we can do that."

"We don't have to make any decisions tonight." She exhales softly. "Did you meet with Bethany? Was she able to help you with the legal stuff?"

I'm grateful that she changed the subject. I know she's not overly interested in hearing about my meeting with Bethany. I know Zoe just wants to help me accept that I'm not Charlie Tomlin's daughter. "I like her a lot. She'll help me figure everything out."

"I'm really glad." She motions towards the door of the bedroom. "You can get yourself something to drink in the kitchen if you want. I'm sorry I'm not better company. I'm wiped today."

I could tell she was exhausted the minute I walked into the bedroom and saw her resting with her head on the pillow. Beck had let me in and then he'd taken off to work at his studio for a few hours. He wasn't comfortable leaving her alone so far into her pregnancy. He made a sweet comment about leaving her in the capable hands of the best nurse he knows. I didn't bother to point out that I'm likely the only nurse he knows.

"I'll make myself some tea. Do you want some?"

"Herbal?" She raises both brows. "Can you bring some of those cookies Beck bought today too?"

"I can do that." I lean forward to kiss her forehead. "I need you, Zoe. You're the only person in my life I know I can depend on."

"I'll always be here for you, Van." She closes her eyes. "I'm not going anywhere."

***

"She fell fast asleep when I went to make us some tea." I giggle slightly. "She's been out like a light since then."

"You should have called me." Beck motions down the hallway. "I would have come back. You need to sleep too."

I do need to sleep but I know that it's not going to come easy. I sat in silence for more than two hours while Zoe slept. I drank three cups of herbal tea and ate a half a package of cookies. I cried and laughed as I replayed the events of the past few months in my mind. I may have a better understanding of who my mother is now, and why I ended up in Rowena Meyer's life but I have a father who I don't know. I have no idea if he's alive or not, but eventually I'm going to have to find out. I owe it to myself.

"I don't think I can sleep." I run my hand over the side of my face. "I have a lot on my mind."

"Zoe loves you a lot." He motions towards the leather couch I've been sitting on for the past few hours. "You're important to me too. I'm a great listener."

I know I can trust him. Anything I tell Beck will stay between us. He'll share it with Zoe because he'll need to. Just as she needs to tell him everything I share with her. I've never met two people who are as close as the two of them. I doubt I ever will meet a couple who are as perfectly matched.

"I wouldn't know where to start, Beck."

He sits. "Sit down, Van. Let's start with the guy that you were seeing. He's a lawyer, right?"

I'm grateful that he doesn't push me right into a conversation about my childhood. I sit next to him, leaning back into the comfortable leather. "Garrett. I met him at the hospital."

"He was in the ER?"

"He got hurt," I say slowly. It feels as though that was a lifetime ago. I still remember the way he looked when they'd brought him in. "He hit a tree with his bike."

His head rolls back with laughter. "How the hell did that happen?"

I'm not going to offer details about Garrett's rambling confessions that day. Beck doesn't need to know that the man I've been sleeping with was chasing a woman with perfect tits. It's irrelevant at this point. "It was an accident. He wasn't paying close attention to where he was going."

"Zoe told me that he's representing your sister," he stops as his eyes scan my face. "I meant that she told me that he's representing your birth mother's estate."

"He is." I look past him to the wall where one of his brilliant watercolor paintings is on display. "He told me today that he's been friends with my mother's family for most of his life."

"He knew your birth mother?" He lowers his voice slightly. "You just found that out today?"

"We've both kept secrets," I admit. "I didn't tell him that I was Charlotte Tomlin right away. I should have."

"Maybe." He shrugs his shoulders. "I don't think there are any hard and fast rules in a situation like this. From what Zoe's told me, you're doing the best you can."

I've been doing the best I can for me. I haven't given much thought to what's best for my relationship with Garrett. "I care about him. I know that he cares about me."

"When Zoe and I first met I made a huge mistake." He brushes his hand across the thigh of his jeans. The light above us catches on his wedding ring. "I almost lost her. I literally almost left the country."

"What happened?" I'm surprised by his confession and I'm certain the tone of my voice shows that. "Zoe's never told me about this."

"She hasn't?" Shock edges the question. "I'm surprised she hasn't."

"Me too."

"I met Zoe at Easton Pub." He crosses his legs at the ankle. "I'd never seen anyone as beautiful. I was in love with the woman within two minutes of meeting her."

I smile at the tender confession. Zoe's told me about the night they met several times and in her version, Beck was drunk and rambling on about a woman he once loved. "She told me you met at the pub."

"I had to see her again so I went back to the pub." He looks right at me. "I took her for a hot cocoa."

I've read about Beck online and I know his sordid past. The man used women without much thought before he met Zoe. He was notorious in the art world for bedding any woman who cared enough about his art to show up at one of his gallery showings. Everything changed when he met my best friend.

"She does love cocoa." I giggle under my breath.

"I wanted her in my life so badly I suggested we be friends." He shakes his head slightly. "I actually told her we should be just good friends."

"You friend zoned Zoe?"

"I was an idiot." He rubs his chin. "I was such a fucking idiot. We hung out and talked and I fell in love with her more every minute we spent together."

"What happened then?" I can't help but push. I thought I knew everything there was to know about how the two of them fell in love.

"I thought she only wanted to be friends too, so I knew I had to bolt. I was so in love with her. I couldn't stand not being with her in that way." He tilts his head to the left. "I was ready to move to London. I wasn't going to see her again and she showed up at my studio one day."

"Did she come to stop you from moving?"

"I don't think she knew I was leaving. She thought I was sleeping with someone else."

"What?" The instant I spit out the word, I realize how loud my voice is. "I'm sorry."

His lips purse together. "Zoe came to my studio and asked me point blank if I had feelings for her. She actually asked me if I ever thought about kissing her."

It's totally a Zoe thing to do. She doesn't hold back. She speaks her mind and chases after the things she wants. It's the reason her life is in such a content and balanced place right now.

"I'm not surprised."   I inch forward on the couch. "Zoe really loves you."

"If she wouldn't have come and told me what she felt that day, Van," he stops as he takes a deep breath. "If she didn't ask me straight out how I felt, everything in my life would be different. I would have gone to London and I would have lost her forever."

I stare at this face. I see all the emotion he's trying to share in his brilliant blue eyes. He's telling me what I've already known all along. I can't let my pride get in the way of what my future may be. I need to talk to Garrett. I need to tell him exactly how I feel.

NINE

"You're still wearing your scrubs." He rubs his hand over his eyes. "What time is it? Has something happened to your mom?"

That's one of the main reasons I'm standing at his door. He understands how much I love my mom. He knows that in spite of everything that's happened that I'm still fiercely protective of her. He gets that. He gets me.

"My mom is okay," I say quietly. "I'm sorry I'm here so late."

"Come inside." He pulls on my hand to sweep me into his apartment. "Did you need something? Has something happened with Connie?"

"I don't talk to her," I say it calmly and with no emotion. "I'll probably never talk to her again."

He crosses his arms over his bare chest. He's only wearing dark sweatpants. I'm certain I woke him. It's after midnight.

"You don't need to talk to her." His tongue darts over his bottom lip. "Tell me why you're here. What do you need?"

You. I just need you, Garrett. I need you to need me too.

I want to say those words, but I can't. I'm not even sure why I got in a taxi outside Zoe's apartment building and told the driver to bring me here. My heart made those decisions for me.

"You're upset about today, aren't you?" He rubs his hand down his face. "Christ, I just threw all of that at you. I didn't handle it properly."

He handled it beautifully. He was compassionate and kind. "I don't think there's a good way to handle something like that. I'm really glad you told me."

"You are?" He leans his head back so he can scratch his neck. "You're not mad that I kept that from you?"

If we were going to start weighing our secrets, his would be a feather compared to mine. "I can't be mad at you. Look what I did. I didn't tell you I was Charlotte."

He looks at me, his green eyes slowing floating over my face. "I never imagined Charlotte would grow up to be as beautiful as you. I used to kiss your little hand when you were a baby."

A sob overtakes me before I have time to feel it coming. I grab hold of my mouth with both hands, wanting to hold in the sound and the emotions that are falling out of me.

"Vanessa." He pulls me into his chest. His large arms circle my body. "Don't cry. Please. I'll take care of you. I'll take care of everything."

I want to believe him. I trust in his words. I know that if he could, he'd wipe my slate clean and shield me from the uncertain future that I'm facing but the unavoidable reality is that he can't do that. I have to face the fact that I'm Charlotte Tomlin and that the father who mourned the loss of the baby in the park, wasn't my father at all.

"I don't know what to do." I rest my cheek against his chest. "I just don't know who I am anymore."

He leans back, cradling my chin in his palm. "You are Vanessa Meyer. That's who you are. You're the woman I can't stop thinking about."

I'm not sure if he knows how desperately I need to hear those words. I can't tell as I look up into his eyes but I do know that he wants me just as much as I want him when his lips brush softly against mine.

***

I pull his pants to his knees the moment we enter the bedroom. I know we should be talking. I have so many things that I want to explain to him, but right now, all I want is to feel him close to me. I want him at a primal level, and I can tell, by how hard he is that he feels exactly the same way.

His hands are in my hair before I have time to react. His fingers skillfully freeing my hair from the ponytail I tied it up in hours ago when I started work.

"Yes," he hisses out between clenched teeth as I take the large head of his cock between my lips.

I run my hands up and down the thick root, taking more of him in with each gentle thrust of his hips.

"I'm missed you so much." The words are labored. "I've been aching for you, Vanessa."

I moan around his cock, twirling my tongue against the side. He fills my mouth so completely. I close my eyes, wanting to get lost in this moment. I don't want to think about what's waiting in the world that is beyond his bedroom door. None of that matters right now. The only thing that holds any importance is his pleasure.

"Suck it hard." He groans as he arches his back.

I give him exactly what he wants. I push my knees apart and take more of him. I stroke him with my left hand while I cup his heavy balls in my right hand. He's so exposed and open. His body takes over because of its need for release. He pumps himself into me, slowly and methodically. The only sounds in the quiet room are my moans and each of the deep grunts that escape him every time he plunges deeper into my mouth.

"I want to be inside of you." His hands are pulling hard on my hair. "I want to come."

I want it all. I want to taste the sweetness that he'll give to me when he falls into his climax. I suck harder, taking him deeper with each stroke.

"Vanessa. Christ." The words are heavy and measured. "Stand up. Now."

I hesitate only briefly. I feel bereft when he grabs me and pulls me to my feet. His hands flash past me, pulling at my clothes, freeing me of them in an instant.

"I'll get a condom." He breathes the words into my mouth before he kisses me deeply. "I have to be inside you. I'm aching. I need you."

I don't move as I watch him walk across the room. He pulls a condom out of a package that's tucked into the top drawer of a dresser. He stares at me as he rips the package open and sheaths his cock. His hand races over it before he moves towards me.

I see the untainted desire he has for me in his face. I feel it the moment his hands are on my breasts. His mouth follows and as he pulls my nipple between his teeth I cry out. I feel my body melt into his and I let him lift me before he pushes me back onto his bed.

"I can't be without you." His lips skim over the tender flesh of my stomach. "I can't breathe when I'm not talking to you."

I pull his head up. As much as I want to feel his lips and tongue on my core, I want him inside of me more. "Please, Garrett. Please."

He doesn't hesitate for even a brief moment as he pushes my thighs apart with his hips. His lips find mine and as he claims my mouth in a deep and wet kiss, he plunges his cock into me.

I cry out from the painful bite of pleasure. I reach for his thighs, wanting to pull him completely inside of me. I cling to him as he rocks himself into my body.

"It's so fucking good," he says hoarsely as his hands cradle my face. "You feel so good."

My body is on fire. I'm nearing the edge already and as I cling to him, he drills himself into me over and over, each thrust harder and deeper than the last.

He uses my body, chasing a release that I know will shatter him. I can see it in his face. His eyes haven't shuttered at all. They've clung desperately to mine as he's fucked my body, giving me as much as he's taking from me with every drive of his hips into mine.

I tense, knowing that I'm on the brink of an orgasm that will swallow me. He senses it and just as I call out his name as I fall into the depth of my pleasure, he pumps his own release into me.

TEN

"Don't waste your breath, Vanessa." He kisses my forehead as I rest my head against his chest. "Don't do it."

"What are you talking about?" I dart my head up so I can look at his face. He's at peace. His hair is a mess. There are small beads of perspiration on his forehead and upper lip and he looks happy. He looks exactly as I feel.

"You're going to tell me that it's late and that you need to go home to sleep." He motions towards the clock that is sitting atop the bedside table. "You were just about to say it."

I tap my hand against his chin. "You think you know so much. Maybe I wasn't going to say it."

Don't lie." He scoops my hand into his, his lips brushing over the soft skin of my palm. "You were just about to say it. I felt your shoulders tense. They do every time we're laying here after we've made love and you're getting ready to leave."

I've never been with a man who can read me as well as he does. He understands my body in ways that I don't. He knows what I'm thinking before I say it.

"You're going to sleep here with me." He holds my fingers against his cheek. "I need you to stay with me. You need it too."

"I need to understand a few things." I don't want anything hanging in the air between us. It's stifling and restrictive. We can't go back to the place we were before he found out that I'm Charlotte, but we can move forward and away from it.

"Now?" He holds my hand against his cheek. "Don't you want to sleep?"

"I don't," I lie. I'm exhausted. This is the first night when I feel as though I can actually sleep. I know that it's because I'm with him. The scent of his skin and the comfort of his body cradling mine will lull me into a deep sleep. I know that but I want to clear the air.

"You're a terrible liar." He kisses my hand again. "Tell me what we need to talk about. I want you to understand everything."

"You said you visited Francesca often," I start in the only place that makes sense to me. "That was after you moved to New York from Boston, right?"

He takes such a deep breath that my body shifts on top of him. "My parents would bring my sister and me to visit the Tomlins often. We visited more frequently after you were kidnapped."

"I wasn't kidnapped," I correct him. "Francesca gave me away."

He rubs my shoulder softly. "You read that in the letter she wrote, didn't you?"

"You read it too," I point out. "She made it very clear. She didn't want me so she gave me to a dark haired woman that she met at the park."

"Vanessa." He buries his face in my hair. "I haven't read that letter."

"You didn't read the letter?" I pull back to gain a better view of his face in the dim light of the room. "Why not?"

"There are very strict instructions in her will." His left brow pops up. "I promised her I would honor everything in that will. She only wanted you to read that letter."

"You have to read it." I'm pushing against his chest now, trying to gain leverage not only for my body but my emotions. "I can't believe you didn't read it."

"It's your letter." He holds tight to my hand. "If you want me to read it, I will."

"I want you to. You'll understand what happened that day."

"Tell me what happened." His gaze narrows. "Tell me what the letter says."

I nod. I know if I told Bethany that I was about to share all the details of that letter with the lawyer representing Francesca's estate, she may advise me to keep my mouth shut. Legalities don't exist in my mind right now. I don't care if there are consequences for myself, but I know that I'm not the only person engrossed in this conversation.

"If I tell you about the letter, is that going to complicate things with the estate and Connie?"

The hint of a smile floats over his lips. "It's your letter, Vanessa. You can tell anyone you choose about its contents. I'm not going to share anything with Connie."

I take comfort in his words. I don't doubt him at all. I know how he feels about my sister. I can't imagine that he'd run off to gossip with her about me. That's not who he is. "She was very sad. Francesca wrote in the letter that she was sad."

"She was sad that she gave you away?"

I pull my bottom lip between my teeth. "I have a picture of the letter on my phone. I can get it and read it to you."

"No." He pulls softly on my shoulder. "I want you to tell me what you read in the letter. I want to hear it from you."

I know that he's doing that to save me the pain of having to look at my mother's handwriting again and the words she chose. Parts of the letter were blunt and lacked emotion, and other parts screamed of the unwavering pain she'd been in since that day in the park.

"Okay," I agree softly as I reach for his hand. "She wrote that she didn't expect to get pregnant. She wanted two children for most of her life and then when she couldn't conceive after Connie was born, she accepted that she'd have one daughter, and then…"

"Then you were born," he interrupts.

"Yes." I move back slightly, trying to get more comfortable although I know it's not possible given the subject at hand. "She wasn't prepared for the stress of another baby. She wrote in the letter that she hired a nanny to care for me but Charlie would only allow the woman to be at the house three days a week. He expected Francesca to care for me the rest of the time on her own."

"What else was in the letter?"

I look briefly at his face. His expression is full of expectation. I feel a sense of shame in confessing everything Francesca wrote in the letter to me. He knew the woman his entire life. They shared a special bond and all I shared with her is DNA. Ironically, the man I just shared one of the most intimate experiences of my life with, knew my birth mother much better than I did.

"We don't have to talk about this." He rubs his hand over my cheek. "If it's too hard, we can stop."

The selfish parts of me have been craving those words. Sharing the painful details of the letter with Garrett isn't lessening the hurt that I'm feeling. It is helping me to accept what I read and maybe, if I tell him everything Francesca wrote, he'll be able to better comprehend why I don't want any part of her estate.

"She wrote that she met a dark haired woman at the park one afternoon." I glance down at his chest. "That woman was my mother."

"Rowena," he says her name with little more than a whisper. "Francesca wrote about her?"

I ignore the question. I don't want to be derailed when I'm gathering the nerve I need to share everything I read. "She spoke to my mother at the park. Francesca called her the dark haired angel. She didn't know her name. She only knew that my mother wanted a child. She wrote that my mother told her as much when they were sitting on the bench watching Connie playing on the swing set."

His only reaction is a gentle shift of his body beneath mine. He pulls me closer to his chest.

"Exactly a week later, Francesca dressed me in a beautiful dress and took Connie and I back to the same park." My pulse quickens. "She saw my mother there, sitting on the bench alone again."

His eyes close briefly. "It happened that day, didn't it?"

"Yes." I nod softly. "Francesca motioned for my mother to join her by the stroller. She took off her rope bracelet and the gold chain she had around her neck. She tucked them both into the blankets around me."

"She told your mother to take you?"

The words sting as he says them. The pain isn't lessened by the fact that I first read them in my mother's handwriting. The frankness of them sends my heart reeling today as much as it did that day I sat on the floor in the lobby of Garrett's office, reading the letter for the first time.

"She told her to take me when she walked away. She told my mother to give me a beautiful life and that if she sold the necklace it would help her pay for expenses. Francesca told her to give me a kiss for her each night before I fell asleep."

He doesn't respond. His eyes just sink into mine and I see the sorrow that is overwhelming him. He knew Francesca. He grew up visiting her and he helped guide her through the legal maze of planning her estate when he grew into a man. He was more a part of her family, than I had ever been.

"She wrote that months later she realized how much she missed me." I sigh deeply. "She hired someone to try and trace the steps that the woman in the park had taken, but nothing became of it so she accepted that I was gone and that I would never come back."

ELEVEN

"Can you meet me for dinner tonight?" he asks quietly as he buttons up the light blue dress shirt he just pulled from his closet. "I want to see you tonight."

I adjust the drawstring at the waist of my pants. I pulled my clothes back on after we'd shared a shower after just a few hours of sleep. "I can't tonight. My mom is going back to the center today."

"That's great news." A wide smile races over his lips. "Do you want me to come with you to help get her settled?"

The offers shouldn't feel as misplaced as it does. We haven't delved into the legal intricacies of what happened between my mother and Francesca in the park more than two decades ago but I know that in the eyes of the law, my mother still kept a baby that didn't belong to her.

"I can put in a couple of hours at the office and meet you at the hospital by noon." His hands deftly fasten the black belt he's wearing. "I really want to meet her."

"I need to go to see the police this morning." I scratch the tip of my nose. "I'm meeting Jonah down there at ten."

"I thought we agreed that I'd go with you." He stops mid-motion with a cufflink in his hand. "We talked about that, Vanessa."

He's right. We had discussed it the day Connie gave me the letter. Once I'd had that information in hand, I'd taken the copy of the letter on my phone to Jonah. He read it and felt that it would help my mother's case. He'd rescheduled the meeting with the police for me so I could gather myself together. I was grateful for his understanding then but now, I'm happy to be moving everything forward. I want this cleared up as soon as possible for both my mother's sake and my own.

"I can handle it," I say shakily. "I need to handle it on my own."

"Did you talk to Bethany about it?"

I turn to face him directly. "Why would I do that? Bethany isn't helping me with this. She's only representing my interest in Francesca's will."

"You know that you can't share that letter with the police, Vanessa." He clenches his hands together. "Jonah advised you of that, didn't he?"

My pulse quickens almost immediately. "I'm going to share that letter with the police this morning, Garrett. It's going to help my mother's case."

"You didn't have a legal right to look at the letter when you did," he points out calmly. "If you show it to them now, it may cause problems for your mother in the future."

I don't want to absorb his words as a veiled threat, but that's becoming increasingly more difficult. "I am taking Jonah's advice."

"Jonah isn't aware of all of the circumstances." He taps his foot against the hardwood floor of the bedroom. "You shouldn't have made a copy of that letter. Legally it shouldn't be in your possession until the will has gone through probate. A judge can dismiss it as evidence if charges are ever brought against your mother."

I feel an overwhelming sense of déjà vu. This is exactly what happened the last time I was in this apartment with him. He pulled out his legal jargon and pushed me into a corner. He's doing it again, whether he realizes it or not. I tap my teeth together as I wring my hands into a tight fist. I don't want to explode emotionally. "You're telling me that I can't use that letter to help my mother?"

"Not yet," he points out. "As soon as the will goes through probate, I'll put it back in your hands."

"What am I supposed to do until then?" I try in vain to control my tone. "How am I going to help my mother?"

"Vanessa." He clears the space between us with just a few long strides. "Postpone the meeting for a few more days."

"Why would I do that?" I push my hands into his chest. "You just told me that I can't help my mother the way I want to."

"You may not be able to help her," he begins as he rests his hands on my shoulders. "I think I know someone who can though."

"Who?"

"My mom." He smiles wide. "I think my mother can help your mom."

TWELVE

"Wait." Zoe's left hand darts into the air between us. "You're telling me that you're going to meet Garrett's mom tonight? I thought you weren't even talking to him."

I haven't had a chance to bring my best friend up to speed on my life. Yesterday, after I'd left Garrett's apartment, I'd gone to visit my mom in the hospital. Ben arranged for an ambulance to transport her back to her room at the center in Brooklyn. I'd ridden with her, holding her hand as she stared at the EMT's face. Once I had gotten her settled, I'd gone home and had fallen into a deep sleep.

"I saw him yesterday," I stop myself from confessing the part about us being intimate. "He knew Francesca for most of his life."

"What?" Her voice is so loud that it pierces right through most of the noise in this mid-town café. "You didn't just say that your boyfriend knew your birth mother?"

"Boyfriend?" I toss her a playful look. "I wouldn't call him that."

"What would you call him?"

"It doesn't matter." I wave my hand in the air. "That's not important. What is important is that his mom and Francesca were very close friends."

"That's so random." She nudges her finger against the edge of the plate that contains the last remnants of the pastry she just finished. "What are the chances of that?"

"A gazillion to one?" I joke. "They went to college together and he visited the Tomlins a lot when he was a kid."

"He's been friends with your sister forever?" She can't mask the obvious disdain in her tone. "He has horrible taste in friends."

I laugh out loud. "They're not close. He doesn't like her."

"That's reassuring." She winks at me. "Does he have any idea who your biological father is?"

It's a question that I wished I had thought to ask when I was tucked next to Garrett in his bed. I don't think he'd hold back if he knew the answer, but I also know that he's adamant about his promise to Francesca. I can't say I'd be shocked to learn that he's withholding things out of a sense of loyalty to her.

"He hasn't said anything about that," I answer truthfully. "I'm kind of hoping that his mom might know something."

"I bet she does." Her face brightens instantly. "I tell you everything. You tell me everything. Best friends usually do that."

I smile at the thought that Francesca and Garrett's mom shared the same bond that Zoe and I do. "I'll find out soon. I need to meet them at a restaurant in Chelsea in less than an hour."

***

"My son is smitten with you." Paulina Ryan's voice is the epitome of grace. She's beautiful. Her eyes are the same shade of green as Garrett's. She's tall and her brunette hair is pulled tightly into a perfect knot. Her make-up is flawless and the dress she's chosen screams of her elegance. I stare at her, wondering if Francesca carried herself with the same quiet sophistication that this woman possesses.

"Mother," Garrett reaches past her to catch my hand in his. "Don't scare her away."

I wasn't sure what to expect when Garrett suggested I meet him and his mother for dinner. I tried to call him earlier so we could compare notes about what was on and off the topic list for tonight. I don't even know if he's filled his mother in about who I am.

"Garrett tells me that you're a nurse." She sits back down at the table, as I lower myself into a chair next to her. "That's a very admirable profession for such a young woman."

I catch Garrett's eyes hoping for a clue about what I should share. I don't see anything even mildly helpful, so I jump into the discussion with no abandon at all. "That's how I met your son. He was brought into the ER in an ambulance."

"He what?" The wine glass in her hand wobbles slightly. "You were sick?"

"He was injured," I interject before Garrett has a chance to respond. "He ran into a tree on his bike. He knocked himself out cold."

"You did that?" She taps his forearm with her perfectly manicured fingers. "Tell me that you didn't do something that reckless."

"He was trying to catch something in the park," I continue on. "He talked about it when I was attending to him before the doctor examined him."

"What was he chasing?" She leans her elbow against the table. "Was it a wild animal?"

"It was." I try to keep a straight face. "It was much too fast for him though. He couldn't catch it."

"That's a shame." She breathes in a heavy sigh. "Garrett is very athletic. He's very strict about his workouts. He rarely lets anything break his focus."

"That day a couple of things did." I motion towards my own, less-than-ample, chest.

Her brow furrows slightly. "Do you want a drink, Vanessa? Are you old enough to drink?"

The question instantly yanks me back into the reality of the evening. I glance at Garrett. He's staring at me. His hand wrapped tightly around the short glass that is filled with amber liquid.

"I'm twenty-four," I offer back because Garrett doesn't. He hasn't told her that I'm Charlotte. If he had, she would have known my age.

"She's younger than you." She turns towards him. "She's much younger than you, Garrett."

He tilts his head towards her. "She's the perfect age for me. Everything about her is perfect."

A low sound escapes her lips. I know that sound. I've heard it enough in the ER when a patient is displeased with the care they're receiving. It's the gruff and muted groan of someone who wants to speak their mind but is holding back.

"You don't agree, do you?" I tap my finger against her hand. "You think Garrett should be dating someone more mature than I am?"

She's instantly taken back. Her body language gives her away as she pushes back against her chair, her arms folding stoically across her chest. "My son doesn't always think clearly when it comes to the women he spends time with."

188

I didn't come to this restaurant to get schooled on the dating habits of Garrett Ryan. I need to change the subject, fast. "Your son told me you live in Boston."

"I do." She brings the wine glass to her lips and takes a leisurely swallow. "I prefer it to New York."

"My mother has a lot of friends in Boston, "Garrett finally decides to dive into the conversation. "She's always busy doing something."

His mother throws him a look that is a mix between *what the hell* and *shut up*. "Where do your parents live, Vanessa? Were you born and raised here?"

I feel a sense of disappointment wash over me at the confirmation that Garrett hasn't told her who I am. I knew it, based on how removed she'd been throughout our conversation but to hear her ask me such an impersonal question stings. "I was born here in New York but raised in Maine."

"You're back in the city now?" She waves her arm towards the window. "Do your parents still live in Maine?"

"My mother… my birth mother died. My mother she lives in Brooklyn and I have no idea where my father is."

The onslaught of information is enough to volley her to down the remainder of the wine in one gulp. "Your family situation sounds complicated."

I stare at Garrett. He's mouthing something to me but between my racing pulse and the low light in the restaurant I can't make it out.

"There's something I think I should tell you." I motion for the approaching waiter to stop when I spot him out of the corner of my eyes. "I thought your son would tell you but apparently he hasn't."

"You're not pregnant, are you?" She spits the words out with such force that I see small droplets of saliva fly through the air. "Tell me you didn't get this one pregnant, Garrett."

"I'm not pregnant." Anger edges my tone. "I'm Charlotte Tomlin."

THIRTEEN

"She's fine." I push on the hand of the hostess. I'm trying to give us all room to breathe. "She's completely fine."

No one else in the restaurant may believe it based on the scream that flew past Paulina's lips when I told her who I was. I have no idea if she was excited by the news or if it shocked the hell out of her. Either way, she started hyperventilating enough to draw the attention of most of the wait staff and the bubbly, blonde hostess.

"I think we should call an ambulance." The waiter suggests. There's no doubt that he's wondering what's going to become of his tip now that our table has essentially halted everyone's meals. "I can get your check while I do that."

"She doesn't need an ambulance." I toss the words at him. "She needs another glass of wine."

"Mother?" Garrett wraps his arm around her. "Are you okay? Tell me how you're feeling."

She doesn't answer. Her eyes haven't left my face since I told her I was Charlotte. She's been studying my eyes. I've watched her gaze float over my nose and my chin. I know she's trying to draw her own conclusion from my features but judging by the blank look on her face, she doesn't know what to make of my ill-timed pronouncement.

"She'll be fine," I try to reassure him. "Her pulse is slowing now. Her breathing is normal."

His eyes flash briefly to mine before he looks back at her. "I was going to ease you into it. I was going to tell you during dessert. Vanessa didn't know that."

I didn't know anything. I took the bull by the horns because Garrett was sitting on the sidelines sipping his bourbon while he was under the mistaken assumption that I can read lips. "I thought you were going to tell her before I got here."

"You can't just throw things at her." He nods towards his mother. "You have to ease her into things. It takes her time to adjust."

I shrug my shoulders. "I didn't know that, Garrett. You didn't think that it might be important to have a game plan before I met her. Why didn't we do that?"

"Charlotte?" she says my name so softly that it's barely recognizable. "It's you, isn't it?"

I turn to look at her. "Yes. I'm Charlotte."

"I can tell." Her hand leaps to my cheek as her eyes fill with tears. "You're just like your mother. You're exactly like your mother."

***

"She made these bracelets for all of us." She holds the rope bracelet gently in her hand. "I remember when she did. Connie had to make something for art class."

"I didn't know that." Hearing Connie's name breaks the moment. "I didn't realize they were Connie's idea."

"Connie wanted to make them and then when your mother bought all the supplies, Connie changed her mind." She shakes her head slightly. "She was a difficult child."

I want to know more about that but this isn't the time or the place to delve into my sister's shortcomings. "Francesca still made them, even though Connie didn't want to?"

"She did." She smiles brightly when she hands the bracelet back to me. "She gave me one, and my daughter too. Connie had one and your mother, of course."

"Do you remember when I was born?" I've been trying to quiet my need to know more, but it hasn't subsided at all. "Were you in Boston then?"

"I was." She glances at Garrett. "You came early. You were three weeks early and your mother had to rush to the hospital in a taxi all alone."

A flash of panic washes over me at the image of that in my mind. "Where was Charlie?"

"I can't recall." Her brow furrows. "He might have been out of town with work. I just remember that your mother had to leave Connie with a schoolmate's family so she could go to the hospital."

The details only add to my confusion about my time with the Tomlins. I want the stories she's sharing to give me a feeling of peace about the decision that Francesca made in the park, but so far, I'm only have a sense of loss over the family that I never got to be a part of.

"You came so fast." She chuckles loudly. "Your mother barely made it into the maternity ward before you were born."

"I had no idea," I say even though it's painfully obvious to both Paulina and Garrett that I know nothing about my birth or the woman who gave me life. "Was she happy when I was born?"

Her hand leaps to the back of her neck. "Tell me what you know about her. What has Connie told you?"

I glance at Garrett. He nods slowly and I know enough to read between the lines of the gesture. "Connie only told me how upset my mother was before she died. She didn't say a lot about when I was a baby."

She swallows hard as she rubs her hand over the back of her neck more briskly than before. Her eyes are glued to my face. "Has anyone talked to you about the day in the park?"

Garrett rakes his hand through his hair. The gesture catches my eyes and I look directly at him. I want him to help guide me. I need his reassurance that I'm not pushing his mother into a place where she'll panic again.

"When we realized that Vanessa was the Tomlin baby," he pauses as he reaches for my hand. "We had to do a DNA test for legal reasons."

Her lips part slightly and her breathing stops. "You did?"

"It's part of the process." He nods. "We got the results back a few days ago."

Her hand moves to her chin. "You know, don't you? You know about Charlie."

I look at her for a long moment before I speak. "I do know, yes."

"I'm sorry." Her shoulder rolls forward as a sob escapes her lips. "I'm the one who told her to tell him you weren't his daughter."

FOURTEEN

"I'm sorry that she couldn't tell you more." He rests his hand on my thigh as the taxi races away from the restaurant. "I thought she'd be able to share more details with you."

I stare out the window, my eyes catching on the pedestrians who all seem in a rush to go somewhere in the late evening. I don't want to look at him. I wanted him to push her more in the restaurant but she had broken down when she talked about Charlie. I could see the regret in her eyes and although I just met her tonight, I know that she's holding tightly to the secrets that Francesca shared with her.

"I think she knows a lot more than she told me," I mumble under my breath as much to myself as to him. "I think she may know who my father is."

"No." He squeezes my thigh. "My mother would tell me if she knew. She would have told you on the spot, Vanessa."

His belief in his mother's absolute desire to do the right thing is touching. He seems oblivious to the fact that she knew that Charlie wasn't my father. Maybe it's that unwavering trust that a child has in their parent that makes him see only the best in her. Francesca told her things that best friends share with one another. She has more answers to my questions and if Garrett isn't going to help me get them, I'll need to find them on my own.

"You're coming back to my place, right?"

I hadn't said anything to the contrary when we got in the taxi. I sat in silence as Garrett gave the driver his address. "I'd like to go home."

"Are you tired?" His hand touches my chin. "I can just hold you while you fall asleep."

I turn to look at him. "I haven't seen Carla in more than a week. I promised her I'd bring her up to speed on my mom. I should go home to talk to her."

I see disappointment flash across his eyes but he doesn't express it in any other way. "I understand. Maybe we can have dinner tomorrow?"

"I work the late shift tomorrow." I lift my index finger to his bottom lip. "Don't say you're going to come see me in the middle of the night again. I don't want you to do that."

"You do want me to do that." He grabs my hand with his. "You love when you walk into the cafeteria and see me there. You know that you do."

"Do you get your arrogance from your mother?" I tease. "You do, don't you?"

He leans forward until his lips are touching mine. "Don't talk about my mother right now. Kiss me, Vanessa. Just kiss me."

***

"Hypothetically speaking," I stop to turn around to look directly at Zoe. "Hypothetically speaking, let's say that Beck wasn't the baby's dad. Would you tell me who was?"

Her mouth actually drops open. "You think I cheated on Beck?"

I laugh loudly. "I said this was hypothetical, Zoe. I'm not talking about you specifically."

"Oh," she swipes her hand across her forehead in jest. "I was going to ask you if you knew something I didn't about my own baby."

"It's Garrett's mom." I stretch my legs out in front of me. "I seriously think she might know who my biological father is."

"You do." She bolts to her feet. "Did you ask her who it is?"

"No." I push on her hand to motion for her to sit back down at the kitchen table. "You should finish your lunch."

"I'm not hungry anymore." She grabs hold of the back of the wooden chair as she takes a seat. "I don't think there's any room in there for food."

I giggle. The baby is due within the next two weeks. Each and every time my smartphone chime rings to alert me to a new message I hold my breath hoping it's Zoe or Beck telling me that they're on their way to the maternity ward at the hospital.

"I think you should ask her point blank what she knows." She pushes the half-eaten sandwich away from her. "Is she still in town?"

"Garrett said she was staying at a hotel on the Upper West Side." I stand up and scoop her plate into my hand. "I could stop by there this afternoon before work and pay her a visit."

"Take flowers." She calls after me as I head towards the sink. "Tell her you just want to thank her for the dinner last night."

FIFTEEN

"Is Garrett here with you?" She cranes her neck to stare down the empty hallway towards the elevator.

"I came alone." I motion towards the hotel room. "May I come in?"

"I just assumed when they called up from the front desk and said I had a flower delivery, that it would be an actual flower delivery."

I push gently past her. "I wanted to surprise you. You were so gracious to me last night."

She doesn't stop me so I take that as an invitation to walk into the living room area of her suite. "This hotel is beautiful. Do you always stay here when you're in New York?"

She reaches for the large bouquet of flowers. "I'll need to call down to the desk so they can bring me a vase."

I wait in silence as she picks up the phone near an ornate, paisley fabric covered, chair. She talks briefly to someone on the other end before she hangs the phone up gently.

"I typically stay at Garrett's but he told me that wasn't an option this time." Her brow rises as a small smile pulls at the corner of her mouth. "I take it you spend time with him there?"

She's asking me, in a not very roundabout way if I'm sleeping with her son. "I do stay there, yes."

"Do you care about him?" She motions for me to sit. "Tell me how you feel about my son."

I should have known that I wouldn't be the only one asking questions when I planned this unannounced visit. "I like Garrett a lot. He's been very good to me."

"He's a kind man." She sets the flowers on the coffee table. "I raised him to respect women."

She wants credit for having a hand in the man that Garrett is today. I can't blame her. I'd hope, if I have a son one day, that he'd carry himself with the same compassion and respect for others that her son has. "He's one of the most remarkable people I know."

A soft knock on the door interrupts her just as she's readying herself to speak again. "It's the vase. I'll get it."

I don't move as she thanks the person behind the door. She mumbles something about wanting to arrange the flowers and I nod in agreement. She takes her time as she places each blossom into the vase individually. She arranges the bouquet with precision before she finally places the arrangement on a small desk near the window overlooking Central Park West.

"Why did you come to see me today, Vanessa?"

Her back is to me as she asks the question and I don't hesitate before I respond. "I want to know more about my mother."

"Do you think I have more to tell?" She turns so sharply on her heel that the red dress she's wearing catches the air and floats around her knees.

"I believe that you do," I counter. "I don't know a lot about my mother or my birth father. I'd like to know anything you can tell me."

"I see." The words are clipped are empty. "It's such a long time ago. I'm not sure my memory has held up."

I'm always bothered when people throw those words around so thoughtlessly. I've assumed that the instant irritation I feel is based on the fact that my mother is caught in the empty void of her own existence. Alzheimer's has stolen her from me and although her memories are no longer composed or marked with clarity, they are there; hidden within parts of her that no one will ever reach again.

"Please try and remember," I coax gently realizing that lashing out won't gift me with anything but another rousing episode of anxiety like I witnessed last night at the restaurant. "This is very important to me."

"Is there anything in particular you want to know?"

Let's see. We can start with the name of my birth father. Or maybe we should begin with the reasons why my mother felt it necessary to hand me to someone she didn't know.

"When did Charlie find out that I wasn't his daughter?" I ask hesitantly. "Was it soon after I was born?"

She rubs her index finger over the bottom of her nose. "It was about two weeks before you disappeared."

It wasn't what I wanted to hear, even though it's exactly what I was expecting. "You said last night that you told my mother to tell him?"

She nods. "I did do that. I found out and I told her that she had no right keeping it from him. Charlie was a good man."

The inference being that Francesca wasn't a good woman. "Are you certain she told him?"

"I know for a fact that she did." She pulls on the hem of her dress as she sits next to me. "He came to see me the day he found out."

I should ask if he was upset, but it matters little now. He must have been devastated. Jonah had told me how much Charlie loved me.

"He told me that he didn't care." She pats my knee. "He said he loved you no matter what. You were his little one and would always be his little one. That man loved you more than the air that he breathed. He loved you until he took his very last breath."

SIXTEEN

I've finished the bottle of water that Paulina got for me after she told me about Charlie. I hadn't been able to form any words to respond to her. I had imagined that Charlie would have walked away from me once he knew the truth, but to hear that he only loved me more, made everything I feel that much more jumbled and cloudy.

"You weren't expecting to hear that Charlie adored you, were you?" She trails her hand over the skirt of her dress. "Did you think he stopped loving you?"

"I wasn't sure," I answer truthfully. "I spoke to a friend of his and he told me how much Charlie loved me."

"I don't know if any man could love a daughter more than he did." She pulls her hand to her chest. "He wept for years after you disappeared. Did you know that he'd visit the lead detective assigned to your case at eleven each morning?"

"No." I shake my head. "I didn't know that."

"He did. He also hired so many private investigators to look for you that he lost track of them all."

They're words that offer comfort that I desperately needed. "What about Francesca, did she look for me?"

She traces her index finger over her bottom lip. "It was much different for her."

"How so?" I ask without any thought. "How was it different?"

"Back then," she stops herself as her gaze falls back to the flowers. "Back then we didn't really understand what a woman goes through after she gives birth."

I sit in silence waiting for her to continue but the conversation has stalled. "Do you mean the physical impact of having a baby? You told me the delivery was quick. She didn't have a caesarean section, did she?"

Her eyes slide over my face. "No. I'm talking about her mood."

"Oh," I say with genuine surprise.

"They have a name for it now. Post-partum depression, I believe. Your mother suffered severely from that."

"Severely?" I parrot back. "She was very depressed?"

"She was depressed, overwhelmed, she often couldn't get herself out of bed. She had good days and bad days." She sighs deeply. "I'd often take the train in from Boston to spend a few days with her. I'd help with you and Connie, cook some meals, try and get her upright and into the shower."

"Did she see a doctor about it?"

"Your mother was so proud." She clasps her hands together on her lap. "She never saw doctors for anything. It's one of the reasons we lost her so young. Her cancer was so far gone when they found it."

I hear the sadness in her voice. I know she cared deeply for Francesca. I can see it when she speaks about her. "I don't know what Garrett has told you about me or about what I know about my disappearance."

"He stopped by last night after he took you home." She gestures towards the door of her hotel suite. "He questioned me about that day in the park. He asked if I knew what happened."

I don't want to push her into a corner but I sense that I'm going to have little choice. "What did you tell him?"

"I told him the truth." She breathes heavily. "I'll tell you the truth too."

I wait in anticipation as I watch her straighten herself on the couch. I can't tell what she's thinking. I haven't known her even a day but I sense that she's uneasy.

"I loved your mother very much." She nods slowly as the words leave her lips. "She told me things I promised I'd never tell anyone."

"I've made those promises to my best friend too," I offer.

"Does she have children?"

"She's having a baby soon." I smile as I glance down at my watch. "He will be her first. He's due any time now."

"You'll love him as much as you love her." She taps her finger against the arm of the couch. "The moment you see him, you'll love him as if he's your own."

I smile through tears. "I can't wait to meet him. I love him already."

"I loved you too." She reaches for my hand. "I loved you very much, Charlotte."

"Please help me understand." I squeeze her hand in mine. "Please."

"She didn't tell me right away." She leans back slightly. "It was years later when she called me late one night and told me that she had given you away to a stranger in the park."

"She gave me to my mother." I look down to her hands and to the plain gold band on her ring finger. "Francesca gave me to an amazing woman in the park that day."

"I prayed for that every night." She wipes a tear from her cheek. "I prayed that the person she chose would love you as much as all of us did."

"She loves me more than anything," I say quietly. "I don't think I could have had a better mother than her."

"Francesca would have found peace in that." She pulls in a heavy breath. "She was weary from all the guilt. She carried it with her forever."

"Did she tell you why she did it?"

Her head turns slowly toward me and it feels like endless moments before her eyes focus on mine. "She said that she saw too much of him in your face. You looked just like your father and you were a reminder of what she'd never have."

"What she'd never have?" I bite my lower lip, trying to ward off the anger I feel inside. "She gave me away because of my father?"

"She had an affair with him." Her hands clench together in her lap. "It was everything she never had with Charlie. It was romantic and passionate and she planned on leaving Charlie for him."

"But she didn't," I state the obvious. "She was married to Charlie until he died."

"A few months ago, before she died, your mother told me about him." She swallows hard. "She told me about the man she had the affair with."

SEVENTEEN

"What did she tell you?" I don't even try and mask the obvious excitement in my voice. This is the main reason I came here today.

"When her doctor told her that she was pregnant, she knew right away based on the timing that the baby wasn't Charlie's," she says wearily. "She met with the man she was having the affair with. She met with your father and told him about the pregnancy."

I dread the next words that are going to come out of her mouth. Just based on the facts surrounding my childhood, I already know that his reaction isn't a positive one.

"What did he say?"

"Vanessa." She turns slightly on the couch, pivoting her body towards me. "I promised your mother I'd take this to my grave with me."

I nod as I feel tears well in my eyes." I understand."

"It's all so far in the past and you've said that you had a happy life. You should focus on Garrett now and spending time with the mother that you do have. If you create new memories with them, you won't have to focus on the past anymore."

I listen to her incessant ramblings about a life that she knows nothing about. I push my hand towards her, wanting her to stop. "My mother has Alzheimer's. It's very likely that she is going to be charged with my kidnapping. I doubt like hell that whatever I have with your son can move forward because we're constantly thrown into a pit of mistrust since neither of us has answers about my past. You know nothing about my life. Nothing."

She sobs loudly and for a brief moment I feel the desire to reach out to comfort her based solely on the fact that she's Garrett's mother. "I didn't know your mother was ill."

"She's very strong," I point my finger in the air. "She's holding on but she won't be with me that much longer and then I'll be alone again. She can't create any new memories with me. She can't remember any of the memories we've already made."

I watch as her shoulder fall forward. I can see her resolve weakening right before my eyes. "He was married. She didn't know that he was married too."

"My father was married?" I shoot back. "He was married when I was born?"

"When she told him that she was pregnant he cut off all contact with her." She covers her face with her hands. "He didn't come back around until he read your birth announcement in the paper."

"What happened then?" I reach to touch her forearm. "Please tell me what happened then."

"He followed her to the park one day." She closes her eyes as her hands drop from her face to her lap. "He saw you in the baby carriage and he told her that he was going to sue her for custody."

"What?" The word can't contain everything I feel. "My father was going to sue her for custody?"

"He threatened her with that." She pushes the air in her lungs out between her lips. "He told her that he was going to tell his wife about you and they'd sue for custody."

"I didn't read about any of that in the articles in the paper." I'm startled by her confession. "Why haven't I heard about this before?"

"He never came forward after you disappeared." She shrugs her shoulders. "He never went to the police. He never contacted the media. He didn't say a word to anyone."

"What about his wife? She must have known. Why wouldn't she have said something to someone?"

"She didn't know back then, Vanessa. She only found out about you a few years ago when your father finally confessed to the affair." She doesn't volunteer anything beyond that.

"How do you know that?" I ask, sensing the probable answer already.

"I know the woman. I know your father." She scrubs her hand over the back of her neck. "He went to college with us. Your mother fell in love with him then. I don't think she ever stopped."

"You know my father?" I pause. "Does he know about me? Have you told him about me?"

"I haven't told him a thing." She stops to rest her hands in her lap. "I think you should be the one to tell him."

EIGHTEEN

"The entire time I when I was pregnant, I wished for one thing." She kisses the top of the baby's forehead softly. "I wanted him to have Beck's eyes."

I stare down at Zoe and Vane. He's wrapped tightly in a blue blanket, a small cotton cap covering his head. Her labor had been hard. They'd come into the hospital during my shift last night and I'd raced up to visit her when I was on my break. I had texted Garrett to tell him that Zoe was in labor and I couldn't meet him for our late night cafeteria rendezvous. He's understood. I hadn't asked if his mother had shared any details of our visit. It mattered little at this point. I had left her hotel suite with my father's name and a hug.

"You knew the baby's name, didn't you, Van?" She looks up at me, her eyes heavy with exhaustion. "Did Beck tell you his name?"

"You were in labor for more than twelve hours," I point out. "I think the lack of sleep is causing you to be paranoid."

She laughs softly. "Did you know he'd be this beautiful?"

"I knew it." I run my fingers softly over his cheek. "Look at you and Beck. You're both gorgeous. He would have to be the most beautiful baby in the world."

"I think he is." She moves him slightly away from her chest. "I just fed him thirty minutes ago. Do you want to hold him while I close my eyes?"

It's an offer that's too sweet to refuse. "You know I do."

She supports his tiny head as she gently pushes him into my waiting arms. "Beck went home to get the camera. Tell him I'm asleep when he gets back."

I should tease her about Beck being able to see that with his own eyes the minute he walks into the room. Now isn't the time for that though. This is a moment that Zoe and I are going to treasure for the rest of our lives. I want it to be perfect in both of our minds. "I'll tell him, Zoe."

She doesn't respond as she rolls slowly onto her side and pulls her hands towards her face. I step back towards a bench that runs the length of the wall opposite the bed. I sit slowly, not wanting to wake the beautiful baby boy I'm cradling in my arms.

"You have the most amazing mom and dad," I whisper to him. "They love you so much and when you're older I'm going to tell you all about how they couldn't wait to meet you."

I stare at his tiny hand as it brushes over his face. Zoe had insisted I be in the delivery room with her and Beck and as he held her hand and offered words of encouragement, I'd wept at the sight of a new life entering the world. I cried as I held her after when she told me that she didn't think she could be this happy and I'd felt like the luckiest friend in the world when she told me his name. Vane Beck.

"You met your dad a little while ago." I reach down to push my index finger into his small palm. "I'm going to meet my dad soon too."

I replay the moment in the hotel room when Paulina told me my father's name. I had repeated it over and over again before I left the room as she hugged me tightly. I thanked her for the gift she'd given me and she promised that she'd visit me soon and she'd bring pictures of my mother and Charlie.

"Look at you," Beck's voice pulls at me from the doorway of the room. "It's Van and Vane."

I whimper as I try to hold back a flood of tears. "You have the most perfect son in the world."

He nods as he walks towards us, a large bouquet of flowers in one hand, and a camera in the other. "I have the most perfect son and wife in the world."

"You do," I motion towards the bed. "She's asleep. She wanted me to tell you that."

"Of course she did." He chuckles. "I'll hold him if you want to take off."

I feel bereft before I even hand him to Beck but I know that this beautiful boy belongs in his dad's arms. "You can probably take him home tomorrow. I'll text Zoe in the morning to see how she is."

"You'll come by whenever you want." He brushes his lips against my cheek. "You're part of the family, Van. You'll always be part of the family."

NINETEEN

I kiss Garrett softly the moment he opens the door of his apartment.

"You should have told me you were coming over. I would have dressed more appropriately." He tugs at the collar of his dress shirt. "I'm wearing way too many clothes."

I laugh as I step past him and into the room. "I wanted to surprise you."

"You're full of surprises lately." He grabs my elbow to stop me in my tracks. "My mother said you stopped by her hotel room yesterday. You brought her flowers?"

"I was thanking her for dinner." I turn to look at him again. "I was being polite."

"You were fishing for information." He yanks me into his chest. "You went behind my back to do it."

I look up into his face. "You knew that I would."

"You're right." He pushes his soft lips into mine before he pulls them across my cheek towards my ear. "That's why I told you the name of her hotel. I knew you'd go down there to interrogate her."

"Interrogate?" I parrot back.

"Call it what you will." His hands race down my back before they cup my ass through the fabric of my jeans. "You got what you wanted, didn't you?"

"I knew she had answers." I press myself into him, feeling the outline of his erection. "I could tell when we were at the restaurant that she knew more than she was saying."

"I talked to her too." His hand dips below the waistband of my jeans. "I told her how much I cared about you."

"How much do you care about me?" I pull back to look directly at his face. "How much?"

"You know how much, Vanessa." His hand jumps to my face to cup my jaw. "You can feel it whenever we're together."

"I do feel it," I admit as I look up into his eyes. "I care about you too."

"You're falling in love with me." His voice is raspy and deep. "I know that you are."

"That's your arrogance talking," I bite back. "You can't really know what I feel."

"It's not arrogance. It's honesty."

"Honesty?" I push back. "What does that mean?"

He leans down until his lips are resting against my cheek. "It means that I've never loved a woman before and I know that I'm falling in love with you. I know that you feel exactly the same way about me."

The space between us both physically and emotionally is miniscule. There's no distance there at all. I can literally feel his heart beating within his chest. "What if I am falling in love with you? What does it mean?"

"It means you're going to let me show you why I'm everything you're ever going to need. I'm going to start showing you right now."

"You are?" I lean back as I feel his lips glide over my skin.

"I am."

***

"Garrett," I call his name into the darkness of the room. "It's so good. I feel so much."

His hand glides through my wet folds again. I've already come twice beneath his skilled tongue and now he's drawing me closer to the edge with just his fingers. "I want you to come again, Vanessa. I want you so wet before I slide my cock inside of you."

The roughness of his voice only pushes me closer to my release. I grip my thigh together, wanting to take everything I can from his touch.

"Open your legs," he growls. "Spread them apart."

I do. They fall open as he slides two fingers into my channel. "I'm so close again."

"You're very close." His lips feather over mine. "I can feel it. I can feel how much your body wants me."

I push my lips into his again. I'm desperate for any taste of him that I can get. I pushed against him after he ate me, telling him that I wanted his cock in my mouth, but he'd refused. He wants to control me tonight, and I want it too.

"If you come for me one more time, I'll fuck this beautiful body." His fingers push deeper. "Just do it, Vanessa. Come for me."

I grind my hips into his hand. "Touch my clit, Garrett. Touch it."

His mouth leaves mine and in an instant it's on my core again. He flutters his tongue softly over the swollen bud as he slides his fingers slowly in and out of me. I bunch the bed linens into my fists as I come slowly with a deep low moan.

I close my eyes when I feel him shift off the bed. I listen intently as he opens the drawer and I gasp when I feel him above me.

"I love when you're inside of me," I say under my breath. "I want it."

I feel his sheathed cock when he pushes the head along my cleft. "I love being inside of you. I love being close to you. It's the only place I ever want to be."

I scream into his shoulder when he pushes himself into me balls deep. He's not gentle tonight. "I want to stay here. I want to be with you."

He grinds his hips into mine, the rhythm hard and fast. "One day soon I'm never going to let you go."

"Don't," I plead through a moan. "Don't let me go, Garrett."

"I can't." The words fall into each other as he ups the pace. "Goddammit."

I arch my ass off the bed, wanting to take even more of him within me. I can't speak. All I can do is moan.

He rallies back on his heels as he pushes his head back. "Too good. It's way too fucking good."

My hips pump in unison with each thrust of his and just as I feel the climax hit me, his lips cover mine in a deep and lush kiss.

TWENTY

"You're even more beautiful than Vanessa said you'd be." Garrett holds my mother's fragile hand in his. "She's told me so much about you."

"I'm not sure that she can hear you." I rest my hands on his shoulders. "The doctors don't know for certain how lucid she is at any given moment."

"She knows I'm here." He cranes his neck back to look up at me. "I know I saw her smile when I kissed her cheek."

I stare at her. I've been back to visit her more often since she was released from the hospital. I've read to her from the magazines she bought once or twice a year when I was young. I've sung the songs she used to sing to me when I was a child and I've told her about my discoveries the past few weeks.

"When I was a little girl she used to take me to cheap night at the movies." I laugh at the memory of it. "It was on Tuesdays and we'd go to the early show at seven. We only did it once a month though."

"I bet you two snuck in your own popcorn and snacks, didn't you?" He brings my mother's hand to his lips. "You'd take Vanessa to the corner store and let her pick out the candy she wanted and then you'd hide in your pockets."

"We did that," I confess. "It was a big part of the fun."

"What else did you two do?" he asks my mother. "My guess is that you'd braid each other's hair and paint each other's toenails."

"My mother has the most ticklish feet in the world." I gesture towards the floor. "She would laugh uncontrollably if anyone touched her feet, including her."

"I'll have to give her a foot massage the next time we come." He leans forward. "Vanessa and I have to go now. I promise we'll be back tomorrow. We'll bring you another bouquet of flowers."

"We just brought her one today," I protest. "We don't have to bring one every time we come."

"We do," he says decisively. "The flowers brighten the space. We'll bring daises tomorrow. We'll put them by the window."

"Daises are her favorite." I try to hold back the tears I'm feeling. "She's always loved them."

"We'll bring them to her for as long as we can. We'll do it together."

***

"Why don't you want me to go in with you?" He gestures towards the glass door. "I can help you with this."

"You went with me to the police station yesterday," I point out with a tap on his chest." You've visited my mom and you helped me decide about the will. Don't you think you've done enough?"

I know what his answer is going to be but from where I'm standing he's gone out of his way to help me find my way out of the maze that has been my life the past few months. He sat next to me, and Jonah, while I explained to the police detective who I was and what my birth mother had done. Garrett had offered his mother's name to the detective with her blessing. She wanted to help. She was willing to share everything that she knew and once I have the letter Francesca wrote to me in my hands again, I can give that to the police. The detective had compassionately explained that the investigation may take months, if not years, and my mother's frail state would be taken into consideration.

"I doubt like hell that your mother will be prosecuted for kidnapping, Vanessa." He pushes my hair back from my shoulders. "I'm glad you're going to claim your part of Francesca's estate. It's your right to have it."

It may be my right but I've struggled with whether I should take anything from a woman who gave me away. I'm not doing it because I have big plans for the money. I plan on working as a nurse until I'm old, and grey and retired. I'm not doing it to hurt Connie. I will never have a relationship with her. I'm doing it because of the last line of the letter Francesca wrote to me.

I'd change everything, my dear little one, if I could. I wish I could live my life again. I'd never have let you go.

"I should go in and talk to him now." I pull on the collar of Garrett's suit jacket. "You'll wait here for me, won't you?"

"I still think you should have called him first." He fidgets restlessly on his feet. "What if he's not happy to see you?"

It's a risk I know I have to take. "I'm going to walk in and play it by ear. I haven't decided what I'll say to him yet."

"I've never met anyone like you, Vanessa," he whispers the words into my cheek. "You're the bravest person I know."

"I'm scared," I admit as I cling to his shirt. "I'm scared but I have to do it. If I don't, I'll never know."

He takes a step back and holds me at arm length. "Go in. I'll be right here."

I nod before I pivot on my heel, grip the handle of the door and pull it open.

TWENTY-ONE

I've never had a father. Rowena Meyer would often tell me that a girl doesn't need a dad in order for her to grow up to be a strong and independent woman. I believed those words because they were the only thing I had to cling to on Father's Day when all the other children at school were making macaroni covered soup cans to give to their dads. I had to stay home when the father and daughter dance was held in the sixth grade. I had no one to take me and even though I didn't tell my mother, I had cried myself to sleep that night.

I watched my friends, as they'd race into their father's arms when they were picked up from school and I mourned the moments I knew that I'd never have in my lifetime. I wouldn't get to share that first dance at my wedding with my father and I'd never get to sit next to him when he taught me to drive. I wouldn't hear him grumble when my first boyfriend dropped me off an hour past curfew. They are the simple moments that all of my friends had taken for granted.

On my third birthday, I closed my eyes as my mother lit the candles on my birthday cake, and I wished for a dad. I didn't care if my mother married one of the men she infrequently dated or if my birth father charged through the door to reclaim me. I just wanted to smell the cologne that my father would wear and I wanted to see his worn shoes when I walked through the door of the apartment in Maine after school.

Now, as I walk into this crowded restaurant in mid-town Manhattan I spot the back of a man's head. It's covered in short salt and pepper hair. I recognize his face the moment he turns to the side. It's the same profile that I saw on the Internet when I'd tentatively typed his name into Google.

He was a man who had created a wonderfully enriching life for his wife and his son. He'd built an empire from the ground up and without either of us knowing, our paths have already intersected in many ways.

I knew he'd be here today. I read the stories that were splashed across the financial papers about the newest opening he was attending. His son was standing beside him in the picture they provided. He's tall, handsome and just a few years older than me. I have a big brother. I have cousins and a nephew and a niece. I'm part of one of the most prominent families in all of Manhattan.

"The bar is through there." A hand waves past my face. "We're gathering all the press in there. You can help yourself to a drink."

I don't blame the woman for her thoughtless words. It's natural that she'd assume I'm here for the opening. The way I'm dressed only adds to that. I'd chosen a navy dress with a black blazer and dark heels. I want to look beautiful when my father sees me. I want him to see only the best in me.

"I'm not here for the opening," I say quietly. "I didn't come for that."

"We're not taking reservations yet." The woman gestures towards the front desk. "We have other restaurants in the city though. I can have someone help you find a suitable spot for dinner."

"I don't need a table." I shake my head. "I wanted to talk to the owner."

"Bruno?" She points towards him. "He doesn't have time for one-on-one interviews today."

"It's not an interview," I call after her as she disappears abruptly into the crowd. "It's personal."

"I'm his son." A deep, melodic voice is behind me. "Can I help you?"

I pull in a heavy breath as I turn slowly. I have to look up to meet his eye. "I just wanted to talk to him for a minute."

His mouth opens slightly as his blue eyes study my face. His fingers leap to his lips. "I'll get him. Don't you move an inch. I'll be right back."

I don't turn around as he brushes past me. He saw the same thing I did. It was there in his eyes when he looked at my nose and the shape of my chin.

I swallow hard when I feel a hand on my shoulder. I know it's him. I know it's my father. The tears start before I have time to even attempt to halt them.

"Miss?" His voice can't contain all of the emotion he's feeling. "Can you turn around?"

I look towards the door and in that instant I see Garrett standing there. He came inside. He ignored my request for him to stay outside and I'm grateful that he did.

I nod at him with a weak smile before I turn slowly.

"Charlotte?" The name whispers against his lips as his eyes meet mine. "It's you."

"I was Charlotte," I say without thinking. "I'm Vanessa now."

"Vanessa," he repeats my name slowly. "I thought you were gone. I thought that she'd hurt you."

I scan his face quickly. I see all the pain of the last twenty-four years there beneath the stoic expression. "You thought she hurt me? Francesca?"

"Yes." He sobs as he clings to the arm of his son. "She hated me so much. I thought she hurt you. I told the police. No one believed me."

"She gave me away." I reach towards him. "She didn't hurt me."

"She's here, dad." His son reaches for my hand. "She's okay. Look, dad. She's so pretty."

"She's the prettiest girl in the world." My father holds out his arms. "You look like me. You look like your brother."

"I do," I laugh as I stare at his face. "I do look like you."

"I'm Hunter." The younger man holds tightly to my hand. "I'm Hunter Reynolds. I've been waiting forever to meet you."

"I've been waiting forever to meet you too."

EPILOGUE

One year later...

"It was a beautiful service, Vanessa." Garrett holds tightly to my hand as we stand in the middle of the small chapel at the funeral home. "She would have loved the flowers and the music."

"You're right." I reach up to adjust the daisy that I'd pinned to his lapel jacket earlier. "I miss her already. It's going to be hard to get used to a world without my mom."

"I'll help," Hunter is next to me now. "I'll do whatever you need me to do, Van."

We've grown increasingly close since I walked into the opening of his newest restaurant a year ago. Bruno calls me every week and we spent at least a few minutes a day texting. I met his wife once when Garrett and I had dinner with the entire family. We're all still adjusting but Hunter and his wife, Sadie, have embraced me with open arms. Sadie is a doctor and she's working at the same hospital I do. We became fast friends as soon as we met.

"It's just going to take time I think." I pat my brother on the chest. "Maybe if you let Cory and Olivia sleep over sometimes that will help."

He smiles at the suggestion. "You can take care of your nephew and niece whenever you want. They love you. You tell me when and I'll drop them by."

I crave time with the two of them. They bring a light to my life that I desperately need. It's the same with Vane. He is one of the most important people in my life. I can't go more than a couple of days without seeing him.

I stare down at my left hand. Garrett had proposed more than two months ago during a visit to my see my mom. He'd knelt on the floor in her crowded little room and told me how much he loved me. He did it so she'd know that I'd always be taken care of. He gave her the gift of peace, even if her reaction that day was muted. I knew that she felt the same joy that I felt when he'd slipped the pear shaped diamond ring on my hand.

We'll get married next summer in the church in Maine that my mother would take me to every Sunday. It was the place she found solace and I know that if she could have chosen where I'd begin my life as a married woman, it would have been there. I'm doing it to honor her and the life that she gave me.

"If I could have helped her, I would have." Garrett's arms are around me. "If I could have given you one more day with her, I would have done anything to make that happen."

I believe him. I know that he wishes for that as much as I do. He stood by my side as we watched her take her last breath and he carried me to our bed that night as I wept into his chest. He'd held me for as long as I needed and he planned every detail of her service with me.

"My mom had to go back to Boston after the service," he whispers into my neck. "She wanted me to tell you that she loves you."

"I love her too." I lean back into him. "I love you more."

"You'll always love me, Vanessa." He skims his lips over my cheek. "We're going to have a beautiful family and no matter what happens, I'll always love you and you'll always love me."

I know it's true. It's been our destiny since he kissed my hand when I was an infant. I was made to love Garrett Ryan and he was made just for me.

PREVIEW OF CHANCE

A Full-Length Standalone

"You're telling me that I've never fucked you?"

You'd think I'd walk away at this point. It would make sense for me to turn on my heel and march out of his apartment. I'm not even sure why I'm here.

Today started out like any other day. I woke up and then I brushed my teeth after I had a glass of orange juice. I cursed myself for doing that and vowed that tomorrow I'd drink the orange juice after I brushed my teeth. I dressed in a navy blue pencil skirt and a pale blue blouse. I'd let my dark brown hair fall in waves down my back and I'd hurried to make the train before it sped uptown. I walked through the door of my office at precisely two minutes before nine. It was the same routine I followed every single day.

I spent my morning in meetings with the development team and I had lunch with the owner of the company. He'd been focused on his phone. It's normal for him. He can't resist his wife and whenever she texts or calls him, the world, as he knows it, halts on its axis.

Once I got back to my office, I settled in at my desk to go over last month's budget. It was exactly five minutes to two when my phone rang and I dropped everything to get in a taxi to come here. I'm in a spacious apartment on Park Avenue, sitting across from the one man who has popped in and out of my life since I was a child.

"Caleb," I say his name as I cross my arms over my chest. "What the hell was the emergency? Why am I even here?"

His finger darts into the air to silence me. It's a gesture that he knows I can't stand. He's pushing me and if I thought it would benefit me at all, I'd push him right back. I know his game though. I know exactly what's going on.

"I have to go." His deep voice fills the room. "I'll call you later, baby."

I shake my head slightly as he ends the call. "If you called me down here so I could listen to you talk to some woman who can't remember being fucked by you, I have better things to do with my time."`

"I didn't fuck her." He pushes his chair back from the desk as he crosses his long legs. "If I had, she'd remember it."

I cover my face with my hands. "I have a lot to do today. I have to get back to my office."

"Why haven't you quit that job yet, Rowan?" He throws up one hand. "I need you to work with me. I'm prepared to sweeten the offer."

"What offer?" I fumble inside my purse for my smartphone. "You know I'm never going to work for you."

"I know that you will one day." He stands quickly, pulling his large frame up. "Tell me what they're paying you at Corteck and I'll double it."

"I'm not telling you how much money I make." I scan my phone, reading the new emails that have come in since I left the office almost an hour ago. "When have I ever told you how much money I make?"

"When you worked at that fast food place right before you graduated from high school," he points out. "I told you my professor assigned a project about young people in the workplace and you let me interview you."

"You were such an asshole." I don't look up from my phone. "You were twenty-two, Caleb. You should have been partying hard. Instead you were harassing me."

"I was curious." He rounds the desk. "I wanted you to come and work for me then, don't you remember?"

I do remember. I remember how envious I was that he was able to work for his father and that he was pulling in more money than my parents were making combined. Caleb Foster has never had to do an honest day's work in his life and he's still trying to get me to pick up the slack for him.

"I like my job at Corteck. I work in a real office." I scan the home office we're sitting in. "Don't you ever actually go into the office building that has your last name plastered all over the front of it?"

"You mean that one you pass every day when you go to your job at Corteck?"

"I need to leave," I say briskly. "Don't keep calling me down here for nothing. I have a job to do."

"One day you're going to ditch all that so you can work with me." He grabs my arm as I walk past him.

I stare up into his face. His body may have changed since we were children but the same glint in his dark eyes that I saw when he chased me around the playground is still there. His short hair is darker now than it used to be. There's no denying that he's gorgeous. He knows it and he uses it at every opportunity. He's tall and muscular and if I didn't know him as well as I do, I might even label him as emotionally dangerous. It's the reason I've always avoided getting romantically entangled with him. Caleb breaks hearts whether he's aware of it or not.

"I'm leaving." I pull my arm free of his grasp. "Don't call me again unless you actually need something from me. I'm tired of you wasting my time."

'You don't mean that Rowan." He moves in step beside me. "You don't actually mean that you'd rather I don't call you."

"I mean exactly that." I pat him on the chest. "You can't just interrupt my life for your bullshit."

He presses the call button for the elevator. "It's not bullshit. I'm hurt that you think that's what it is."

I sense the grin on his handsome face before I see it. "Why am I even here? You could have offered me the job on the phone."

"You always say no when I ask you on the phone."

"That's because I'm never going to work for you." I push the call button again. "Is the elevator broken again?"

"It looks that way." He gestures towards a door a few feet from us. "You can take the stairs or you can wait until they fix it."

"I have a lot to do today. I can do the stairs."

I follow him through the doorway into a long and narrow hallway. "Do you want me to walk down with you?" He raises a brow.

"I'll be fine." I reach to open the door but it doesn't budge. "Is this broken too? You'd think a place on Park Avenue would have a better maintenance man."

"The door is fine." He grabs hold of the door handle and gives it a quick twist. He swings it open effortlessly. "You're sure you don't want me to walk down with you?"

"Of course not," I brush past him into the stairwell. "Promise me you're not going to keep calling me for nothing. I have important stuff I have to tend to."

"More important than me?" He swings his arms in the air as he walks into the small stairwell. "Don't try and tell me that our friendship doesn't mean everything to you, Rowan."

"It doesn't." I laugh as I look up at him. "You know that it doesn't. I have to go."

"Wait." His hand pulls on the edge of my skirt. "There is something I need to tell you."

My eyes open wide. "Why do you insist on wasting my time? It's just a game to you. You're lucky my boss doesn't care when I leave in the middle of the day."

"This isn't a game." He swallows hard. "I do need to tell you something. I have to tell you something. I just don't know how to."

I've known Caleb Foster my entire life. I know the instant when something is wrong. A sudden darkness has overtaken his face. It's not just the lighting in this dim and musty stairwell.

"Row." His jaw tightens. "I'm sorry, Rowan. I can't believe I have to tell you this."

"Tell me what?" I grab onto the lapel of his jacket. "Just tell me. You're scaring me now."

His hands clench at his sides. His lips move slightly but nothing comes out.

"Caleb, tell me."

He sucks in a deep breath, cups his fingers around my chin and looks directly into my eyes. "Promise me you'll still be my friend when I tell you. Promise me you won't stop talking to me."

"I promise," I whisper softly. "I'll always be your friend."

"You're the only person I can tell this to. You're the only person who'll understand," he starts before he pauses to pull in a deep breath.

Coming Spring 2015

PREVIEW OF EMBER

A Three-Part Series

"If you're coming back to my place I need to buy some condoms."

The fork in my hand stops in mid-air. I don't look up. I can't. I've barely taken one bite of the roasted squash salad the waiter brought me not more than four minutes ago. This is New York City. This is the place where I thought I'd find the love of my life. What the hell was I thinking?

"You're up for coming back, right?"

My head darts up and I study him. This might actually be the first time I've seriously looked right at him. I'm on a blind date. Maybe the term itself holds more meaning than the literal. Obviously, I had no idea what Larry looked like before I walked through the doors of Axel NY a half hour ago. More than that, I couldn't have predicted that we'd be talking about sex before I'd finished my first glass of wine.

"I don't know you," I say bluntly. "Why would I go home with you?"

It's a question that borders heavily on rhetorical. I don't think that Larry's bright enough to weave those tangled pieces of subtly together. He's an assistant to a paralegal. That says a lot about his drive in life considering he looks like he's in his mid-forties. He's also dying to be fucked. He's not shy about it at all.

"We're on a date, Bridget ..." The words linger there on his thin, smug lips. He doesn't add to them because why would he? Those words have clearly and succinctly spelled out every intention that he has. They aren't masked in anything but the truth. Larry wants his dick to see some action tonight and I'm apparently the main attraction in that circus.

"It's just a date," I explain. "I'd like to get to know you first."

"Why?" He pushes the food from his fork into his mouth and chews.

"I'm not interested in a quick fuck."

His unruly brow cocks. "I heard you were up for just about anything."

Fuck you, Zoe Beck. Fuck you for whatever the hell you said to him when you arranged this date.

"I have no idea what my friend told you about me," I pause while I contemplate how to put this delicately. I stare at him. The wayward piece of kale that is stuck between his front teeth is only adding to the allure that is Larry.

He leans forward on the table. The patch on the elbow of his inexpensive suit jacket brushes against the linen tablecloth. "This place isn't cheap. I brought you here because I thought you were a sure thing."

A sure thing? A fucking sure thing?

I wince at the words. "The only sure thing tonight is that you're going home alone."

It's obvious immediately that Larry is contemplating those words with all the grace of a pack of wild dogs. His hand slams heavily against the spotless white linen tablecloth. "I didn't buy you that expensive salad for nothing. The least you can do is blow me."

No, the least I can do is tell him to fuck right off. "I am not interested in you."

"I'm not interested in you either." He flings his napkin at me and it lands squarely in my squash salad. I was actually going to have another bite of that. "I like brunettes."

Touché. "I like men with hair."

Ouch. I can feel Larry's pain from across the table. Obviously no one, including all the brunettes he's been with, has pointed out the bad comb over that's happening on the top of his odd shaped head.

'We're leaving now."

I actually look to the right and the left to see who Larry is talking to. I'm gathering that he's still engaged in a conversation with me even though I'm trying desperately to ignore him. People are starting to stare and I have no aversion to a little extra attention, but tonight, I don't want to be the main attraction in Larry's sideshow.

"Get up." He grabs tightly to my bare bicep and yanks hard.

I cry out sharply. Considering the fact that most of my body is still stuck next to this table in a chair my arm can't leave with Larry. "Let go of me."

"Is there a problem?" A deep, husky voice asks.

I turn towards it even though Larry is still trying to separate my arm from my shoulder to take as a consolation prize. I look up into the dark eyes of a brown haired man. He's staring down at me with a noticeable look of concern on his face.

"Hey," he calls across the table at Larry. "Enough. You're hurting her."

"Get lost." Larry loosens his grip only momentarily. "My girlfriend and I don't need your help."

Wait. No. Hell no.

'I'm not your girlfriend," I growl at him. "Let go of my arm already."

"You're coming with me." Larry pulls harder and I can't help but cry out in pain.

Within an instant my arm is free and the lapel of Larry's jacket is firmly entrenched in the fisted hands of the handsome man with the dark eyes.

"Are you okay?" He cocks a winged brow. "Did he hurt you?"

"I'm fine." My voice is quiet and small. Maybe I'm not as fine as I thought. I lean my hands on the table, suddenly feeling dizzy.

I hear movement behind me before I sense someone crouching next to me. "He's gone. Are you sure you're okay?"

I turn to the left and look into the same deep brown eyes. "I'm fine. He just shook me up."

"He may have torn something in your shoulder." He presses it lightly with his fingers. "I'd get it checked out if it's sore tomorrow."

"Are you a doctor?" I know he's probably on a date with someone. The dark suit he's wearing doesn't hide his muscular frame.

"No." A small grin pulls at the corner of his mouth. "I'm a firefighter. I'm Dane."

"Bridget," I say with a wince as I try to move my arm to shake his hand.

"I'm taking you to the ER now." He pulls on the back of my chair. "Come with me."

I don't protest. Why would I? He's a fireman and he wants to rescue me. I may actually have to thank Zoe for this date, after all.

Coming soon

THANK YOU!

Thank you for purchasing and downloading my book. I can't even begin to put to words what it means to me. If you enjoyed it, please remember to write a review for it. Let me know your thoughts! I want to keep my readers happy.

For more information on upcoming series as well as updates, please visit my website, www.deborahbladon.com. There are book trailers and other goodies to check out.

If you want to chat with me personally, please LIKE my page on Facebook. I love connecting with all of my readers because without you, none of this would be possible. www.facebook.com/authordeborahbladon

Thank you, for everything.

ABOUT THE AUTHOR

Deborah Bladon has never read a romance hero she didn't like. Her love for romance novels began when she was old enough to board the bus, library card in hand to check out the newest Harlequin paperbacks. She's a Canadian by heart, and by passport, but you can often spot her in New York City sipping a latte and looking for inspiration for her next story. Manhattan is definitely her second home.

She cherishes her family and believes that each day is a gift for writing, for reading, and for loving.

10145244R00130

Printed in Great Britain
by Amazon.co.uk, Ltd.,
Marston Gate.